Henry Noel Brailsford

The Broom of the War-God

A Novel

Henry Noel Brailsford

The Broom of the War-God
A Novel

ISBN/EAN: 9783337031480

Printed in Europe, USA, Canada, Australia, Japan

Cover: Foto ©Andreas Hilbeck / pixelio.de

More available books at **www.hansebooks.com**

Heinemann's Colonial Library of Popular Fiction.

THE BROOM
OF THE WAR-GOD

A NOVEL

BY

HENRY NOEL BRAILSFORD

*" All the flotsam and jetsam of humanity, the ragged edge of Society,
swept up by the broom of the war-god."—P. 243*

LONDON

WILLIAM HEINEMANN

1898

To
MY FRIEND
J. E. M.

CONTENTS

THE BROOM OF THE WAR-GOD

CHAPTER I

THEY PLACE THEMSELVES IN THE HANDS OF FATE

ALL the world in Lamia had adjourned to take coffee. In the lower town a few tired women sat on the door-steps nursing their babies and talking listlessly, mechanically, as if to stop required too much effort. But the Prefect, and the garrison, and the fat storekeepers, every man who boasted trousers of European cut, had adjourned to the *café* in the square. The needs of the time demanded their presence. A company of that famous Philhellenic Legion had come among them—Italians doubtless, the brave brothers from across the sea, the first of the promised two hundred thousand who were to join in the crusade against the Turk. They can drink like the orthodox, they can talk like Hellenes, these men from Italy—he adelphè Italía! And they had asked for rations and rounds of ammunition for a dozen men. That demanded talk, and coffee, and cognac. " Five Turkish coffees, waiter!" The

waiter had answered "tora," which means in Greek
"instantly," and in English "you must wait five
minutes." Already matters were arranging themselves, affairs marched, they were aiding victory
here in Lamia. For there on the walls Marco
Botsari waved his sword, and Colonel Manos and
hero Vassos and Smolenski flanked him, all from
Athenian prints and all crowned with laurel. Beside
them hung a map of Crete, and already it was
labelled "The Great Hellenic Island." And yonder
on the roof the stork plumed her wings in safety
and the swallows flew in and out of their mud nest
in the corner of the coffee-house over the counter.
And words did not halt yet on the tongue of a
Hellene. Yes, yes, all went well. "A glass to your
health, Prefect, and *zéto pólemos !*"[1]

Outside in the great square it grew dark. Already
the lights were lit in the two hotels, first in the new
Hôtel de France whose patrons were always coming
to-morrow, and then in the Grand Hôtel d'Europe
where they had always departed yesterday. The
little shrine on the Acropolis had remembered St.
George and his lamp-wick sputtered fitfully across
the dusk. His name is writ in oil all over Greece.
It is a type of the country, that Acropolis of Lamia.
Nature has raised a frowning rock, Venetians have
put bastions upon it, and modern Greece has built
a one-storeyed barrack. The artillery come there
for training, for it is a pleasant town, Lamia, near to
the sea and the vineyards of Phocis ; it has good

[1] ζήτω πόλεμος : *Vive la guerre !*

cafés too, and a little theatre of Orpheus. A merry place for the lads to train in! The guns are all in Athens; but they are safer there.

Inside, the two waiters in shirt-sleeves were bustling about. They were gleaning news, hailing old patrons from the country, discussing the business of strangers, and incidentally they lit a paraffin lamp or set down a little cup of Turkish coffee, a syrup of ground coffee and sugar boiled together to be drunk between sips of water. And here was a customer calling for a chibouque, surely a legionary. A quick little fellow with an oily skin and a black moustache attended to his affair with great dispatch —he was the business man of the establishment.

" Does the stranger belong to the Legion ? "

" Certainly."

" Bravo, a gallant fellow."

" Is the stranger an Italian ? "

" No, an Englishman."

" Ah ! " and the little fellow drew a deep breath of reverence. A countryman of the great Lord Byron then, and perhaps a lord himself!

" Inglesi," " Anglos," a murmur ran through the *café*. The Prefect ceased to canvass that affair of the rifle, the grocer foresaw a chance of interesting a stranger in the misdoings of his wife—a real stranger this time, a Frank from over seas—and his heart beat with hope. Everywhere the mouthpiece of the hookah had a rest, hands were arrested halfway in a gesticulation, the "stranger" had the ear of the house. He was a tall spare fellow and his

uniform of olive green hung loosely about him.
His head was too long for the *képi*, and the peak
was tilted upwards, showing a rough brow bronzed
a deeper hue on the bulging temples. His nose
had been broken and the coarse nostrils gaped
above a bristly moustache of an uncertain colour
between brown and red. The sunken blue eyes
had an air of pathos and appeal as if they protested
against their burial in this uncouth head. For the
rest, the man's lips spoke of gross passions, and his
large prominent ears suggested the half-breed, the
pariah, the man who has lost the civilisation of his
race. Obviously he had northern blood in his veins,
for his coarseness was muscular, while a Levantine
turns to oil when he degenerates. Yet he spoke
Greek fluently, eloquently, with a natural turn for
metaphor and a command of telling adjectives.
Who was he then—this Englishman ?

But he had ordered two chibouques—" Ki !
Yanni " (John)—and the waiter called his acolyte
to bring the little lumps of coal which must be
placed on the slowly burning tobacco in the bowl of
the native pipe. The stranger was soon pouring
out his explanations. The Prefect had placed a
chair beside him and had pledged him in *ouso*.[1] He
was reading a paper in French which the Englishman held out to him. It was a passport, and certi-
fied that Wilfred, Conte di Coletti had performed
his duties in Crete like a good soldier, and it bore

---

[1] *Ouso* or mastique : a clear native spirit, somewhat potent,
which tastes of aniseed.

the magic name of Vassos. Coletti explained that he was an Englishman from Smyrna, that his father owned a gold mine there, the very gold mine which had enriched King Crœsus. "Coletti" was a good English name, he said, though his patent of nobility was Venetian. He spoke Greek too? Oh! yes, Greek, and Turkish, and French, and Italian, and English; he had lived on every shore of the Mediterranean.

Then the talk veered to Crete. Coletti turned to a handsome lad beside him in the uniform of the Legion, a young Frenchman with more of the Greek in his features than any man in the room, a frank and beautiful face with its straight nose and long chin and exquisitely modelled upper lip.

"Dis donc, Émile, tu étais aussi en Crète?"

And then the Prefect, proud of his halting French, began to question the lad. Ah! yes, he had been in Crete, and his eyes glowed as he thought of danger and glory. "Malaxa—Akrotiri"—he spoke the words as a lover might murmur the cherished name of his mistress. They seemed to tell all he would say. Ah! how they crept towards the blockhouse from rock to rock, first standing up to shout insults to the Moslems, and then "ping, ping," and he raised his arms as if they still held his beloved rifle. "La hausse à neuf cents mètres, 'ping, ping,' a cinq cents mètres, ping, ping," and he felt himself moving again towards the doomed tower. "Malaxa! Malaxa!" and he fell silently again into his glorious dream of that engagement, which meant nothing to him but the excitement of firing, and nearing the enemy amid the whirr of bullets.

And Akrotiri? He laughed his contempt of that fleet which had bombarded the heights where he stood. "There were the Austrians and there the British," and he drew their positions in water on the table with his finger. "And the English shells! Mon Dieu, Monsieur Wilfred, I congratulate you on your countrymen," and again he fell to imitating the roar of the guns and noise of an approaching shell, as it cuts its way through the air with the hum of a resolute mosquito. He was incapable of describing his experiences, he could only re-live them.

He had been taken prisoner too by the Austrians when he was running the blockade. Ah! les sales bougres! they took his arms and locked him up for three days and flogged him for singing the *Marseillaise*.[1] But he was free now, and off to the wars again—zéto pólemos—psámmi —neró—physíngia. He fired off all his Greek as a *feu de joie* and emptied his glass. They sufficed for his need, those five words. What more does a soldier want? He must be able to give three cheers for the war, and then he can live on bread and water and cartridges.

Then the Prefect turned to the third member of

[1] Such was Émile's story, but I am not sure that he quite understood what happened to him.

the group, who had sat silent hitherto, watching
the scene through his eye-glasses. He might have
been an Englishman or a German. He was
shorter than his companions, but more stoutly
built. He had an air of reserve and shyness
which he tried to cover by a show of superiority
and cynicism, yet at bottom he had not enough
respect for himself to be able to dispense with
that of others, and when he spoke he seemed
anxious to conciliate. He listened to the talk of
others with a certain delight. He found their
conversation pleasant because he thought his own
better. His features were an irregular mass of
contradictions—the symbols of a character at war
with itself.

"And the comrade, was he also in Crete?"
inquired the Prefect.

"No," said he, "I have been less than a week in
Greece——" but he was not permitted to continue
his explanations. With that eagerness to recognise
a generous action and to give credit for a disinterested motive which is not the least of the
saving qualities of a Greek, Coletti was already
haranguing the company in Greek. He spoke
excitedly, turning to "the comrade," displaying him
to the coffee-house with a gesture, and then thump-
ing the table to emphasise the quality of his wares.

"I tell you Mr. Graham's a gentleman. I'm
a rough fellow myself, but I know an educated
man when I see him. You take the word of
Wilfred Coletti. He's knocked about the world

a good deal in his time, has Wilfred Coletti, and he knows a thing or two. And mind you, an English gentleman's not like your Italian vermin. There was one of them with us in Crete. A marquis he called himself, and a Socialist. But what does he want with a title if he's a Socialist, I'd like to know? No, no, none of your Socialism for Wilfred Coletti. But I soon showed him who was master there. An Englishman's not going to be put upon by any one. Thought he would boss the show, did he? Wanted to make Émile here his scullion. But I won't see a friend abused wherever I am. I soon pinioned him, and put a pistol to his head, and showed him who was boss in that show. I know them, those Italians, all cowards and thieves. Isn't it truth I'm saying, dear friend?" and he turned with an odd gaze of affection to Graham. " But he doesn't understand. He doesn't know modern Greek. But he knows ancient Greek, mind you. He's a teacher in St. Andrews in Scotland."

"Wha's talking aboot St. Andrews here?" said a new voice, and Coletti's speech came to an end, that quaint revelation of chivalry mixed with the coarsest race prejudice, of English domineering with the sentimentality and want of reticence that belong to a Levantine.

"Is it you, dear friend?" Coletti was saying presently in an odd English, flavoured with memories of the Greek, and the Turkish, and the French with which it jostled in the speaker's

brain. He gripped the two hands of the new-
comer and his eyes anointed him with the unction
of his joy. He knew half the floating population
of the Levant, this Sandeman among the number.
Sandeman was a Scotchman, chief engineer on
board the *Albania*, a Glasgow-built boat, owned
by a Greek firm, which had been pressed into
the Government's service as a transport, and was
plying now between the Piræus and Stylis. He
had come up for a good dinner in Lamia, and a
jolly night to follow. He was a little spare man,
with a sharp, weather-beaten face, keen grey eyes
and red hair.

"And our young friend here's from Scotland,
eh? Div ye ken Glesga? Hoo's a' in the Saut
Market?" and without waiting for an answer he
sat down, continuing to address Graham.

"There's five o' us here, a' guid men. There's
Polyvio here. He's a decent fellow, Polly, and
there's Thamson, the second engineer. He's a
puir crittur, Thamson, but there's nae harm in
him. And Col—what's his damned name? Oh,
aye! Coletti—a queer deevil, Coletti; but ye must
na mind him. Then there's you, a' dinna ken your
name, but that's no maitter, is it?"

"Oh! no," said Graham, hardly restraining a
laugh, and settling down to enjoy a rare feast of
eccentricity.

"Ye're a rum enough looking chap, onyway, but
we'll say nae mair aboot that. We're a' freens
here. An' there's me—Tam Sandeman, the best

man amang ye. Man! I've had a damn guid dinner, and guid wine til't. An' noo we'll talk Philosophy. See there noo, there's Thamson looks as if he wished himself oot o' the door a'ready. Man Thamson, ye're a puir crittur. Ca' yoursel' a man, and ye canna talk Philosophy! But we'll no mind *him* onyway."

'E knew wot was right and wot was wrong, did Thomson, and that was enough for 'im, damn 'im if it wasn't.

But the Scotchman had him on the hip.

"Man, ye're an awfu' fuil, and what's waur, ye dinna ken it. It's no the question whether ye *ken* what's richt and what's wrang. What a'm speerin' is whether ye can *dae* it?"

And he went on to talk of predestination and the fore-knowledge of God.

"Dae ye mind o' the time when ye was a wean, man? Noo dinna say 'aye' if ye don't. Weel, ye mind o't. Guid! Ye're no just siccan a fuil as ye look. Weel, if a' could ha' keekit into your soul when you was a wean, and seen a' that God sees, a'd ha' seen a' that ye was ever to dae in a' your days. And ye've been a wild lad in your time, a'm thinking. But never mind that, ye couldna' help it. Ye did just what God made ye do. And no' a sin mair or a sin less could ye hae committed, though ye'd tried till the sweat ran aff o' ye. That's Philosophy, onyway, and it doesna' maitter what havers ye were comin' oot wi'. Noo fill up your glass, man, and listen to Philosophy."

But Coletti had been looking puzzled, unhappy ;
an indignant instinct of the free Englishman revolted
him against this strange tyrannous doctrine.

"I don't know nothing about Philosophy," said
he, "but I've got a feeling that tells me that I
ought to do what my heart says is right, and that
I can do it, and that I'll be punished if I don't."

"Ye believe in God maybe?" said Sandeman ;
"ye're a queer kin' o' heathen, but ye'll grant me
that."

"Yes."

"An' God kens a' that ye're gaun tae dae, ye
damned sinner."

"Of course."

"Then hoo the mischief can ye help doing a'
that He kens ye'll dae ?   Man, ye're the biggest
fuil ever I met.   But ye can drink wine a' the
same," and he filled up his glass.

All opposition was over now.   Coletti was
scratching his head unconvinced, but too un-
skilled at this sort of talk to find an argument,
and Thomson the Cockney had settled down
sulkily to listen to Sandeman's "nonsense."   He
was used to the thing, they had often drunk
together before.   And Sandeman ran on triumphant, cudgelling the brains of his victims with the
reverent name of "Philosophy."   He had already
disposed of the freedom of the individual, and now
he went on to adjust the destiny of nations.

"It's this way, ye see.   It's noo ae nation and
noo anither that the A'michty exalts.   First it was

the Romans, an' they had their day, but He was soon tired o' them, sick tired o' them. An' then it was the Greeks, or the Egyptians, a' dinna just mind which, and *they* had their day, and God was soon done wi' them. And then it was us yins, and maybe we've come till the end o' oor tether, an' we're gaun doun the brae like, an' syne it'll be the Russians——"

"Our fleet can meet the Russians and the French any day," said Coletti indignant, feeling that now at last he was on sure ground.

"Man, it's easy seen *you* ken naethin' o' Philosophy. What's fleets got to dae wi' Philosophy? You drink your wine and listen to your betters. Weel, an' the Turks hae gaun their ain gait lang enough. And the A'michty has just lookit on, an' seen it a', and bided His time. They micht murder Armenians an' outrage women-folk, but God's done wi' them noo, an' they winna get leave to bide. And noo it's the Greeks that hae got to rule. Doesna' maitter though they're a wee nation; doesna' maitter though they arena' ready for war. God's finished wi' the Turks, an' *they* maun go. If the time o' the exaltation o' the Greeks has come, they've got to win, they couldna' be beaten if they tried."

And so he ran on, repeating his doctrine endlessly, dinning it into the heads of his listeners. To the imagination of Graham he seemed a very figure of Fate as he sat there dominating his companions, unworthily superior, reckless in his mali-

cious childishness. And when he closed his ears the
impression grew on him that some blind force was
governing this irresponsible rabble—the Prefect
and the grocer playing at patriot, their superiors
playing at war, Émile in his gay quest of adventure, Coletti upholding the British name with all
the heat of his alien blood. Then as he rose and
left his companions, the clinking of his side-arms
against the benches reminded him that he too was
part of this mad world. A memory flashed through
his mind of his drive through the streets of London
on his way to Charing Cross and the East—how
all that organised wealth, that materialism which
rested on brain and character, had conspired to
mock his enthusiam ; how the taunt of "folly"
seemed to leer at him from the eyes of the police-
men, the clerks, even the porters in the station,
each filling some place in that gigantic organism
which throve without ideas, and was civilised
without Hellenism. "Folly," "folly" had rung in
his ears as the train left the station, and then he
had settled down in his corner and written in his
notebook, "The only expiation of folly is to be
resolute therein."

CHAPTER II

A GALLERY OF PHILHELLENES

GRAHAM was too much excited by the whirl of emotions within him and the fantastic memories of his evening in the coffee-house to go straight to his quarters. He made across the square to the guard-house where his company was lying, but the first bench that he passed invited him, and he sat down to think. The warm darkness seemed to move about him like an aromatic cloud. It covered up the strangeness of the scene : those odd little shops, with their inscriptions that echoed the classics, became mere human dwellings ; that reveller engaged in tracing interesting patterns as he reeled among the trees was merely the village ne'er-do-weel. One could not see that his loins were girt with a cartridge-belt and his shoulders decked with bandoliers. The burly figure yonder opening that house door was nothing but a bourgeois returning to his wife. Graham did not know that it was the patriotic grocer who carried the Greek colours in his buttonhole, and nursed a double rage in his heart against his erring wife because he had missed a chance of extorting a condemnation of her from a stranger. The darkness levelled distinctions, ignored the war, forgot nationality.

No sound came over the square except the ringing of a little bell turned by clockwork which served to guide the thirsty to a wine-booth; the donkeyman had already vanished into the dark crying his oranges and lemons, and the humbler tradesman who went afoot with *stragália* [1] was covering up his wares, for was not that Demetri staggering home? There would be no more demand for the little salt brown beans that made the resined wine so tasty.

It was a charitable darkness. The persons of the farce dropped their masks. They moved about, black human figures, neither petty nor frivolous, black human figures waiting for the horrors of a war that was coming. A sense of pity and forgiveness, of a simple sadness in the tragedy that called for no clever phrase to express it, came over Graham as he sat on his bench, thinking without words. Yes, yes, it was Fate that moved them, those black masses on legs, those things in the dark without eyes. And he abandoned himself to the fancy. It seemed the road to rest, to walk towards Death in this fashion, with grown-up children about one, with " Folly " for the rule of life. The responsibility of living ceased to oppress;

[1] Little beans with a salt taste, esteemed a great delicacy when roasted. They stimulate thirst.

one marched like a beast of burden.   It was well
to make war, to fight for an idea, to lie in one
grave with crusaders.   Why trouble to organise, to
drill, to fortify? One can die without these things.
It is the dying that counts.   And when death ends
the stage, why ask from what hostel we set out,
what motive put us on our way? It all comes to
the same in the end.

And then came Coletti and seated himself on
the same bench.   The fire-eater, the Jingo, the
Cretan volunteer, he too grew vague in the darkness.   The wine had simplified him too.   He
talked with enthusiasm of Greece.   He used the
direct language of a man who does not reflect,
who has not realised that his every emotion is
matter for praise or for blame.   He loved Greece,
he would give his life for her, he was no mercenary,
no adventurer like those Italians.

Then he dropped into song.   It was one of the
klephtic war-songs, a nasal ecstasy chanted in a
high falsetto voice while the head swayed to and
fro and the eyes were now closed and now flung
towards the moon. Graham heard the national
music for the first time.   The figure before him
might have been some negro witch-doctor reciting a charm, so utterly did he lose himself in the
purposeless gestures of the song, the unmelodic
contortions of the tune.   A long vowel would
drone for a while like the keynote sounded by a
bagpipe, and then a wild succession of spasmodic
shakes would follow, as if the bitter complaint of

an enslaved people too long repressed had at last broken forth. It was not the energic song of a brave nation resolved to conquer, but the wail of a nervous race excited by petty tyrannies till they must seek relief in some effort, hopeless though it should be. "We can endure no longer, the goad of our masters has pricked us, we must leap, we must run, we must fire our rifles, we will even die, for we can hold our peace no longer;" such seemed to be the burden of this klephtic war-song. It was the tune that had led them when they waged the desultory war of independence, and again it sounded through the Greece of to-day, impatient under the emotional strain of watching Crete agonise beside her.

Next it was a love-song that he sang. Graham could catch some of the words—the conventional symbolism that occurs in every language. Coletti was flattered when his hearer showed some curiosity. Yes, it was a love-song, his own composition. It compared his mistress to a rose, the fragrance and the grace of her, and then her way of shutting herself up at night, and ah! the thorns which would not let him pluck her. She was a Greek and she lived in Smyrna. He had gone one night and sung that song under her window with hired musicians to accompany him on their lutes and their guitars. And next day he went to his father to ask for money—he must make her presents—but not a piastre would the old man give him, so he packed up his bundle, and was off to the

c

wars.   He had gone again to sing adieu to his
lady:

> Under the walls of Larissa soon shall I lie.
> Pity me, lady.
> 'Tis you, O cruel one, beautiful, drive me to die.
> Pity me, lady.
> Are not my salt tears enough, why must I bleed?
> Pity me, lady.
> When I return, a corpse, then you will heed.
> Pity me, lady.

Coletti wrote the words for Graham in his notebook, using the Latin alphabet and a phonetic
orthography all his own.   His knowledge of Greek
was purely colloquial, though it was his mother
tongue.

As Coletti went on with his song Graham could
reconstruct the scene.   Coletti at first whining,
painting himself a corpse, working on the pity of
the girl.   Then she had wept, "yes, wept, poor
girl," said Coletti, "think of that"—wept, and bade
him stay in Smyrna!   And then in his triumph
he had flung all his silver contemptuously to the
lutanists and burst into the klephtic war-song—
adding impromptu verses—Beloved Greece, his
adopted country, 'twas for *her* he would die.   She
called him to her.   *She* shed no craven tears at his
departure.   "Adieu, lady, adieu; I shall return
alive and crowned with laurel."   And then he had
turned on his heel, and spat upon the door-posts
of his mistress's house.   Bah!   She would not send
him to the wars.   She was no wife for a brave

man. He loved the Greeks, yes, but these Greek
women were not like English-women. And he
was an English subject, "remember that, dear
friend; I could show you the papers if you wished."
Ah! no! the lady for him would send him bravely
to the wars, but only an Englishwoman could do
that—or perhaps a Frenchwoman, and he went on
to talk regretfully of the little milliner he had left
behind in Marseilles, and to wonder if their child
was a boy or a girl.

Graham had heard enough. He began to saunter
towards the barracks. A queer jingle ran still in
his ears—" Piastres for presents—he would give me
none, so I'm off to the wars." " 'Tis you, O cruel
one, beautiful, drive me to die." No, that was not
how it ran, it was " for Greece " he would die ; but
was he to die at all, and was it as a corpse or laurel-
crowned that he would return ? But what was that
over there ? Two dim figures were reeling together
out of the *café*. " Scots wha hae wi' Wallace
bled," sang one of their voices, and then it dropped
into prose.

" Man, ye're an awfu' fuil, Thamson; it's no that
we were singing—it's ' *zeto polemos*.' Man, can ye
no cry ' *zeto polemos* ' ? "

" Oh ! damn the *polemos*, to 'ell with the *polemos*,"
said the other voice; " you 'old your —— jaw,
you're screwed you are—damn the *polemos* I says."

" An' noo we'll talk Philosophy," resumed the
other. " A'm no screwed, a' can talk Philosophy.
An' if a' was sch—sch—schrewed a' was predestined

to be screwed, ordainit and foreknown to be sch—
sch—schrewed by the omnipotence o' God A'michty,
but a'm no screwed.

> Oh ! Willie brewed a peck o' maut "——

And then the darkness covered up the two
figures. "There goes Fate, screwed, predestined to
be screwed," thought Graham.

Inside the garden of the guard-house a group of
legionaries were sitting. The sentry box outside
was vacant, but one of the men seated on the bench
within had his rifle somewhere near him, and his
belt, with its bayonet attached, was lying on the
grass at his feet. He was evidently on duty. His
comrades sat round him, smoking cigarettes and
talking in groups. An officer from the barracks
on the Acropolis was with them, and the Prefect
in plain clothes. The officer was a stout old fellow
with a brusque manner and a burly carriage ; he
wore a simple uniform of dark blue, and on his
collar was a single star that indicated the rank of
sub-lieutenant, and a golden wing which showed
that he belonged to the artillery. His hair was
grey and his voice trembled as if with age and
hard living—subalterns usually have grey hair in
the Greek army, it is as infallible a sign of their
rank as the single star. A stranger who knew
nothing of Hellenic politics might take that single
star for a long-service decoration.

As Graham sauntered towards the group their
talk became more excited. A little cross-eyed
Italian was haranguing them in French. He had

served with Cipriani at the front before war had been declared, he had marched and fought for three days, killing innumerable Turks and burning their villages. But the cold had been too great and he had returned to Athens. Then he went on to curse the Government. No pay! no rations! Everything to-morrow—and then those eternal delays. "The War Office is disorganised," he said; "procrastination will ruin everything. Ma foi! How much longer will they keep us here in Lamia, half-way between Athens and the front! The Turks will come and drink coffee in Athens before we start."

His grumbling went no further. Coletti was upon him, blind with rage. "He says the Turks will come and drink coffee in Athens, the traitor;" and mumbling something about "Italian vermin," he dragged the little fellow by his collar to the place where the officer and the Prefect sat, hardly separated from the privates. "Kyrie axiomatike,"[1] he began, "he wants the Turks to come and drink coffee in Athens." Soon they were all talking together, Coletti emphasising the purity of his patriotism and the low motives of Italian volunteers, the little legionary half squealing between fear and rage, the old subaltern puzzled, in his ignorance of French. The Prefect got up and deliberately struck the culprit thrice on the side of the head, and then the officer, accepting his lead, bade Coletti tell him that there must be no traitors in the Legion, and

[1] κύριε ἀξιωματικέ : *Monsieur l'Officier.*

that he would have discipline at all costs. Graham too had come up, endeavouring to explain, but while he persuaded the Prefect that no treason had been spoken, the little culprit still spitting out his rage had gathered up his kit and was gone, declaring that he was a volunteer and would join the Garibaldians.

The incident was scarce a five minutes' wonder. Talk was soon in full fling again. Émile, "the Cretan," was now the centre of interest. "How many Turks had he killed?" asked some one, eager to be incredulous. Poor Émile fell into the trap. He soon had an imaginary rifle to his shoulder—"ping, ping!" a Turk fell at every report; and then there were the prisoners and the wounded, the good God alone knew how many of them they had shot down after the fight. This was the confession for which the others had waited. They were jealous of this gallant lad who had seen the enemy already, who had fought too as an irregular. As for them, they might perhaps hear cannon some day, but it would not be the big guns of the six great Powers ; they too might march against the Crescent, but it would be in files and companies, carrying an uncomfortable uniform, and restrained by the word of command of some detested officer. And this lucky Émile had shot the wounded. They shouted round him, they bayed at him. Was that how Frenchmen behaved? asked an Italian, thinking of Tunis. "And he professed to be fighting for the Cross," exclaimed Grassini,

the Socialist and Atheist. Émile too had his
rough retorts at his command, and soon fists were
shaken in the air.

Graham, weary of the whole affair, sick though
he was of these mutinous volunteers, these jealous
Christians, was driven from his attitude of spectator.
Hitherto he had spoken little, hardly venturing to
pronounce even a silent judgment upon them,
acutely conscious as he was of his ignorance of
things military. But to-night a sense of responsibility came to him, he found courage to judge and
to act as an educated man among the unschooled.
He rose from his seat in time to stand between
Émile and his persecutors. " It is shameful to
quarrel among ourselves while we are marching
against the common enemy," he said in his stiff
French.

" Yes, yes, he is right," answered Grassini ; " we
must not quarrel when we are fighting for liberty.
Ah ! it is a glorious cause, we must keep our hands
pure, no shooting of wounded in such a war ! "
And then Graham took Émile's arm and led him
away.

" I only did what the others did ; I don't want to
be better than the comrades," said his *protégé*.

Together they ascended the stairs that led to the
long dormitory of the guard-house. At the door
they met Lieutenant Chanteloup, the French officer
who had charge of the little company on its march
to the front. He was a dignified man, perhaps
forty years of age, with melancholy eyes and a

gentle smile. Hé seemed more concerned for the comfort of his men than for their discipline or fitness for the war. He went about fingering a little medal attached to his watch-chain. He had once shown it to Graham ; it was in the form of a cross, and the inscription was a token of gratitude from Louis Philippe to his ever loyal subjects of the ancient house of Chanteloup. And then he had grasped Graham's hand, and looked into his eyes, and muttered in his inarticulate nervous manner : " So we are going to these new crusades together—I congratulate you."

To-night he had finished his inspection of the dormitory. Everything was in order, and he was about to return to his hotel. At the top of the stairs Émile and Graham saluted and would have passed on, but Chanteloup held out his hand. He seemed to hesitate as if uncertain what to say, and then with a grave inquiry after Graham's health he turned and walked down-stairs. In his own mind he was debating a question between discipline and kindness. He knew what it meant to pass a night in a room infested with vermin, surrounded by un-educated men, tormented by their foul talk and filthy practices. He had a spare couch in his own room, Graham was really his social equal, but would it be good discipline, would it not create ill-feeling in the little company ? Then as it were a light from his own romantic world, the world of a Catholic and a Legitimist, a world without windows, fell upon the image of Graham in his mind—his fellow-crusader—yes, he should have his sofa, and he turned round once more and made his offer. For a moment Graham hesitated, and then the warm pressure of Émile's arm on his decided him. "*Merci mille fois, mon lieutenant*, you are very kind, but one must get used to it," and the pair passed into the dormitory.

Already some of the company were stretched on the planks that served for beds, and had rolled themselves in their military blankets. Graham found Yorghi, the thief of the company, on the next bed to his own. He lay on his stomach snoring, and a noisome stench came from him. He slept in his uniform, that uniform which he never abandoned; it was some sizes too big for his ill-shapen carcase. Two pairs of uniform trousers were hidden there, and a shirt of Graham's, with sundries innumerable. No one interfered with him—indeed, his trade furnished a welcome amusement, but everybody had decided that he should be delivered over to head-quarters when the company reached the main body of the Legion, and the more sanguinary even talked of military law. And meanwhile Yorghi lay there on his stomach with his booty safely beneath him. Only his boots had been removed, and the sight of the festering sores on his feet and ankles, the work of vermin and the penalty of filth, added a touch of pity to the loathing with which Graham regarded this

fellow-Philhellene. He had barely undressed and
arranged his blanket when the room began to fill
up. Some of the men undressed and were treated
to disgusting familiarities by their fellows, others
sat down on their plank-beds, and lit their pipes,
and a smell of coarse tobacco filled the room,
welcome in the main to Graham, for it overpowered
the human odours that had prevailed before. In
one corner Grassini was delighting his compatriots
with a stentorian rendering of airs from *Tell* and
Fra Diavolo. At the other end of the room a low-
caste Greek from Smyrna, Louis by name, was
entertaining the company to a humorous account
in Levantine French of a disgusting *contretemps*
which had befallen Émile in Athens, when the
pair had visited a woman of the streets. For a
while Graham lay struggling with his disgust.
"'Tis a soldier's life," he said to himself, "it is
well to lay aside for a time the restraints and
refinements of civilisation. That is a brave noise
that Grassini is making—an honest fellow, rude
enough no doubt; but he will fight well, he will
charge with dash, he will never think of the shot and
shell; and you, Graham, with your nerves, where
will you be then? And even Louis—bah! to
think of him sickens me—even Louis has humour;
he is gay and unconcerned. And you, Graham,
were you not thinking of death and of fate
an hour ago?" So he reasoned, but always
some new abomination occurred to interrupt the

sermon which he industriously preached to himself.

At last he abandoned the attempt, his brain was too weary to succeed in its sophistical task; he was too tired for self-deception. He turned on his side, and closed his eyes, and drew the blanket over his ears. A longing to see beauty came over him. Must he succumb to this hideous reality around him? He tried to revive those facile dreams that had danced so prodigally before him some weeks earlier. He tried to think of his adventure as one might think of some quest in the *Morte d'Arthur*, Malory's book, that had been his chosen reading in boyhood. But such things are quaint imaginings that may beguile an idle hour beside a Highland stream, while the clouds print their fancies on the sunny face of the hillside, and the trout leap in the shallows. The reality was too vivid, too hard in outline to melt into such dreams.

Or again he thought of his mother's stories of friends of hers who had fought with Garibaldi, and he recalled his boy's sorrow that he had been born too late to join them. Was the dream of a great free Italy any fairer than this inspiration of Hellenism? But now Grassini was talking Italian, and he was reminded of the crew of Garibaldians with whom he had sailed from Brindisi to Patras; drunken gaol-birds, filthy and truculent, ten of the twenty deserters from their own army. Garibaldi

helped even less than King Arthur. And now the
cry for something beautiful became conscious in
him. It struck him with a sort of shame that he
had heard no music since he had left St. Andrews.
The slow movement of Beethoven's Violin Con-
certo came into his mind as Joachim might play
it, with its serenity that is not cold, its tenderness
that is not plaintive, a thing completely beautiful,
a satisfaction in itself so perfect that thought need
never stray outside it. Again and again he played
it for his mind's ear, till peace came to him. The
room was quiet now, none spoke, and the smell of
tobacco was gone. A cool air blew in from the
window, and the wind moved in the leaves of the
fig-tree outside, and its branches brushed against
the wall.

Suddenly the calm was broken by the report of
firearms. It came like a fit of neuralgia which
invades a dream, an unreasoned succession of
pains which arise one knows not how or why in
places whose existence one forgets. From the
market-place came a regular fusillade; six sharp
cracks would come from the same spot, and one
knew that some one had emptied his American
revolver; or again it was the well-known sound of
the service-rifle, from a distant street, or far off on
the hillside. The whole room was awake and on
the *qui-vive* in an instant. Men rubbed their eyes
and sat up gasping. "*Les Turcs! hoi Tourkoi!*" the same cry of terror came in half-a-dozen

different tongues. Graham alone knew the meaning of the demonstration. Twelve o'clock had struck; it was Easter Sunday according to the Greek calendar, and the people were celebrating the Resurrection. He explained the meaning of the noises to his companions, but they seemed too flurried and excited to heed him. He kept silence for a while, uncertain whether he despised the Greeks outside the more for wasting cartridges in time of war, when every round was priceless, or the legionaries within for their panic. He felt disposed to lie quiet, and analyse the scene, interested but indifferent. Then some one—it was Émile—mentioned Lieutenant Chanteloup, and the name recalled him to his duty. Was he not here simply because for an instant he had felt his responsibility and accepted it? He got up and obtained a hearing.

One by one the men got back on to their planks again, some grumbling and swearing, others laughing at some obscenity or other. It was as if an unwary traveller had kicked the earth from a dung-heap by the roadside, and the corruption which had lain asleep and harmless had infected the air once more. Graham sought relief no longer in music. With the new motive of responsibility before his mind, his thoughts wandered to this strange demonstration, and the legend that lay behind it. In the silence of the night in this ancient place, among a people ready to die for the

Cross, the meaning of the symbol came home to him. It seemed a new thought, daringly original, this conviction of the beauty of pain, and the deity of him who will suffer gladly. The paradox burnt itself upon his heart, and he fell asleep content with the great beauty of the old thought that had come to him by chance.

CHAPTER III

"WHEN do you think of starting, sir?" said Graham to Lieutenant Chanteloup.

They were sitting drinking coffee in front of one of the little restaurants in the square of Lamia. It was ten o'clock on Tuesday morning. Two days had gone by since that night in the guard-room. For Graham they had passed wearily. Yorghi—thief and old soldier—had been too busy making merchandise of his stolen goods to find time to drill him, and he had been reduced to wander about the little town alone. Already it began to wear a sombre aspect. Every lady in the place had a brother, or son, or husband at the front. News came irregularly, and if a day had passed without a letter, and there were rumours of fighting, the sister, and wife, and mother put on mourning. The streets talked of death, now gaily, when a girl in crape met her gallant, some elegant fellow in a cavalry uniform, now wearily, when a mother with a babbling child beside her, proud of its new clothes, went listlessly about her shopping,

31

—but not always in prose, for sometimes through the sunny air came the majestic throb of the *Funeral March* heralding the coffin filled with flowers in which a soldier's body should have rested, the poor body that now lay rotting in some Thessalian pass, mutilated and dishonoured by the Turk.

But at this hour all was quiet in the square. Noon begins early in Lamia. There the sun will always grant noon when the heart wills it. The black rocks of the Acropolis gleamed like armour in the blazing light; the square was deserted, and when a man had need to cross it, he went hurriedly, scarcely erect, like a fugitive running the gauntlet where the fire is hottest. Under the ruined mosque with its silent minaret, some soldiers were bargaining with a peasant who had wine in his donkey's panniers, and across the way a group of legionaries gazed into the show-case of the photographer's booth. There were portraits there of the last thieves crucified in Lamia—three naked figures riddled with shot wounds, new and old, roped to their crosses. Civilisation triumphed: it photographed the vanished barbarism, exulted in these corpses safe there in the clutches of the new science. Stiff saints in the churches serve as models to virtue, and rigid sinners in the little booth may frighten vice.

"When do you think of starting, sir?"

"That depends on when M. Ferrari and Coletti get back from Stylis—they won't be more than a couple of hours I hope. I told them to drive."

"Have you news yet from head-quarters, sir?"

"Yes, those reports of a disaster were only too true. There's been a big engagement at Mati—somewhere on our side of the frontier. The Greeks fought like heroes—ah! it is a pitiable story—but they were hopelessly outnumbered, and they have fallen back on Pharsala. It was the Prefect who told me, poor old man; there were tears in his eyes as he left me; he said he must go to provide arms for the *franc-tireurs* who are going up from this district, and then he turned round—'You see me, sir. I am too old to go with them, am I not? But they say that two hundred thousand Italians have left Rome to help us! Ah! it is only for the moment, this defeat.' They are a brave race these Greeks!"

"So we are going to take part in the second battle of Pharsala, lieutenant. *Absit omen!*"

Chanteloup smiled and thought for a while. He seemed to lose himself in reverie, and then, as if speaking to himself, he murmured, "Nous allons arriver à un moment plus que critique—plus que critique," and as he said the words he rose, smiling with those grave eyes of his, and straightened himself as if to assure himself that he was ready to face the crisis, gladly but wittingly as a brave officer should. He paced about for a while, and then sat down again beside Graham. A little

D

news-boy was running round now from *café* to *café*. The boat had come into Stylis then, and Sunday's papers from Athens were for sale. Graham bought a *Soteria*.[1] It was lying on the table between them, and Graham was translating the telegrams. Yes, all was true. In the language in which he had read of Salamis and Marathon— the same language, but how strangely debased— he now spelt out the tale of the futile bombardment of Prevesa, and the retreat from Mati. And then he turned to another page. A sentence from Demosthenes in leaded type headed the leader. It spoke in burning words of the great race struggle ; of the war for the Cross ; of the fate of a nation trembling in the balance, and for the first time Graham realised the tremendous issues at stake. And now Chanteloup was looking curiously over his shoulder. Like most educated Frenchmen he knew no Greek.

" That looks like a poem," he said ; "what is it ? "

" It's very odd," came the answer ; "yes, it is a poem, *Christian, Stand Firm* is the title."

"Ah, that is it, is it ? 'Christian, stand firm,'" and he paced about for a minute, while Graham, his curiosity thoroughly aroused, began to study the poem. Chanteloup was back before he had translated the first verse. His step was firmer now, and there was a ring of decision in his voice

---

[1] A cheap Radical paper which, in the contemptuous words of a Greek officer, "spoke against the King."

as he said—"*Au revoir;* at one o'clock we start
from the street corner yonder—you will tell the
others." These chance words flung at him from a
half-penny broad-sheet in an unknown tongue, had
brought that touch of imagination which his nature
was craving. They linked his dreams to the
present, and from that day forward throughout
the campaign, amid weariness and disaster, his
heart was closed to impressions. A command
was laid upon him, the more imperative because
it had come unsought in all its abruptness and
unreason.

As for Graham he sat still at his table. He was
in the centre of Lamia there, and one by one the
waves of that disaster which had broken over the
Greek army fifty miles to the north came rolling
towards the little town. First it was a little group
of legionaries who straggled across the square and
seated themselves at a table beside him. Their
faces were new to him, and they were talking
German.

"Du, Schweitzer, what think'st thou to do?"
said a tall, yellow-haired fellow, with the accent of
a Berliner. He had the air of a man who has
suffered much, and whose sufferings are highly
interesting to himself. The other, the Swiss, was
a smaller man, with refined features, but he seemed
sodden with drink. A third proved to be a Norwegian peasant who had lived many years in
Prussia. All three were travel-stained; they carried

neither blanket nor haversack, their uniforms were torn, and the sun had bleached the green almost to yellow.   The Norwegian had no boots, and his feet were swathed in rags that had once been white.

"Du, Schweitzer, what think'st thou to do?"

"Drink *schnaps*."

"Ach! my good friend, be for once reasonable."

"Leave   me   in   peace!   Waiter!   quick,   a cognac!"

"*Herr Je!*   Is the creature crazy?   Schweitzer, I've come so far with you, since you are my good comrade.   I didn't leave you in the lurch when the Turkish cavalry came after us, now did I, Schweitzer, you'll grant me that?   And now I insist on knowing where you're going.   Schweitzer, you shall answer me.   Where are you going?"

"To the devil."

"*Himmel!* to think what I've done for the fellow, and he won't answer me.   Schweitzer, if *you* go back to the army, of course I won't *abandon* you, but——"

"Go back to Athens if you want to, I'm not going to desert——"

At this point Graham came forward and joined the party.   The Berliner seemed surprised to see a man in the familiar green uniform.   The conversation began, as all conversations begin in the Legion, by an inquiry as to the nationality of the new-comer.   That over, Graham begged for news

of the Legion. The Norwegian sat still, too tired
to speak ; the Swiss imbibed cognac and ill-temper ;
the Berliner alone was in his element.

"Alles ist verloren—die Legion zerstreut und
zersplittert.   Ich   rathe   Ihnen   nicht   weiter   zu
gehen——"

"Everything   lost !   The   Legion   scattered !"
What could it mean ?

"You'll go no further now, will you ? I've seen
more than you of how things are managed.
You'll come back with us, won't you ? *Hören Sie
mal.* We've been marching three days—three
days without food or sleep, and the Turks were
after us the whole time. Again and again we saw
them—cavalry down in the plain. If we hadn't
thrown everything away and kept to the hills, we
shouldn't be alive now. *Du Lieber Gott !* Once
in a lifetime is enough for me ! I'm back to
Athens."

"And where are the others ? "

"God knows ! It was every man for himself!
We three stuck together, but everything's lost.
The whole army's in flight, and the Legion's
annihilated. And there's a European war now.
Forty thousand Russian and German troops have
occupied Larissa. We escaped over the hills to
Volo, walking day and night, and then we got on
to a steamer which brought us here. *Herr Je !*
If we hadn't kept our heads and stuck together,
the dear God alone knows where we should be.

The Greeks are annihilated.   The Turks are three to one, and every regiment's led by German officers. The whole army has thrown away its rifles.   There is no longer an army.   If we hadn't kept our arms we'd have been dead men.   Twice, thrice we had to turn and fire on the cavalry.[1]   But the first essential of a good soldier is to keep his rifle. I've been a sergeant in the Prussian army and I know my business.   You'll come back to Athens with us, won't you ? "

"No, I'm going to Pharsala.   The army is there now.   There's a French lieutenant with us, and we are going to start in a couple of hours.   You'll come too of course!   I don't believe the war is over yet."

"Well, well, it's sheer folly, but I'll never leave a comrade in the lurch."

Further questioning proved useless.   Graham could form no clear idea of what had happened— some terrible disaster clearly.   The official accounts must have minimised the mischief.   But he seemed an honest fellow, this Berliner.   Then came a feeling of disgust that he had missed the great battle which had evidently been fought. He cursed his luck as he thought of those days of useless waiting in Athens, and the red tape which had kept him there in enforced inaction.

[1] The Berliner's Turkish cavalry were probably inoffensive peasants fleeing astride donkeys, or perhaps war-correspondents hurrying to send their "stuff" from Volo.

But now there was a chance of hard fighting.
His blood warmed as he thought of the prospect
of joining a forlorn hope, and sharing in the
desperate resistance that would be offered at
Pharsala.

His excitement set him in motion, and he found
himself sauntering through the narrow streets behind the square. For a moment he fancied he
could recognise *his* mother and *his* sister in those
figures clothed in black which walked ahead of
him, and the haunting cadence of the military
funeral hymn came into his ears with a homelier
pathos. A wave of self-pity swept over him.
And now he was standing before a monument
and mechanically reading the inscription. It com-
memorated the martyrs of the War of Independence,
the men who had fallen " for Faith, and Fatherland,
and Freedom." " Christian, stand firm !" said a
memory, and he turned away shivering as it were.
He saw himself standing aloof while a band of
heroes marched onward. This faith was not his,
this fatherland an alien country, and yet he thrilled
at the thought of either—thrilled as a musician
may as he hears a marvellous air which he can
never play. He thought with envy of Chanteloup.

A turning of a lane brought him once more into
the square. It was animated now. A long pro-
cession was passing through it. It never halted,
and he could only see that it came from over the
mountains and went towards the sea. There were
carts and carriages, mules and packhorses, men on

foot and men in the saddle. Here was a covered carriage, the roof piled with portmanteaux and trunks, and inside it one caught a glimpse of a delicate girl fashionably dressed. Her face was pale and she had been crying. Then came a cart drawn by a yoke of oxen. Its wheels were of solid wood and almost hexagonal in shape. The oxen went stolidly in the rear of the carriage and another cart pressed on behind. They were laden with boxes and cradles, with flasks of wine, with tables and chairs; this carried a spindle, and that a plough.

Old women and men sat among the wreck of their fortunes, gazing before them with eyes that saw nothing, and burying their heads in their hands. Here was a little girl, tripping gaily along, playing hide-and-seek behind a wagon, now standing still, now dancing on, an active little fairy with shapely brown legs. Another went timidly, holding her mother's skirt with one arm and clasping a cat in the other. The men had rifles slung over their shoulders and the women carried babies. No point of colour lit up the dismal train. The men's kilts, once white, hung limp and yellow over their yielding knees, the women went in brown or black, and there lingered no touch of coquetry or fashion even in the draping of their shawls.

Here was a village pastor holding the rope by which he led his sorry beast. He was chanting some fragment of ritual to himself; the monotone

was shaky and uneven, and when he attempted
the ornate conclusion, the little tune that gave out
a " Kyrie " or an " Amen," his voice broke in a sob.
But his wagon passed, and Graham still stood
absorbed in the monotony of suffering that paced
before him. Each cart meant the wreck of a
homestead.

Every mother guarding a baby, every father
with a daughter at his side, seemed to swell the
indictment against the pitiless foe, who spared
neither mother nor maiden, and massacred man
and child alike. The very name of Turk had
sufficed to empty Thessaly. They knew from
what terror they fled, these peasants. Sixteen
years ago the very soil on which he stood had
belonged to the Moslem, and the Muezzin's call
had come with the dawn from that minaret. That
woman yonder had heard it in her maiden days,
and now, bent with toil and motherhood, she
had turned to flee from it. Graham caught her
eyes as she passed him. Her baby cried, and she
put it to her breast, and it lay there resting on a
child yet unborn, and the mother of both, thin and
worn, staggered wearily on, keeping her place in
the regiment of the disinherited.

But Graham turned away, he had no need to
look yonder. He had found a motive that made
war holy. He went back to a *café* table and
scribbled a note of farewell to his mother. It
might be his last letter to her, but he could think
of her without remorse as he faced the risk of

death. The vision of that woman who had looked at him remained with him, and he knew that he carried arms for no alien cause, no remote ideal. He thought of Chanteloup without envy, and he felt no need of a Faith.

CHAPTER IV

A GENTLE SHEPHERD

SIX weary figures were stumbling up a street in Domoko. It was night, and only a star here and there lit up the gloom. They seemed to be within a labyrinth of curtains. They had been winding through mountain chains all day. They had left behind them the sea and the broad plain with its gaiety of clear air and sunshine. Each hour of the waning day had tightened another fold of that mountainous robe about them. They had marched straight forward towards the darkness, and here it was at last, the goal of their wandering, sheer night in Domoko. Those houses that one divined somewhere to the right and the left were the last wall that shut out day. One would never know what was inside the prison—strange things perhaps. There was Émile on his face, his rifle rattled on the stones, and a string of eloquent French oaths came down the hill, jolting over the cobbles as it were. A stumble and a run, and another stumble —the panic of the unknown had seized Graham too. The Berliner was creeping along at the side,

43

feeling his way with his hands. *Donnerwetter!* He had tumbled over the steps of a cottage, and his rifle too went clattering down the hill. "Die erste Bedingun*k* beim *j*uten Soldat ist das Gewehr immer fest zu halten," thought Graham; it had been the German's last articulate remark, it seemed to sum up the art and science of war in his mind.

But here was a light at last. The Greek corporal who led the little party thundered at something with the stock of his rifle. It gave back the sound of wood: it must be a door. "This is the best house of the three," said the corporal; "they're sure to give you a good supper here." It was Yorghi who slunk round to the door at the words, and the Berliner who hustled after him. "Ic*k* will nie einen Kamerad im Stich lassen," quoted memory in Graham's mind, as the German vanished into the yard. "Adieu," sang out Yorghi's voice already in the porch of the villa. "That's what your host's silver spoons will say to him to-morrow," muttered Émile, realising that he had missed the most desirable quarters. Then the corporal returned and explained that the next house was up a lane to the left; Émile and Louis followed him, while Graham and the sixth of the party waited, leaning on their rifles. They were on the top of the hill, they seemed to have climbed above the innermost ring of those curtains. A dim, grey light hung about them, it seemed to quiver over the mountain tops to right and left. As they waited there, sleep almost came upon them. Their eyes were half closed as they peered over their rifles, while the points of fire strewn upon the hillside, where fugitives had pitched their camps on their way to the sea, lengthened out till a warm glow ran round the horizon.

It seemed that half-an-hour had passed when the corporal, who was acting as quartermaster, returned. Graham and his companion—a Greek American named Nicholaïdes—were certainly not impatient. Their march from Lamia over the hills in the blazing afternoon sun had wearied them out. A civilian is not accustomed to go laden with rifle, and blanket, and haversack, and with a hundred and fifty cartridges disposed upon his person. It was more because they were too tired to resist that they at last followed the corporal to a little hut some yards from the roadside. Here he did not go through the formality of knocking. "Alexi! Alexi!" he shouted, until at last the door was opened by an old man in shepherd's costume. Some conversation followed, and then the shepherd beckoned all three within the house. A passage which also served as a store-closet led to its single room. It was an oblong room with whitewashed walls, toned a rich brown by the peat-smoke. It had two small windows with diamond panes at either end, and the greater part of the mud floor was occupied by a raised platform. In the centre of the wall opposite the door was a little alcove where stood a picture of the Madonna and the infant Christ in

gaudy blue and gold. Furniture there was none
except a wicker basket turned bottom upwards to
serve as a table. For a while the corporal stood
leaning against the wall chatting with the shepherd.
Nicholaïdes and Graham used the interval to stack
their rifles in the corner, unfasten their belts and
those bandoliers that had galled their shoulders
for ten weary hours, and then flung themselves
down on the sheepskins which their host had
spread for them on the platform.

Graham had fallen asleep, when he was roused
by the voice of the old man beside him talking to
Nicholaïdes. The host was sitting on the floor in
tailor fashion, pouring some clear liquid from a
large bottle cased in wicker into little tumblers.
With a movement full of gracious dignity he
handed a glass to Graham and another to
Nicholaïdes, and then he gave the toast, solemnly
and with a touch of pathos in his tone. Graham
felt himself checked, rebuked as it were. The
simple courtesy had nothing of triviality in it.
The custom-staled clinking of glasses which an
Englishman performs with a wink at his own folly,
or a *gauche* show of reluctance, while he leans
back in his chair, left the host still grave and
dignified. He did not seem to feel the traditional
ceremony an inadequate vehicle to convey his
welcome. He was glad to see the young soldiers,
he wished them health and success, he would touch
glasses with them in the name of good fellowship.
He chose the well-worn phrase, the conventional

gesture, he was sincere in his simplicity, convincing in his observance of custom. The artless ritual retained the dignity of those things which criticism has not breathed upon.

The spell of this welcome was working on Graham. The sheepskin seemed luxuriously hospitable, the room homely and familiar, with its lamp that shed orange light and brown shadow, for in the dimness one thought only of the sparse radiance, incurious of the foreign things it might reveal. The little room grew catholic, and the old woman busied over the fire upon the floor might speak in Ersc or Gaelic, or in the language of Rembrandt's models. And to Graham's ears, while the two Greeks talked, came a charmed murmur of familiar words with a burden of Homeric memories.

It was Nicholaïdes who called him back from his dream, addressing him in English. "He wants me to tell you that he has only a little house, and he is poor, but he will do his best to entertain us;" and while the strange language was spoken, the old man watched the two faces intently, eager to learn how his message would be received. He seemed more than satisfied with the answer, and filled his guests' glasses again with *ouso*, and then went to prepare supper. It was a plentiful meal of coarse food that he set before them, apologising again for his poverty. There were hard-boiled eggs, dyed crimson, a relic of Easter, black bread too, with roast lamb killed to celebrate the close of Lent. During the meal he left the room, but came back for a talk with the strangers when their wants were satisfied.

He brought a supply of rugs with him for the strangers, and threw them down with a kindly contempt. As for himself, he said, he never used such things. He could not sleep under a roof, he went out every night on to the hillside. The clear air of the mountains—it was that which made him hale and hardy. He was seventy-three years of age, and never had a day's illness. But he knew that townsmen liked to sleep in houses. He found that out a month ago in Athens. He had gone down to see the committee of the Ethnikè Hetairia. He wanted to organise a band of irregulars from Domoko to go and fight at the frontier. In '78 he had been captain of such a band, and many a time before he had led revolts against the Turks. They thought him too old for the work this time. It was a cruel insult—but still, they were very kind to him. A young fellow from the University took him over the Acropolis and the Museum, and they gave him quarters in a splendid hotel. Well, when night came he took his sheepskin cloak and lay down in the courtyard, but the proprietor came and explained that he ought to be in his bedroom. Ha! ha! he tried it for an hour, but he crept out again and dodged that proprietor and slept outside after all. He supposed people could get used to sleeping indoors if they did it all their lives. It's odd what one *can* get used to, if one tries.

"So you were a Turkish subject once," said Nicholaïdes, with something of that nervous curiosity akin to terror which a Greek of the towns displays at the bare mention of the Turk.

"Yes," said old Alexi after a pause, and then his face lit up with a look of pride that was almost merriment. "Do you see the ceiling?" and he pointed to a flat roofing of wicker-work which covered the spaces between the rafters. "Well, I built that the last year that the Turks were here. My daughter was fifteen then, and a tall, well-grown girl—eh, mother?" and he nodded to the old woman who had joined the group, and was squatting quietly on the floor, looking proudly into her husband's face.

"And one day a Turkish sergeant came to my house with three of his men. In they came, with their rifles, as insolent as could be, and called for lamb and *ouso*, and they sat here drinking till the evening, and called me 'Giaour,' and 'dog of a Greek,' and as they went away the little one came home. 'She's just the sort the Pasha likes,' said the sergeant. Well, I knew what that meant, so I worked all night and built that roof, and next morning I took my wife and my daughter up, and pulled the ladder after me.

"Sure enough about the same time in the morning they came again, swaggering into the room, the sergeant with five men this time. But they just looked about them and saw the muzzle of my rifle pointing through the wicker-work. Ha, ha!"

E

he chuckled to himself and drained his glass, "but this time they said, 'Good-day, Alexi,' as meek as could be, and went out the way they came in."

By this the old woman had begun toying with her husband's hands as if she would convey some hint to him, but he released himself and grasped hers playfully. Then she spoke: "The strangers have been walking all day, Alexi; they are tired, we must let them sleep." Nicholaïdes protested, but the old man, ever courteous, rose as if to go; then he sat down again, excusing himself for a few minutes longer.

"I shall be busy with the sheep very early next morning as soon as it is light. I shall not see you again, but the wife will look after you." And then he seemed to hesitate. At last he ventured to ask the names of his guests. It was a breach of antique etiquette, which forbids such questions until the strangers are about to depart, but then the old man would not be there to speed them on their way, and take toll of them in the currency of curiosity in payment for his hospitality. It was not about Nicholaïdes that he was most eager to inform himself—a handsome gentleman of leisure, who carried his forty years with the air of a young man of twenty-five—a man of pleasure who spent his summers in the islands and his winters in Athens, whose father had been a pushing merchant in New York, who left a competence to his indolent son which sufficed for his easy bachelor life— no, there was nothing here to stimulate curiosity;

but the other was a Frank, a foreigner, and old Alexi had never talked with one before.

"Ask him from what country he comes," he said to Nicholaïdes.

Graham startled him by answering in Greek.

"From England!" exclaimed the old man. "*Kala!*"[1] He seemed delighted. Was it not nearly the furthest point from which a stranger could come?

"Then you must live in London?"

It was a damper to his spirits to learn that his guest did not come from London after all. He could hardly understand it.

"But you came through London on your way here?"

"Yes."

"They told me in Athens that several of the London papers were Philhellenic."

"Yes, there's great sympathy for Greece in England."

"And in London too?" asked Alexi anxiously.

"Yes, in London too."

"*Kala!*" said Alexi again with unutterable satisfaction; and Graham thought of the current cant about the responsibility of the Press. So some obscure scribbler in Fleet Street could influence even the Ethnikè Hetairia, and give a fillip to an old insurgent in the remotest hamlet of Thessaly!

Alexi was thoughtful for awhile. "Can you write Greek?" said he at length.

[1] Κάλα : Capital!

" Ancient Greek," answered Graham.

Alexi looked puzzled.

" You see, we all learn it in the universities in England."

"*Kala!*" said Alexi once more, beaming with gratified patriotism, and then he begged his guest to write something by which he might remember him in years to come. It was a quaint request, but Graham's heart had warmed towards the brave old man. He took a card from his pocket-book and wrote on the back with great deliberation, trying, as best he could, to modernise his school-room Greek, and then he handed it to Alexi, inscribed with a few words of thanks for his enter-tainment, a prayer for the success of Greece in the war, and, at Nicholaïdes' suggestion, a sentence explaining that he was an English volunteer in the Philhellenic Legion.

Alexi spelled it out with difficulty ; some of the words puzzled him, and Graham had to explain their meaning through Nicholaïdes. Then holding the card under the lamp, the old man noticed the name and address in "Frankish" print on the other side. "Ask him to write that in Greek," said he to Nicholaïdes, and when that was done, with another comprehensive "*Kala!*" he grasped the strangers' hands and went out to sleep at the sign of the stars, among his flocks, wrapped in his sheepskin cloak. And the cold wind from the mountains blew round him and brought him happy dreams, till he fancied that he had killed the very Turkish sergeant who had coveted his daughter—nay, that he had brought the head to a stranger from London who had watched his prowess, and would write about it in those English Philhellenic papers.

CHAPTER V

OBITER DICTA

As for Graham, it was the rhythm of marching feet which rang in his ears when the little room was dark and silent. The tyrannical cadence possessed his very blood, his pulse seemed to beat to that weary tune of "left—right—left—right," his thoughts jolted to its measure, his recollections swung themselves before him with a sort of military jerk. It deadens the brain, it dulls the imagination, it dominates the ears, more persistent than the throbbing of the screw, the swaying of the vessel which haunt the seafarer during his first day on land. Graham could think only of the march, the faces of his comrades came before him with a see-saw motion, Coletti—Émile—left—right—Schweitzer—Berliner—left—right. And so in fancy he swung again along the road from Lamia. The green-uniformed company jerked its way over the moors like a caterpillar on a leaf—a long living thing which moves in ripples and rhythms up and down with its many feet. Only the dust-cloud which circled about them went freely, with graceful curves and irregular impulses.

At first they had combated the monotonous pulsing with music. The metre of their going acquired a meaning when one sang to it. Émile, and Coletti, and another Frenchman named Érin started the *Marseillaise*, and the Berliner retorted with *Die Wacht am Rhein*, and Graham joined impartially in both, and then came the familiar airs that recalled his student days in Germany, when the Schweitzer led off with *Vivat Academia* and *Es zogen drei Burschen*. All this was in the first hour of the march, when everybody trod lightly and the men squared their shoulders and straightened their backs in the pride of carrying arms. And when they were tired of their singing they fell to talk. Ferrari, the sub-lieutenant, walked beside the front rank chatting amiably. He had served in the Italian navy, had held a commission in the Argentine army, and had been through the civil war in Chili. He talked very loudly and bravely, and bragged in very shameless Italian-French sounding all his final consonants; " C'es*t* vrai, ça mes garçons," he would say to emphasise his tale, and to mark where one lie ended and another began.

But the talk soon ran to the future, and the enemy they were marching to meet, these sixteen men treading a road that had seen the advances and retreats of Crusader and Venetian, of Philhellene and Insurgent for four hundred years. They were an item in an army that still waged its secular campaign, a ripple in a Christian tide that ebbed and flowed for ever.   And the enemy too was the same.   " See that pistol, boys?   Pfui!   I shoot myself so, if I fall into the hands of the Turks, wounded or whole.   Don't you trust them.   I love my life as well as another, but I won't trust it to a Turk.   If you 'scape with a whole skin you'll lose your honour, and the odds are that your nose and ears 'll go with it.   My good pistol, you may have to do me that service yet!   Dogs of Turks that they are!   They go over a battlefield and mutilate the dead, and burn the living in petroleum.   Holy Madonna! if I were God I'd court-martial the lot of 'em and the blessed Gabriel should give the word, Ready—present—fire—and all the angels should shoot 'em down—So!" and he fired his revolver into the air—" if I were God."

This effort of imagination seemed to fatigue him. The afternoon sun went through the sky, the very heavens seemed to swoon about him, his outline was lost, he overflowed in liquid fire.   But the tramp of the little company rang out inexorably, left—right—left—right, and the sweat poured from their brows and their *képis* cut cruel circles round their heads.

" Comme il fai*t* chau*d*," exclaimed Ferrari, and then an inspiration visited him.   He wriggled out of his haversack, and handed it to Graham.   " Here, carry that, it's heavy and I'm hot."   Graham shrugged his shoulders and then loaded them. The interests of discipline seemed to require it, but he turned round to the Frenchmen and said slowly in a loud voice—"I begin to understand the Italian reverses in Abyssinia," and then to Ferrari—"You were in Abyssinia too, sir, were you not?"

"Abyssinie? Moi? Non," came the answer, and two minutes later the sub-lieutenant jumped on to the back of a cart which the company overtook.

"Lieutenant God mounts his chariot," exclaimed Érin; "ah! 'if I were God!'"

And then it was Coletti whom Graham saw, boiling with rage against these "Italian vermin." He wouldn't serve under that fellow. He would sew a Union Jack on his sleeve to show to what nation he belonged, he'd fling off his uniform coat, make knickerbockers of his trousers, when he got to Pharsala, and fight with the Andarti. "That's a free life, my dear friend; you go where you please, fight when you please and as you please, and by God, you are respected."

"But a uniform is some protection after all," Graham had objected, "a *franc-tireur* is liable to be shot if he's taken prisoner."

"The Turks shoot all their prisoners. No, no, you'll come with me, dear friend, we'll fight like volunteers and not like conscripts."

"Halte!" cried Lieutenant Chanteloup. "Ten minutes' rest in every hour is the rule in the French army."

The moor had come to an end, and they were at the base of the hills. A little streamlet trickled across the road, and a band of fugitives had camped beside it. The lean horses were unharnessed and grazed mechanically. Three ducks in a basket had smelt the water and were struggling to escape. Now a neck, now a foot, and now a wing was thrust through the wicker. The peasants sat round, careless of the din, leaden of aspect; an old man was carving a doll for a little four-year-old who stood at his knee clasping a rag, which had done duty hitherto. She looked critically at the new treasure, and then dangled the rag with an air of passionate fidelity, as if to assure it that it should be first favourite still. The old man chattered contentedly the while, glad to sit in sunlight busied with an easy task. His son, a stalwart fellow of forty or thereabout, was oiling a rifle; he got up to beg some cartridges when the soldiers halted. His wife bent over the fire making coffee, a baby was tied to her back in a shawl. The children were standing shyly in a line watching these men in green coats who talked some queer jargon that was not Greek. Coletti was singing, his rifle on the ground, his arms making eloquent gestures towards the children—

> " Regardez ça, regardez là,
>   Comment trouvez-vous tout ça ? "

was the rollicking chorus set to a merry catch.

" Blue eyes and brown eyes," said the song, "eyes for every taste," and he pointed to each shy little girl. The mother bent over the coffee muttering a single word again and again : " Zeitoun, Zeitoun," and she shook her head and sighed. It was the

Turkish name for Lamia. No one had used it for sixteen years, was it to be current once again?

> "There are blue eyes, there are brown,
> There are eyes for every taste,"

sang Coletti again, and the mother of the eyes said " Zeitoun."

And then as Graham ran over the history of the day, the throb of marching feet seemed to slacken. The company had left the road and went scrambling over a hill path that took them to the head of the Phourka Pass. The double column swayed and wavered, and soon all semblance of order was lost; men scrambled as they could, sometimes slinging their rifles over their shoulders, and clutching with their hands at clumps of grass, resting as they needed it, pushing on when an access of energy came over them. Coletti turned white and sick, overpowered by the sun, and all the while he cursed himself for a fool. Why the devil had he joined this Legion? He had been a free man in Crete and fared better. The Andarti didn't start a march in the heat of the day, at one o'clock precisely. He wouldn't follow these Italians an hour longer. "Go on," he said to Graham, "you'll regret it, and I'll say this, you're no true Englishman if you let yourself be bullied by a parcel of ignorant fools that are no more fit to be officers than I am to be a priest." And with that he flung himself on the grass and went to sleep, and one by one the stragglers filed past him, all eager to follow his

example, all carried onward by the brute tyranny
of that rhythm in their heads.

There was little to interest him on the road,
and Graham wondered how the time had passed.
Physical sensations had filled it—an aching at the
knees, and the hopeless weariness and weakness
that come of heat and dysentery. His companions
were silent now, gloomy and ill-tempered. They
hardly stopped to notice the quaint living creatures
that they passed, here a tortoise, and there a little
beetle that rolled a ball of dung before it three
times larger than itself. Even Grassini had left
talking of the Social Revolution. He dropped to
the rear like Coletti, forswearing officers who
marched across hills at mid-day.

Then it was Yorghi who provided a mild sensation
by firing at a partridge. They had reached the road
once more and fields of standing corn flanked it.
There were men here and there upon the road.
Once they had passed a convoy which carried some
military prisoners to the rear—three black-visaged
fellows in the dark-blue jackets and light trousers
of the infantry. They sat fettered in a cart, filthy
and unshaven. They had fired on their officers in
the camp at Pharsala, so Nicholaïdes gleaned from
the sergeant in charge, and had tried to raise a
mutiny. It was soon after this that the Berliner
had fired into the corn. Suddenly men started up
to right and left, three of them, and one came limping, holding a blood-stained handkerchief to his
thigh. There was a violent altercation. Nicholaïdes

translated to Graham, and Graham to the lieutenant. They had been sleeping in the corn, why
not? It was hot, was it not? "And you have
shot a man. Ah, there he is, the man who did it,"
and he gripped the Berliner's rifle. "Feel it! It's
still hot. A strange thing if one can't sleep peacefully by the roadside of an afternoon without
being shot at by one's comrades. What is he, that
fellow, an Italian?"

"A German," said Nicholaïdes.

"Germanos, h'm, that's natural. Why isn't he
with the Turks? He must be a spy;" and then he
blazed forth in a torrent of patriotic invective, as if
the unlucky Berliner had been the Kaiser himself—
that Wilhelm Pasha who seems to every Greek an
imperial incarnation of the Fiend. "It's the nature
of a Turk to shoot Christians, he can't help it, but
a Prussian is a dog who bites his own master's heels,
what with his fat Vismarki, and his firing on poor
Greek soldiers taking their siesta and harming
nobody. By St. George, I'd like to put a bullet
in his skull, though he is an emperor. Firing at a
fellow asleep in the corn! If I hadn't an aunt, now,
and a grandfather——"

"Where are you going?" asked Chanteloup.

"To Athens," said the soldier. "We shall be
out-flanked at Pharsala. The army is demoralised.
It's at Athens the great battle will be, under the
shadow of the Acropolis, or perhaps at Marathon.
And I must protect my aunt."

Chanteloup turned away, and called the

Schweitzer to him. The Schweitzer spoke two
mother-tongues. "Tell him that there must be no
more firing." And then he smiled and added—"We
are among the main army now; it's there in the
corn all round us."

"Ach was!" said the Berliner. "Das ist ja
un*j*ereimt! Habe gar nix davon *j*ewusst."

"And tell him," Chanteloup went on, "that the
next man who fires will be deprived of his rifle."

"Na nu," muttered the culprit. "Das ist was
anders. Dummes Zeug." It was the only threat
that would have touched him.

Then as it began again in Graham's memory,
that "everlasting demnition" see-saw, it was the
image of Érin that came uppermost. They had
passed on together after this incident. A quarter
of a mile further on they had found the Norwegian
resting by the roadside with his feet, bandages and
all, soaking in the ditch. He was reading a little
book, a homely German book almost square in
shape, with some tarnished gaiety of golden orna-
ment on its "elegant all-linen" cover. It was
Hauff's *Märchen*, and he sat wholly absorbed in
the company of dwarfs and princesses. He was
the only man in the squad who carried a book.
He had stuck to it when he threw everything else
away—blanket, and haversack, and boots—on the
retreat from Larissa. He rose as Érin and Graham
passed him, as thin, and weary, and patient as ever,
ready to stumble on as long as need be till he
could sit down and lose himself in Faery again.

Chanteloup overtook them soon. All pretence of disciplined marching was abandoned, and these three pushed on ahead, with the Norwegian at their heels. The lieutenant made some kind inquiry. Were they tired? They were surprised to find themselves quite fresh now. The heat was over. The sun was setting among the blue peaks of the mountains that doubled themselves in Lake Genias. The plain stretched to right and left untilled—utterly peaceful. A blue haze curtained off the valleys in the distance, and warm winds hurried past to cool themselves on the snowy brow of Othrys. They had seen the last of the sea, they had stopped guessing where Thermopylæ lay, they pitched camps for Xerxes no longer in the broad strath beneath them. They hurried on to their *rendezvous* with Pompey—and the Crown Prince.

"It's a repetition of the great *débâcle*," said Graham. " The Greeks have plunged into the war confident and unprepared. But there's one difference. They have no Gambetta."

" H'm," said Érin, " and not much courage either, I'm afraid. Do you know the story of the Last Cartridge?" And he went on to tell how a little band of infantry-men had defended a country house for hours against regiments of Prussians, snatching ammunition from the dead besiegers. His own uncle had been one of them. And all the way to Domoko he talked briskly and cheerfully. Chanteloup listened attentively, and Érin spoke with some pride and respect, yet withal familiarly, to his

officer, a fellow-Frenchman who shared the same
traditions.   Now he would tell of his work as an
engineer in Madagascar, or again how he had kept
himself for a year as a travelling mechanic in Egypt,
mending engines for the Arabs and the Fellahs up
and down the Delta.   When talk flagged he would
break into song, imitating Parisian street cries,
playing the gamin of the capital so cleverly and
gaily that even Chanteloup laughed, grave aristo-
crat and Catholic though he was.   And so these
four had reached Domoko an hour before the last
straggler of the company appeared, the Frenchman
merrily resolute, the Norwegian doggedly facing
his work, trudging along silent, vacant, but untiring.

And then Graham began to see visions, half
asleep in the shepherd's cottage.   He saw the
mountains like a flock of sheep filing before him,
extravagantly beautiful, now Alpine, now tropical,
and then the little hills skipped like lambs and
passed into a dream ; the pulse of marching died
away in his ears till at last he lay asleep in Alexi's
sheepskin rug.

CHAPTER VI

FINDS FATE AT HEAD-QUARTERS

PICTURE to yourself a strath which lies level and unbroken between two lines of hills. It is the place to which you would flee for temporary refuge after panic. The enemy is far to the north of you on the great plain of Larissa, but you have set a wall between yourself and him. Here your nervous soldiery may re-form, they will not strain their eyes to catch a glimpse of a line of red fezes advancing down some dusty road against them.

It is the plain of Pharsala. The little town lies at the base of the southern range of hills. Its one long street is full of soldiers. They lounge about in groups, besieging the few shops whose owners have not yet fled. A sentry stands on guard at each, and a peasant, distracted between fear and cupidity, serves his armed customers through the window. There is a fountain in the midst of the street, and some evzones kneel beside it washing the sheep's entrails that are to make their evening meal. You may see cavalrymen carrying a mutton chop to a dirty little shop where a dirtier peasant *chef* will grill it for the consideration of a penny.

They are large bearded men in great-coats and top-boots. Their uniforms fit them very ill, they have nothing of that dash and alertness which you associate with cavalry. Others you may see in the same green uniform but with rifles slung over their shoulders. They belong to the regiments for which the Government could not find mounts. Most picturesque in the motley crowd are the evzones, highlanders clad in the national costume. All of them wear pleated kilts of white linen, and shoes of red leather with raised peaks at the toes surmounted by a coquettish bobbin of red wool. Most of them have blue overcoats, but some carry sheepskins slung over their shoulders. The regulation head-gear is a red fez with a tassel, but you will see caps and *képis* of every pattern among them. They walk with the swift dog-trot of mountaineers, with bent knees and slouching back.

From the hills above the town you may hear an occasional bugle-note. The raw levies are being drilled in the cool of the evening, trained to march over uneven ground, to deploy in skirmishing order, to form in companies and half sections, to wheel with precision. They are veterans these men, they have been under fire at Vougasi, or Raveni, or Mati, and now they are learning the rudiments of drill. A train of carts is lumbering over the causeway that runs across the marshy plain between the village and railway station some three miles distant, half-way towards that bulwark of hills which shuts out the plain where the Turk is already master. They are laden with black bread, and sea-biscuits, and coarse salt cheese. From the other end of the town comes the bleating of a flock of sheep driven by a peasant and three evzones with a subaltern astride a donkey. And between the sheep and the provision train lies the army. One can almost feel it panting still like a frightened horse after its panic race. Its officers are trying to feed it into condition after its Lenten fast, for during all the fighting on the frontier no animal food was allowed. It was a holy war, men fed themselves on orthodoxy, and the lazy commissariat dreamed that life was one long Lent.

There are few signs of the pomp of war in this army. You will hear no note of music save the uncertain tremolo of an unskilful trumpeter, or the dispiriting wail of some evzone chanting a klephtic song, for the single military band that Greece possesses is kept busy in Athens playing the funeral march for officers fallen at the front. The men's uniforms are ill made, their colours are sombre, and even the officers make no display of bright plumes or gold lace. The soldiers who lounge about, dirty, unshaven, dispirited, are scarce cousins to the guardsman you have watched in Hyde Park or the cuirassier on the Boulevards. They do not flaunt their uniforms of dull green or sober blue as though they were a king's colours, the badge of honour and of chivalry. They wear them as the symbol that they have left for a time the liberty of

a civilian life. They carry their rifles as a plough-
boy shoulders a hoe.

It will scarce occur to you to single out the
officers from this demoralised mob. You may
have met a company marching through the town
changing its quarters, or escorting provisions. The
men walked in any order that pleased their fancy,
for the most part straggling along, solitary units
with no wish for comradeship or talk. Their
officer is with them somewhere among them, arguing with one or other of his men, allowing
himself to be addressed by his Christian name.
Men with two stars, or three, or one are to be met
with in the street, buying rice, or sugar, or socks, or
stragália, bargaining with the village hucksters,
haggling over prices like any of the rough privates
with whom they rub shoulders. No one salutes as
they stroll through the streets. If your Western
training impels you to raise your hand to your
képi, be sparing in your civilities. Deny them to
any spruce fellow with a shaven cheek and clean
linen. He came not honestly by these *things.
He is one of those who forced his way into the
train that left Larissa for Volo conveying the
women and the wounded. He has slept for a night
in a clean bed in a European hotel, while his men
were wandering without a leader over the weary
plain that stretches from Larissa to Pharsala. But
you will soon lose your awe for the man with the
sabre and stars, you will sit with him in the *café*, you
will find that he differs from his private only in this,

that his purse holds more money to pay for drinks, and he knows more languages in which to chatter. For in his degree he has wealth and education.

In a big house beside the Mosque the fate of this army is being decided. It is the head-quarters of the Crown Prince. Sentries stand at the gate and orderlies and *aides-de-camp* lounge in the courtyard. In a darkened room up-stairs the Prince is sitting. The French blinds are closed, the place has the aspect of an invalid's chamber. Its occupant rarely stirs outside. He is conscious of failure, he knows that defeat awaits him, he sits longing for a telegram from Athens which shall bring news of an armistice and relieve him of a task for which he is unfit. But the wire carries only curt messages from his father in Athens, bidding him decide on the spot as he thinks fit, leaving the destiny of the nation to this young man's discretion. The King is cooped up in his palace, an angry mob surges outside. His hopes are fixed on the little body-guard of naval officers from the warships which lie off Phalerum, waiting in his antechamber to escort him to the sea, if there be need of flight. He has no leisure to think of the beaten army in Thessaly, and the distracted prince at its head. And so Constantine sits patiently behind his shutters, listening fearfully to the steps of the messengers who come and go upon the stairs, and thinking of the demoralised army outside, ready to mutiny, and exact from him the penalty for its defeats.

A map is spread upon the table, and a little
officer is talking vehemently to him, pointing with
his finger to the range of hills north of Pharsala,
that screen that shuts out the Turk from view. It
is Captain Varatasi,[1] a professor in the military
school, who now commands the Philhellenic
Legion. He is a strange contrast to the Prince,
with his tall figure, his phlegmatic air, his listless
blue eyes, the receding chin and prominent ears, a
heavy face of the Romanoff cast, a degenerate type
of a race never famed for courage, for was not
even Peter the Great the veriest poltroon for all his
genius and his heroic physique? Varatasi is a
mere shadow of a man, standing scarcely five feet
three. The left shoulder is raised as if with a
perpetual shrug. The top-boots threaten to engulf
the meagre legs, and the sabre closely girt to the
spare waist seems almost too great a weight for
the slight figure to carry. But the head is large
and beautifully shaped, and the deep-set eyes
have a light that haunts you for ever. They are
mournful eyes, the eyes of a man who has dealt
all his life with inferiors, who despairs of their
frivolity and indolence, yet never relaxes his own
steady endeavour. The nose has an aquiline
curve, and the chin is pointed and protruding.
The lips under the slight reddish moustache are
thin and firmly set. It is a sensitive face with
a certain sad humour in it, and when the melancholy eyes meet yours and the mouth relaxes in a

[1] See Note A. *ad fin.*

smile that is half pity, half tenderness, you would call it beautiful. He was known in Athens before the war as the bravest officer in the army, and yet till this campaign he had never been under fire. The face has a magical ascendency in it which comes of self-restraint and self-respect, and these are the parents of bravery.

The Crown Prince crushed a telegram nervously in his hand, the telegram which threw the responsibility of the campaign upon his shoulders, he averted his eyes from Varatasi, and muttered, " I do not follow you." What did he want, this troublesome captain? An advance beyond that screen of hills? He dare not advance. The army was demoralised. It was eager to shoot him. The people had clamoured for war. They should have it. Was it not equally war whether he waged it to the north or the south? Victory he never could hope for. Europe must intervene. He had merely to keep his army together till she did so.[1]

" See," said Varatasi; " at Pharsala you may be outflanked both on left and right. Smolenski can only hold his own at Velestino. Edhem may easily hold him in check and still have men enough to advance on our right and our centre at once. Why not move your head-quarters to Tekké? The hills stretch away there to left and right, you could not well be outflanked, and at the worst you can still fall back on Pharsala. Trikkala was recaptured to-day, so that our rear is secure. And

[1] See Note B. *ad fin.*

if you fight here the hills behind you are useless, for the railway station is the crux of the position. You see it lies in the centre of the plain. The Turks could command it from the heights of Tekké with their artillery—so. You leave those heights undefended, inviting the enemy to plant his batteries there. Our artillery on the heights behind Pharsala could not touch an enemy seven miles away. If you mean to hold this position you will have to give battle in the plain. Edhem can bring up two men to your one, he can move his cavalry on level ground, and shell you from the heights. If you stay here you must choose between disaster or a shameful retreat whenever the enemy appears. Nothing could be plainer. Will your Highness look at the map?" and he pushed the plan towards the indifferent Constantine.

"I do not follow you. I see no special advantage in the position at Tekké. The army is not fit to advance. And as for the railway station, I entrusted it to you and your Legion. What do you think, colonel?" and he turned to one of his staff, an elegant personage who had won his position by the sword. He had used it with some dexterity to cut firewood at a royal picnic.

"I am of your Highness's opinion," he said. "You have stated the case admirably. The railway is doubtless safe in Captain Varatasi's charge."

"The army *must* advance if it is to regain morale," said Varatasi. "The Turks are still a day's march away, and we might be at Tekké before noon to-morrow. As for the railway station, two hundred men cannot hold it against an army. My contention is that Tekké is the key to the railway."

"Then you shall go to Tekké," said the Prince, rising, "and I will send some evzones to hold the hills."

And then Varatasi went out. As he mounted his horse at the doorstep wearily and awkwardly, the Prince's *aides-de-camp* smiled, and said "Good-evening" with a patronising air. Friday's *Asty* appeared with a reassuring official *communiqué*. The army at Pharsala was being rapidly re-organised, it said. The Crown Prince had full discretionary powers. He had chosen a position well-nigh impregnable, with a mountain chain behind him, and the heights in front were to be secured by a regiment of evzones assisted by the Foreign Legion under Captain Varatasi.

But one man riding in the darkness over the causeway towards the railway station, knew that disaster was impending. He foresaw another retreat, another blot on the honour of Hellas, another impotent plea of outflanking movements from the incapable commander of a demoralised army. His heart was heavy and bitter within him, and unconsciously he smiled that sad smile of pity and resignation which had become a habit with him. It must have been so that Pericles smiled, returning from the Agora in the first months of the Peloponnesian war.

CHAPTER VII

"ANOTHER Englishman for the company, sergeant," said the burly corporal, his mouth full of strange oaths and savoury soup. It was Graham, who had reached the bivouac of the English company of the Philhellenic Legion at last. Another march in the heat of the day had brought Lieutenant Chanteloup and his international squad to Pharsala. They had left Domoko after the mid-day meal, and at nightfall their straggling line had formed outside the little town where the Greek army lay encamped. Past the artillery park, where men were busy watering horses and entrenching batteries, past the hills where the infantry were drilling, and through the teeming crowd of armed men who thronged the village, the little company had marched, in perfect order, dressing its lines as precisely as the rough road would allow, ringing out its left—right, left—right on the cobble-stones with the mechanical regularity of clockwork; Chanteloup and Ferrari in front, Sergeant Baumgarten, the Berliner, walking beside his men. They

74

carried themselves with a certain pride of race, conscious that they represented the great military nations of Europe among the slip-shod soldiery of Greece.

The brief southern twilight had almost faded when they met Captain Varatasi at the entrance of the causeway which led from the village to the railway. It was Baumgarten who recognised him —the "*juter* braver Kerl" of whom he had spoken so often—and Graham who told Chanteloup that this little officer in artillery uniform was Commander of the Legion. He talked courteously with Chanteloup for a few minutes, inquiring into the route he had taken, the prospect of other French volunteers joining the Legion, and the like, and then he inquired as to the nationality of his men. "Are there any Englishmen among them?" said he, and Chanteloup introduced Graham.

"Do you speak French?" The few words were spoken with a perfect accent, in a musical voice which won Graham's heart at once.

"Mais oui, monsieur, un petit peu."

"Bien. You will find a score or so of your countrymen in the Legion under an admirable officer. Your company was the last to leave Larissa." A hint of sarcasm was in the compliment. "It shall be the rear-guard on the next retreat," he had almost added, but the instincts of a good officer restrained him. And he smiled sadly, and took his leave of the new-comers. He was in no mood for talk.

An hour's walk along the causeway brought the little company to the railway. Night had fallen, and a long line of bivouac fires stretched away towards the village and along the base of the hills for three miles to the west. And in the clear sky Orion shone out, watching the latter destiny of the people whose fancy had first given him a name and a history.

The wall of a big farmyard loomed through the darkness beside the road. Camp fires ran round it, and the glare of a huge bonfire came from within. It was the bivouac of the French into which Graham stumbled first. They had built clever little tents for themselves out of blankets stretched on poles. They were too busy welcoming Érin and Émile to give heed to Graham's questions. He passed on to the Germans. The man whom he addressed had just wrung the hands of Baumgarten and the Schweitzer, receiving them back as it were from the dead ; he put his hands on Graham's shoulders, and stared intently into his face. " Nein, ich kenne Sie nicht ; " Graham was not one of the company that had scattered in panic and fled, some of them to Volo, some to Athens, and some on the skirts of the main army to Pharsala. And then a friendly young German American led him into the farmyard to the English bivouac. They were decent fellows, he said, in the English company, he wished that he had joined it.

" Another Englishman for the company," said the corporal, and he flung down a great log beside the fire for Graham to sit upon, and ladled out a pannikin of soup for him from the great camp pot. There were ten or a dozen men seated round the fire, smoking their pipes, the others had already turned in and were lying rolled in their blankets on the straw round the walls. A grateful confusion of homelike sounds and smells overpowered Graham with their welcoming. He had not heard an English tongue since that miserable evening when he left London, and now the familiar Cockney accents filled his ears, brisk, cheerful, and kindly. Even the oaths that he heard all around him, exploding like shells on a battlefield, served to give him the home feeling. Here one seemed to be on easy terms with the mother tongue ; the slang, the vulgarisms, the quaint impure vowels rang delightfully national, blatantly English. And from across the fire where four men were seated apart from the rest came at times a rich flavour of the brogue.

" 'Ow's that for soup ? " said one of the men who sat on the ground by the fire smoking a clay pipe. He was not a conspicuously military figure with his rough beard and ragged flannel shirt. " I won't say that it's *pre*cisely wot I would give you if I was at 'ome in the Mansion 'Ouse, E. C., but what with ye wily Turk a-messin' round, and ye ancient Greek a-takin' to 'is 'eels and hinterruptin' my culinary hoperations, it's the best I can give you or any gent as comes to see me in the circumstances."

" Bein' soup, I call it most souperior, Uncle," said a tall young fellow known as Middle Cock.

He had a lofty air of Cockney impudence, and lived on easy terms with himself. He was one of the fraternity of "cocks," the "bloods" of the company. "I call it most souperior, and if this gent 'ere says anything different, w'y I saiy it's souperfluous."

"You dry up, Middle Cock," said the corporal; "nobody axed you for a 'armony, not but wot we'll be glad to 'ear you w'en this gent 'as 'ad 'is soup, an' finished 'is dessert and 'is champagne."

"'Ave a little cold venison," said Middle Cock, passing a piece of mutton to Graham; "sorry we 'aven't any truffles in the larder just now, but you should 'ave let us know you was a-comin'."

Graham thanked him, praised "Uncle's" soup, but declared himself satisfied, and lit his pipe with a chip from the fire. Middle Cock continued to do the honours.

"Well, and 'ow 'ave they treated *you* since you came out 'ere?"

"Oh! I give them credit for good intentions. We've fared better than their own men, I fancy."

"H'm. You'll be singing a different tune before long. You needn't expect to dine off roast beef and sleep on a feather bed in the Foreign Legion. You'll be 'eartily sick of the 'ole —— business precious soon, I can tell you."

"Oh!" said Graham, laughing, "I didn't come out expecting a picnic."

"Well, I'm free to tell you or any man what I think of ye ancient Greek," retorted Middle

Cock. " They're a parcel o' damn dirty ungrateful cowards. Though I will say this, that Captain Very-tassy's a real good sort. But there ain't many like 'im, and I wish I was well out o' their God-forsaken country. Here's me and my mates flung up our work to come and fight for them, and the Committee in London promises us our rations and paiy same as in the English army, and they paiys us in paiper and feeds us on bread and mutton, and not too much of that, and just when it suits them, and it's a wonder we're alive after it all——" And so he ran on, but in language on whose vigour this poor report is a sorry libel. His imagination had never grasped what hardships any war must entail, and especially a war conducted by the bankrupt and demoralised Government of a fourth-rate Power. Indifferent to the cause for which he was fighting, and careless of the shame and misery of soldier and peasant around him, he converted every trifling inconvenience into a personal insult, and saw a breach of faith in every breakdown of a distracted commissariat that served out yesterday's rations to-morrow.

" I've been doing a think," said Uncle; " I'm not much of a 'and at that, but this is 'ow I figgers things out."

" Come along, Uncle," interrupted Middle Cock, " now we shan't be long."

" Well, this is 'ow it is. I'm an admirer of ye wily Turk, that's wot I am, and I don't know wot I'm doing 'ere. *I* ain't got no quarrel with

'im, no'ow. I'm damned if I want to fight him.
I'd embrace 'im like a brother—bless 'im. 'E's a
man, 'e is. I don't want to shoot 'im. W'y I'd
fall upon 'is neck and kiss 'im."

"I'm ashaimed of you, Uncle," said a little
yellow-haired fellow named Simson, who had been
lying on the ground so far without joining in the
discussion. He sat up now, carefully placing a
letter which he had been reading by the firelight
into a pocket he had cut in the lining of his
uniform. "I'm ashaimed of you, Uncle, talkin' of
goin' about kissin' Turks."

"'E'd look out for a juicier morsel than Uncle,
would ye wily Turk," interrupted Middle Cock.

"I don't saiy that *I*'m pertikler nuts on ye
ancient Greek, but I'll go with any man that's
fightin' Turks. I don't care a tuppenny damn for
Greece, but I'm not goin' to sit by and watch the
Turk outragin' women an' massacrin' Armenians,
an' I'll go with any one who's got the spunk to
stand up to 'im ; whether 'e's a Roossian, or a
Proosian, or a Greek, or a Hitalian, or whatever he
is, 'e's good enough for me."

"He's a brave man is the Turk. I love him
like a brother," answered the Philhellene known
as Uncle, puffing great clouds from his cutty clay,
and twinkling humorously between each pull,
"and as for his 'arems and all that, w'y I wish I
'ad one myself. 'E's no worse than an Englishman
any day. W'y look at them Dooks, they all keeps
as many as they wants, and nobody says nothink."

"Devil take 'em both, that's my motto," said Middle Cock. "I only hope I'll be 'ome in time for the Jubilee. June 22, ain't it? It's time I was ordering my guinea stall seat. A pot of double X, that's what 'd suit me down to the ground—eh, Uncle?"

"You shut up, Middle Cock, I can't stand it. W'y it's a month since I tasted English beer. Don't you make a fellow's mouth water. You make me wish I was in London "—and he gazed for a while into the fire, raking the embers together with his bayonet. Then he seemed to recover his wonted gaiety. He began to shake with laughter. "Well, if ever I get out of this God-forsaken country, and back in London again, I'll cut a dash, you bet. W'y, the girls 'll think I'm a guardsman or somethink. I saiy,, Middle Cock, do you remember those little girls in Athens? When we was goin' into the English Church on Easter Sunday—the daiy we left Athens. 'I don't like them *quite* as much as the Life Guards,' says she. Lor', didn't I stick out my chest same as an old pouter pigeon, and stalk up the haisle, a-clinking my side-arms against the pews. Smart little thing she was, too."

"Well, are we to have a sing-song to-night, in honour of this auspicious occasion?" said the corporal, whose proudest distinction was to be known as "Big Cock." "If you're willing, gentlemen, I moves that Uncle takes the chair."

"'Ear, 'ear," said everybody.

G

"Unaccustomed as I am to public speaking," said Uncle, " I expex every man to support me in calling on Isinglass for *The Balaklava Charge.*"

"'Ear, 'ear. Good old Isinglass," said everybody again, and the owner of that nickname rose with great promptitude, a tall, loosely-knit man with a red beard and many interesting diseases. He had seen service in India, and he sang in the approved canteen manner, which has more resemblance to reciting than to singing. The ditty went with extraordinary patriotic verve, the gaunt figure working its long arms with soldier-like regularity, swung through the pantomime with an air of devil-may-care bravery. "We're rough fellows," he seemed to say—"but in certain sitiwations we comes out strong;" and he looked so rough that one believed the rest. The whole performance was wonderfully convincing. Isinglass in his uniform beside the camp fire, venting his soldierly bombast, seemed somehow to appropriate the glory that belongs to "Cardigan the fearless." There was such an obvious absence of art in his story that one fancied it was truth.

Then came *Comrades, Soldiers of the Queen,* and *The Gallant Fusiliers.* At home they were posting a copy of the Foreign Enlistment Act on every church door, but here in Thessaly her Majesty's faithful subjects, proscribed in that rather wordy document, were singing loyal songs in her honour. Half of the company had worn her colours at some stage in their eventful careers, and they carried with them the old traditions, the old ballads they had sung in camp at Aldershot or on the march in Egypt. They forgot that King George existed, the name of Hellas had no music for them, the Greek army was nothing to them but an ill-organised commissariat department which miserably failed to satisfy their wants.

O'Brian had given the *Cruiskeen Lawn* with inimitable sentiment, Uncle had extorted *Ye Banks and Braes* from Graham, the Cockneys had sung *God save the Queen* while the Irishmen sat silent with pursed lips, trying to look picturesquely disloyal, and then the company broke up. The " Cocks " and " Uncle " still sat by the fire playing cards, and Graham was about to ask them where he should dispose himself for the night, when Simson came up to him, the yellow-haired lad who had rebuked Uncle for his pro-Turkish sentiments. " 'Ere," said he, " I'm the smallest chap in the company, and I've got two blankets over there ; suppose you come into partnership with me, eh ? Keep us both warmer you know. 'Ave a good look at me, now ; I won't take up much room, will I ? "

Graham thanked him, and soon they were snugly bestowed on the straw under the wall. Their haversacks served them for pillows and they wrapped a pair of service blankets tightly round them. Their rifles and bayonets lay at their side. They had only to buckle their belts and tighten their boot-laces if an alarm should come in the night.

"Wonder what they're doing at 'ome to-night," said Simson, when these few preparations were completed. " My word, won't they be buying up all the late *Stars* to get the news about us. Wonder 'ow the cricketing scores is going on. I saiy, Smith, I wonder 'ow Ranji's coming on with 'is thousand, eh ? "

" Don't know," said Smith, a tall athletic fellow who slept beside Simson. He had been in the artillery, but a football club had bought him out. The season was over and he had no work to keep him in England, his old love of war had asserted itself, and the Volunteer Committee had accepted him gladly when he offered himself for service in Greece. " Don't know. I'm thinkin' of my best girl. Poor old girl, I expect she's 'avin' a bad time with me out 'ere."

"'Ad a letter from my tart to-day," said Simson; "she wants me to come 'ome."

" It's about time we was droppin' off to sleep," said Smith. There was something soldierly in the way he closured the discussion.

And then a silence fell upon the farm-yard. The plain of Pharsala lay all about it, a background waiting unmoved for human figures to come and go upon it, eternally passive, stolid beneath the hurtling of conquests. And now the army was stretched in sleep, horizontal between the hills. The Enipeus ran on between its muddy banks even as it ran when Pompey slept beside them. His legionaries had lit camp fires on the very acre where the embers kindled by English hands now smouldered, and in that Roman army there were volunteers who longed for silence and the dark, vexed by the talk of their rude companions. The twang of the Cockneys still echoed in Graham's ears, as he lay trying to recall Catullus' verses :—

> Chommoda dicebat si quando commoda vellet
> Dicere et insidias Arrius hinsidias
> Et tum mirifice sperabat se esse locutum
> Cum quantum dixerat hinsidias.

And then he fell to thinking of Lucan and of Pharsala—Pharsala forever the burial-place of freedom, the gloomy marsh where force engulfs the right, with a cynicism in the very soil of it, a primeval irony that waits for armies.

" Victrix causa deis placuit, sed victa——" but he could not complete the line. He thought of the degraded army in the village behind him.

The Legion slept at last, Simson dreaming of his letter, Smith thinking of his sweetheart at home, Varatasi weary from his fight with destiny, Uncle and Middle Cock longing for English beer, Graham looking for Cato at the end of Lucan's line. A warm wind swept over them all, and brought rain-clouds with it. The fading of the stars was near when rain began to fall. It came in great round drops. They fell upon the upturned faces of the sleepers with a warm caress. It felt good to be awake, the joy of sentience crept vaguely into the Legion's dreams. The dim time of unconsciousness began to pass. The rain-drops were very warm, they kissed the cheek, they wheedled the dead nerves awake again. There was a fascination in counting the drops,—one—two—and three ; how warm and soft they were !

"You there, Simson?" said Smith, and then Graham sat up and looked about him. In the grey morning light he could see a figure crouching over the camp fire.

" Well, if that young fool ain't readin' his girl's letter again," said Smith. " 'E won't stay 'ere much longer, what'll you bet ? "

It *was* Simson, reading and re-reading, and as he read his eyes grew dim and he muttered, " Poor little girl," and then, " I'm a God-damn brute." This was the letter :—

"—— *Road,*
"*London, E.*
"GOOD FRIDAY, 6, iv. '97.

" MY DARLING JACK,

" It's three long weeks since I saw you. Oh ! Jack, do you know what that means to me ? I have never been without you before, and now—I don't know how I can write it—perhaps it'll be months and years till I see you again. But it's wrong of me to write like that, you said you were going to fight for Liberty, and then perhaps there won't be a war at all. It said in the *Daily Telegraph* that the raid of the insurgents was not a *casus belli*. Dear lazy old Jack, do you know what that means ? Do you remember when old Smithers thrashed you for not knowing your ' phrases from foreign languages,' and I cried, and that spiteful Bella Martin screamed out, ' Please, sir, here's Annie Wells took bad'? That was six years ago, Jack, when we were in the Ex-Sixth. Dear me! I'm beginning to feel quite old. That reminds me, Jack, you must be back for my twentieth birthday. It wouldn't be like a birthday at all unless you came in on your way to your work, and wished me many happy returns, and gave me the first kiss of the year. Oh! Jack, you'll promise me that, won't you?

"I saw your father on Monday. He seemed very old and miserable ; he said he had scarcely slept since you went away. He talked a lot about your mother. I think he is always miserable about this time of year, because she died then. He said he knew he ought to put a memorial notice in the papers, but he hadn't the heart to do anything since you went away. Oh! Jack, won't you come home for *his* sake? I know you thought it your duty to go, but he won't live long if you are killed. I can't bear to think of it. Yes, I do think of it, but I *know* you won't be killed.

"I'm going to tell you a secret, but you must promise faithfully not to tell any one. Oh dear me! You aren't here to promise that ; how stupid I am! Well, after I saw your father I went straight off to the *Telegraph* office, and put in this notice :—

' *In loving remembrance of my dear friend Agnes Simson, who passed to her rest April* 3, 1895.
Blessed are the dead that die in the Lord.
Inserted by a loving friend.'

"I don't want your father ever to know who did it, but I think he will be pleased, don't you?

"You used to like my writing, but I can't write nicely on this foreign paper.

"I've got a new blouse for Sundays, It's pink, because you always like me best in pink.

"Tom Williams has been very attentive since you went. He has often been round to see me. He came yesterday evening to take me for a walk in the Park. He said I was getting pale with staying indoors, and reading newspapers. But I hadn't the heart to go out with him. Father said I ought to take up with a hard-working steady fellow like Tom. Oh! I was angry with him for that! Oh, Jack, the horrid things people are saying about you —you wouldn't believe! My own dear Jack, *I* trust you, but oh! why did you ever go away?

"Father is wanting me to go in for a place as Ex-P.T. in Canterbury. The pay is £5 a year more than I get here, but I won't go. I'll be here in the same old place waiting for you when you come home.

"Such a queer thing happened in school on Monday. I was teaching geography to the Third Standard. I asked them what Greece was famous for. A boy said 'currants,' and then a little tot held up her hand and sang out, 'Please, ma'am, volunteers.' Oh! Jack, if you could have seen me blush! I put up the duster to my face, and the chalk all got into my mouth.

"I dreamt that you were back last night, and just

didn't I hug you, and smother you with kisses.
Oh! why did you go and run into danger? I want
to make you so happy, Jack. Don't you care about
it? Don't you want my love?

"I must stop now. There is only one post to-
day, and I didn't know, or I would have written
sooner.

"Good-bye, dear, *dear* Jack, think of me every
night, and kiss my photo, and I will kiss yours.
Oh! why did I let you go? I ought to have held
you in my arms till the train went without you.

"Your loving sweetheart,

· "ANNIE.

"P.S.—I just lie in bed at night and stretch out
my arms, and pray to you to come back.

"P.S.—How is Mr. Smith? Give him my kind
regards, and tell him from me to look after you.

"I only got such a short note from you this week.
Do write soon and tell me everything—*everything.*"

CHAPTER VIII

A CHAPTER OF CONTRASTS

IT was a life of contrasts which began for Graham with his first morning in camp at Pharsala. The night was a time of fear and uncertainty. Men slept in uniform with their arms at their side, but by day one almost forgot that an enemy lay beyond those hills within a day's march of the railway station. The sun was already up, men were going about half dressed talking gaily, lighting fires, and boiling water when Graham awoke from his second sleep. Middle Cock handed him a tin of coffee flavoured with cognac, and then he strolled over to the fire.

"Who's for Pharsala?" the corporal inquired, and a party was formed to stroll into the village to buy coffee, and cognac, and tobacco. Another group was standing round a big Ulsterman with a melancholy countenance, who had just come in from head-quarters, where he had been imprisoned the night before. A sentry had challenged him, and knowing no Greek he had knocked him down. The guard knew no English, and therefore arrested him. They had given him wine thereafter, and patted him on the shoulder with the kindly assurance, "Johnnie good, Johnnie bono," but he refused to be comforted, and his sympathisers considered it a mighty scandal that an Englishman could not knock down Greek sentries with impunity.

"Who says a bathe?" was another cry, and Graham, with the dust of two days' marching upon him, joined himself gladly to a tall red-haired lad named Morgan, who promised to lead him to a deep river pool half-a-mile away.

"Take your rifles with you," said the sergeant as they set out, "there may be an alarm any moment."

Morgan had been in Texas, had shot his man in a saloon; his people had a "place" in Berkshire, and as the war proceeded they seemed to buy up half the county. He entertained Graham with genial superlatives during their walk; he hunted keenly for larks' nests whenever a bird shot up through the clear morning air into the brilliant sky; he had the second-best collection of eggs in England; he was the crack shot of the company, and went about plotting murder against the old bull-frogs that croaked along the bank. Finding by chance that Graham had studied in Oxford he recollected that he was a Hertford man. Then he was the youngest private in the Legion, his age was nineteen, and he had left three beautiful maidens weeping in the old country. Morgan said

many things, and Graham enjoyed his bathe.   He
added a new type to his portrait gallery of Philhellenes.   Some days after this, when a mail came
in for the Legion, it was Graham's duty to hand
round the letters.   He noted the Ramsgate post-
mark on one addressed to Morgan in an old-
fashioned feminine hand.   He saw a vision of a
seaside boarding-house and a widow who had
known better days, and then of little Master
Morgan, a likable cheeky youngster, patronised
by the shady lodgers, smoking the ends of their
cigars, appropriating their tall stories, devouring
the shilling shockers which they left behind.   He
was the contribution of the Whitsuntide tripper
to the cause of Hellenism.

The sun was high in the sky, a white disk amid
vapour, when Graham sauntered back to camp.
Wreaths of mist fluttered over the plain as a gentle
wind blew down among them between the hills,
Kassidiari to the south with its gaunt brown rocks,
Tekké to the north with its green slopes and
rounded hollows.   The Legion was taking its
siesta, and those who were still awake sat mending
their uniforms or talking idly.   Graham joined the
little knot of men who lay chatting on the verandah
of the farm-house.   There was Svendsen, a Danish
lieutenant, Goldoni, a jolly dark-haired Italian
private, who was holding forth about Zola, and a
tall Italian named Montalto, with mutton-chop
whiskers and the mouth of a jockey, who looked
like the caricatures of John Bull in *Il Papagallo*,

cultivated phlegm, talked of *le sport*, and carried a
pocket Dante, for that too was an English taste.
He was an officer in the navy who had come out
to Greece on furlough and incognito. A couple of
Greeks who belonged to the English company
completed the little party. They were the genteel
faction in the Legion.

It was a *causerie* on French literature at which
Graham assisted. Goldoni raved of Zola, and
Montalto championed morality. Mavromichali,
the younger Greek, a handsome fellow of twenty
or thereabouts, with a keen intellectual profile and
an air of vigour and quiet self-confidence, praised
La Débâcle. Palli, his friend, an older man with
dreamy eyes and disdainful lips, could not stomach
the coarseness of the realist, he was all for Pierre
Loti. He raved of *Aziyadé* and *Le Mariage*.
Graham talked of *Pêcheur d'Islande*, and Montalto
joined him in praise of its mysterious sea-scapes,
its primitive fisherfolk, its atmosphere of salt, and
storm, and fog. And then the artillery galloped
past, rumbling its guns and caissons over the road
to Trikkala.

"On va se battre là bas, aujourd'hui," said
Montalto.

"O la la," exclaimed Goldoni, "et nous autres,
nous causons littérature en face des Turcs."

Then came Speropoulo, Varatasi's lieutenant,
with orders that every company must be ready to
march in an hour's time.

"Another retreat," said Svendsen.

"Withdraw that offensive expression," said Palli with much gravity. "You should say a strategic concentration in the rear."

Mavromichali whistled a few bars of Wagner.

"That's from the *Flying Dane*, isn't it?" said he.

Goldoni rose and hesitated a moment, as if preparing a joke. "I'm thinking of the correct newspaper phrase," he said. "'His Royal Highness the Crown Prince placed himself as usual at the head of his troops.' How will that do?"

Inside the courtyard the English company were preparing to roast a sheep for dinner. It was skinned already and beheaded, and its legs were tied to a long pole. Middle Cock and Simson were carrying it up and down with the most solemn air they could command, while Uncle squatted on the ground, drumming on an empty biscuit tin with an old bone, and droning out the "Dead March" in *Saul*. The Ulsterman was flinging logs upon the fire and growling at the tomfoolery of the Cockneys.

"We're to be ready to march in an hour's time," said Graham.

"Wot the deuce is hup now?" asked Simson.

"Only another retreat, I suppose."

"Well, I'm blowed," was Uncle's sententious comment.

"Damned if I'll leave this old sheep before I've 'ad my dinner," said Middle Cock.

"Well, if I'd 'a thought they'd go on in this way, I'd 'ave stayed at 'ome," said Simson; "they

ain't worth fighting for.   That there Crown Prince
ought to be shot."

"Vote we chuck the 'ole —— business," said
Middle Cock.   "The Germans have fixed it up to
clear out to-night.   I'm off with them."

Then Uncle bestirred himself to get some of
the sheep cooked within the hour.   Others fell to
rolling their blankets, cleaning their rifles, and
filling their water-bottles.   Captain Birch emerged
from his improvised tent to see that everybody's
cartridge-belt was full.   Cartridges are a species of
luggage which has a way of being left behind " by
mistake " when men start on a march.   It is in-
conveniently heavy.   "Wot's the blooming use o'
cartridges, I'd like to know?" Uncle would say; "we
never fires any.   We can do without 'em in this
kind o' war."

Then came a request from Varatasi for men to
carry the stores of the Legion, sacks of sea-biscuit
and cartridge-cases, from the house to a cart outside.   Graham felt the need of hard work to
deaden the shame and the dejection that were
overpowering him.   "Better be of some use carrying baggage than sit brooding over the destinies
of nations," he said to himself, as he flung off his
tunic and volunteered for the work.   Speropoulo
noticed him as he shouldered his first biscuit-sack.
He was a kindly, nervous soul, who felt the need
of saying something appropriate at every juncture.

"I shall watch how a 'professor' carries sacks,"
he said.

Two hours passed before the order came to fall in. The men sat about under the blazing sun with their baggage on their shoulders, swearing at things in general. The talk ran chiefly on the retreat from Mati and the Larissa panic. They all seemed to delight in dinning the disgraceful details into Graham's ears—how they had lain all day at Mati behind a hillock in the rear, without firing a shot, while the shells whistled past them, and spent rifle-balls littered the ground beside them. And then had come the order to retreat, and with the darkness the frantic cry, "The Turkish cavalry are upon us." The artillery dashed past them, trampling men to death as they fled. Carriages were overturned in the ditch, women were mixed with soldiers, infantry and cavalry fought for room upon the road. Once they had caught the thud of horsemen sweeping towards them on the causeway. The flying Greeks had doubled their speed, but their own sergeant gave the order to form. Bayonets were fixed, the front rank kneeled, the Irishmen crossed themselves, they all thought that their last hour had come. "Fire!" shouted the sergeant, as the horsemen hove in sight through the gloom, and two troopers fell from their seats, while the rest swept on, swerving to avoid the little band of Englishmen. They were not Turks after all, only Greek cavalry riding for their lives, reckless of duty, trampling footmen and peasants to death in their mad career. And then the firing became general, evzones stood in the ditch blazing away at their comrades on the causeway, too terrified to do much damage. Blankets, and rifles, and haversacks littered the ground, with here and there a wounded man groaning in an agony of fear. The Englishmen marched on steadily, keeping to the fields. They found a deserted house in Larissa, where they slept soundly for a few brief hours while the panic rout swept on to Volo or Pharsala.

In the morning five of them went off to bathe in the Peneus. They were still absent when Varatasi came round to Captain Birch to tell him that the whole army was in retreat towards Pharsala. The Crown Prince had been the first to leave in a special train "in order to reconnoitre the position at Pharsala." His cooking utensils went with him; the money chest of the army, its stores, its heavy guns, all these were left behind. Quietly the Legion waited in the deserted square till the bathers returned. Meantime the Englishmen who were available were on duty in the railway station, guarding the last train reserved for the women and the wounded. Sturdy men, officers among them, had tried to tear them from the trucks, and once more the English Philhellenes had fired upon their Greek comrades.

At last the bathers returned, Uncle, and O'Brian, and the three " Cocks," sauntering along, swinging their towels, chaffing one another.

"I'll not say anything to you for this, men," said Birch, "we may have to die together in a few

H

hours;" and then, sobered but steady, the company
began their march, the last squad in the Legion to
leave the town, the rear-guard of a demoralised
army, with its chief flying on ahead as fast as
steam could carry him.

But this after all was no retreat. When at last
the Legion started it made towards those hills of
Tekké. An Italian officer bustled past, talking to
Lieutenant Svendsen. " Nous sommes les plus
avancés de l'avant-garde," Graham heard him say
in a tone of imbecile pride. It was the Prince's
response to Varatasi's advice. They were on their
way to Driskoli, a little village at the mouth of
the pass, down which the Turkish centre marched
some five days later.

Graham's spirits rose at the news. At least the
Legion would have the place of honour, and however the main army might behave, they in their
outpost must encounter the enemy. He fell to
preparing his mind for the fighting which must
come soon, that very night perhaps. They were
passing through a hamlet on the banks of the
Peneus. Boys were rushing hither and thither,
chasing the lean ponies of the village. Some of
the houses were closed already, and in others the
peasants sat at the door with their household gear
about them, waiting to load the wretched beast
who was evading his tormentors with what little
spirit he possessed.

"They ain't got much confidence in their own
army, anyhow," said Simson; and then they forded

the Peneus, leaving the village behind.   They were in desert country now, marching through the sun-lit silence, a handful of men pledged to face this unknown terror.   The fields were cleared for them to fight in.   "We dare not look upon the thing that you must wrestle with," said the eyes of the peasants behind them across the river.

And then O'Brian beside him began to talk, a brisk fellow with an honest open face and a genial brogue.   He wondered what Graham's politics were, and then assuring himself of a sympathetic listener, he grew eloquent about Ireland.   He for-got his surroundings, he talked as though he had shouldered his rifle in the cause of his country's inde-pendence.   He poured forth her history, from Brian Boroo to O'Neill, and then to Cromwell and to William, and so to Grattan and Emmett, O'Connell and Parnell.   He seemed to live with a legion of dead patriots; he told their forgotten creeds till the swift southern night fell on the Thessalian plain.   He cared something for the fate of Greece ; yes, he was fighting for the national idea, for the freedom of Crete.   He would fight for that cause in Poland, in the Transvaal, wherever a down-trod-den race asserted its individuality.   He was here in the Legion chiefly that he might learn the use of arms, for some day he hoped to march under the green banner of an Irish Republic.   How else could he fit himself for soldiering?   He would never wear the Queen's uniform, indeed it was a bitter-ness to him that even in Greece he had learned his

paces shoulder to shoulder with Englishmen, but
then he knew no language save Erse and English.
This campaign was like to be a fiasco, he feared,
but he was in love with the life, the roving fit was
on him; he thought of joining the French Foreign
Legion when the war should be over, or the United
States army.   He was a journalist by trade, and
secretary of some Parnellite organisation; his whole
life was given to fighting for Ireland, but he was
eager to learn how to wield a bayonet and drill a
company.   It seemed a manlier career than his
old craft of quill-driving and agitation.   And then
he took to argument with Graham, an idealist who
only knew that Berkeley was an Irishman, Mazzini
at least no Englishman.   Sometimes they talked
of nationality, and again of Celtic aspirations, then
of the Land League, or of Clericalism and Healy.
Then he would tell Graham his life history, or in-
veigh against the English character, pointing to
the frailties of Uncle or of Middle Cock to enforce
his denunciations.

And so, forgetting the war, they carried the hopes
and wrongs of Ireland into Driskoli.   It was night
when the company halted on a terrace before the
village store, and lay down to sleep upon the gravel,
hungry and tired.

CHAPTER IX

SATURDAY and Sunday were spent by the
Legion in investigating the material resources of
Driskoli. It had been a thriving village; there
were many well-built houses left empty by their
fugitive owners waiting for the firebrands of the
Turk. Big Cock made a speciality of hen's eggs,
and soon knew the favourite haunts of all the
roosters in the country-side. Middle Cock discovered that a certain barn was haunted by hawks,
and their eggs too made an excellent flavouring for
the rice which could be bought at the village store.
The cool mornings were spent in foraging expeditions to the deserted villages across the hills.
Captain Birch led these in person, losing no oppor-
tunity of licking his scratch company into shape.
Uncle was left behind to cook the company's
sheep, while the rest were busy marching over the
rolling hills, forming in skirmishing order, wheeling
over uneven ground, learning promptitude and
cohesion. The objective of these sorties was
generally a little hamlet where some live stock

had been left by the villagers in their hurried flight. It was better that the fowls or sucking pigs of Thessaly should find their way to the Legion's larder than that they should wait to fatten the invader. There was a spice of adventure too about these expeditions. There was always a chance of encountering Turkish scouts, and once an hour was spent in a fruitless search for a couple of spies who had hid in the standing corn at the approach of the little company.

Yet it was sorry work for an armed force to make war on barn-door fowls. Ever and anon came news of fighting in Epirus, or a victory at Velestino. Smolenski's men had destroyed fifteen hundred Turkish cavalry on Friday, said rumour, and the Legion went on slaying chickens. In the absence of books or newspapers, men took to cooking. It was impossible to sleep all day; it would have been unsafe to walk far from camp, for Driskoli was the most isolated outpost of the Prince's army. No one had energy for sports, and evening was the consecrated time for concerts round the camp fire. Cooking and eating absorbed every one's attention. It was an adventure even to enter the grocery store. You might meet an officer with ideas about discipline, who would remind you that it was the officers' quarters for the time being. There was something romantic in the stupidity of the bullet-headed boy behind the counter who answered "*then echei*"[1] to all your queries. Graham passed his time

[1] θεν ἔχει : There is none.

between attempts to carve himself a pipe to replace the old briar which some Philhellene had stolen, and experiments in cookery with such matérials as he could extort from the grocer's boy by force or fraud.

Another resource was the village well, with its long stone horse-trough fed from an ever-running spring of icy water. It was the centre of the camp. Legionaries came there to wash their clothes, and the evzones posted in the village brought sheep's entrails which they cleaned for the evening meal. Graham used to bathe there twice a day, and most of the Englishmen followed his example. There was no woman within ten miles of Driskoli, and it was surprising how quickly these outpost regiments forgot the decencies of civilisation. The hour that one spent under the cool running water held the only tolerable moments of those tropical days. At first the evzones were amused at this English love of water, but at last they came to look on it with tolerant pity as a practice natural to heretics. The orthodox are anointed once for all with holy oil at baptism; it is a charm against all the impurity of this vile world; but a heretic—well, he no doubt must fly to tiresome substitutes, inexpedient makeshifts.

They were genial fellows, those evzones; they would fill your gourd for you if you stood at the end of a long *queue* waiting at the well, and say "*tipote*"[1] with an air of charming courtesy when you thanked them. They would hunt half a morning

[1] τίποτε: It is nothing; don't mention it.

for a bit of wire, if the Legion had caught a sucking pig in its foraging, and Uncle was at a loss
how to fix it over the charcoal fire. They acted
as hosts to these Franks who had come to Greece
to fight for them, and the most embittered Cockney
would except the "kilties" when he railed upon
King George's soldiery. They even succeeded in
teaching Uncle the name of their regiment, and
henceforward over the "grassy"[1] he would toast
" *to ennaton tagma ton evzonon.*"[2]

Graham saw but little during these two days
of the acquaintances he had made at Pharsala.
Montalto and Goldoni spent their time with the
Italian officers, of whom there were no less than
six. Mavromichali and Palli went about together,
avoiding the English company, of which they were
nominally members.

Graham took his share of fatigue duty, gathering
firewood and carrying water, and the men were
very ready too to employ him as interpreter. The
loneliness that besets a man surrounded by companions with whom he has nothing in common
weighed very heavy on him. His mental horizon
narrowed ; it seemed as though a lifetime had
passed since he had spoken with an educated man
or fingered a book. His thoughts were driven
into a single channel ; he set his teeth, as it were,
and went about his work filled with one idea, the
duty of an educated man among inferiors, and the

---

[1] He meant κράσι or κράσις, wine.
[2] The Ninth Battalion of Evzones.

pride of race which upholds a man of northern blood among peoples less vigorous and disciplined. The gloom of defeat and failure had settled on the Legion; men asked themselves why they had faced death for a worthless nation ; some talked of deserting; some stayed sullenly because they were ashamed to fly. Some few were upheld by an aristocracy of blood that made them willing to stand firm, to endure hardship, to fight to the death if need there were. To them it seemed a task worthy of their race to do bravely in this degraded army.

"Oh, I shall stay as long as there is an army in the field," said Svendsen to Palli one day. "Denmark has sent Greece the wrong man to be king, but she can still breed soldiers who will stand to be shot at."

And as for Graham, a like determination to deserve the name of Englishman had silenced the self-questionings that had racked him in Lamia. He ceased to dream of death ; he grew interested in bayonet drill.

Palli and Mavromichali used to spend the sweltering hours of sunshine in a big barn near the company's bivouac. It was a long building half-filled with hay. They would lie .there alone with the evzone colonel's horse. The sun filtered in with a pale light through cracks in the roof, and filled the place with a wan semblance of theatrical daylight. One could lie there and forget the war and dream of home. It roused memories of childhood to lie on the soft hay. One thought of the old cat one had played with in just such a barn at home, and the little sister with whom one kept house in the darkest corner, for barns are much the same all the world over.

On the third morning of their stay in Driskoli the two friends lay there reading. Mavromichali had made a wager with Palli to find a book in the village. It seemed a forlorn hope; the grocer's boy replied to the strange request with a dumfoundered "*then echei*," [1] but going patiently from one deserted house to another, Mavromichali had at last come upon a heap of rubbish where lay an old Prayer-book. He returned triumphant to the barn. Palli was lying as he had left him, stretched on the straw and dreaming of Paris. There was a tone of mischief in Mavro's voice as he flung down the book, and proclaimed his discovery.

"H'm, it's Greek," said Palli; "I thought you said it was a book."

"You shall listen to it for that, my man," said Mavro, and he began to read from the Psalter in his clear, eager voice: "'*Lord, thou hast been our dwelling-place in all generations.*' It's magnificent, isn't it?"

"Doesn't interest me. I'll recite some Verlaine if you like."

"What a miserable decadent you are, to be sure!"

"'O très haut Marquis de Sade,'" quoted Palli. "Now that's an interesting subject."

[1] There is none.

"I find the God of the Psalms tolerably interesting."

"The only interesting thing about God is the motive that leads us to invent him."

And then they fell to talking metaphysics. Palli scoffed at the very study and quoted Nietzsche. Mavro fell back on Plato, spoke of him with a glow of enthusiasm, an ardour that was half the gratitude of the student, half the love of a patriotic Greek.

"I don't find him satisfying," said Palli.

"But he makes one think, he stimulates."

"You suggest a definition; a stimulating book is one which leaves everything to the reader."

And then there was a pause, till between amusement and disgust Mavro asked—

"What on earth made you come here? You're ashamed of being a Greek; you talk your own language like a courier; you're in love with Paris. What in the name of paradox made you take the resolution?"

"I didn't resolve. *On m'a résolu.*" And then he checked himself.

"Who resolved you?"

"Oh, . . . my doctor. He thought I needed a change."

"On the principle of kill or cure, I suppose. But seriously now?"

"Well, perhaps it was chiefly *pour chasser la décadence.*"

"You're as bad as a stimulating book," said Mavro slowly.

And then came a shrill whistle from outside.

"It's the Turks at last," said Mavro, "that's Birch's whistle; and here are we talking about decadence," and he pulled on his boots, and buckled on his belt and the bayonet that had been lying on the straw beside him. He was a notable figure as he stood up, his eyes ablaze with excitement, the keen Hermes-like face alert with decision and intellect. "Aren't you coming?" he said as he glanced at Palli, still listless on the ground.

"Oh, it will be time enough in a minute. Come back and tell me if it's anything out of the common. The last time Birch blew his whistle it was only to serve out that vile salt cheese. Bah! I want no more of it!"

It was not cheese that was at issue this time, however, but cannon. They lay on the plain across the Tekké hills, a pair of heavy field guns left by the army on its flight from Larissa. His scouts had brought in word of them to Varatasi, and he had determined that they should lie there no longer, a reproach to Greece, a blot on the honour of his own arm, the artillery. He had sent to headquarters for a squad of cavalry, and at last they had come, some fifty of them. In half-an-hour the Legion was on the march. A few troopers rode in front along the sandy road, the Legion followed, a line of horsemen flanked them on either side, and videttes were scattered on the hills to right and left, the eyes of the little force.

Graham had "covered" Mavromichali when the company "fell in," and now they marched side by side. They talked at first about the cavalry. Mavro was learned about the functions of cavalry. He was also a keen horseman, the only "non-English-man" in Alexandria who played polo, he said. He went on to discuss English officers; they attracted him, he counted many friends among them in Egypt. He liked their gallantry, their love of field sports, but he found them desperately uneducated and *borné*. He was nearly going with Colonel Burn-Murdoch to see the last Soudan campaign; he had always had a desire to see war. Then he was silent for a while, thinking of his own motives in coming to Greece, and puzzling over Palli's case. Graham was startled when he suddenly began again. "What do you understand by decadence? I have an uncle who reads Verlaine and raves about the decadents. I've read him of course; some of him I liked, some of him seemed to me such odd French that I couldn't enjoy it, but I can't analyse the attitude."

Graham was like one who seeks to talk in a forgotten language; old thoughts of his own were struggling to enter his mind, but he could not grasp them. The ancient self of his college days seemed to him a shameful thing that he could not resurrect. There came into his mind a half-forgotten epigram that lay somewhere in the very notebook that he carried in his haversack, jostling with cartridges and service cheese, but it stuck in his throat when he tried to utter it. *He that is aweary of the sun, let him light the gas,* said memory at last, but the sentence was only half spoken when a tremor of excitement swept from rank to rank of the Legion. They swung round a bend in the road, and then a halt was called. "A decadent is one who is aweary of—Hallo! what's that on the hill-top yonder?" It was three horsemen who stood rigid against the horizon.

"They have lances, they are not our men," said Mavro. And then the tremor of excitement which had struck the Legion grew articulate.

"Turks," it said in seven languages at once. Émile the Cretan speculated on the corps to which the three videttes belonged. They stood out black against the brilliant sky behind them, but he was posting his companions in the meaning of green turbans and red fezes, crescents on green ground and crescents on red. Baumgarten among the Germans was certain that those were the very men who had pursued him near Volo. "Jewiss sind sie dieselben. Sehen Sie mal, Schweitzer, ein weisses Pferd und zwei schwarze. Wie?"

Then came a vidette galloping madly towards Varatasi, his sabre clinking on his spurs, and his water-bottle beating the stock of his carbine like a drum. There was a hurried consultation, and then the march began again. Still those three figures stood on the brow of the hill a mile away, statu-

esque and immobile. Away to the left came the
crack of a carbine that went echoing among the
hills. It was one of the videttes who had fired.
Men glanced at each other with an eager look
of congratulation. The pace grew imperceptibly
quicker; men took a pride in every detail of discipline. Those who had been out of step before
fell into the steady music of the march, and ad-
justed the rifles on their shoulders till they sloped
parallel with those in front. And then among the
French, Érin and Émile struck up the Greek
National Anthem. One company after another
took it up, some whistling, some singing, and the
triumphant song was borne across the hills to those
three Turks, stolid and black against the horizon.
Slowly they turned and trotted off. "What shall
we see next on that hill-top?" was everybody's
thought.

And then the long line opened out, left the road,
and spread across the moor in skirmishing order,
on the left the Danes and on the right the English.
They carried their rifles at the trail ready to load
at once, and each man watched his neighbour ten
paces from him to preserve the mathematical
beauty of the line. Each of those forty men felt
himself a unit then, facing the unknown thing
across the hill. The singing had ceased, you heard
the tramp of feet in unison no more; a man lost
himself no more in the corporate life of his company. It was not now "the company" which
marched and sang, no longer "the company" which

faced the danger, but each man for himself, alone within his radius of ten paces. And so they marched for half-a-mile, silently, steadily, their ears alert to hear the word of command, their eyes strained for the first glimpse of a red fez upon the hill-top.

Ah! there were the guns at last lying deserted in the sandy road and their empty carriages beside them. The Danes and the English were climbing the hill at last, while the other companies, French, Italian, German, Greek, and Armenian, were busy with the guns.

On the crest of the hill the company formed again. Eagerly they scanned the wide plain before them, but even the three scouts had vanished, not a Turk was to be seen; but they lay in force in that village three miles off, there where the minaret of a mosque peeped above the olive trees. And there was Larissa twenty miles to the north. It seemed less than five in the clear air. There was a gleam of water where the Peneus ran, and on yonder cliff was the Acropolis. Mavromichali was telling Graham the names of the mountains on the horizon, a frowning blue barrier, with here and there a snow-capped summit. There was Olympus to the right, with its triple tiara of gleaming peaks, the fortress of the gods, and far to the left Malouna with its fatal pass. Varatasi was talking to Birch a few paces off. Graham heard the order. "Send half your company to the end of the ridge yonder."

"Section B, left turn," said Birch, and Graham

found himself following the corporal. Varatasi
called Mavro to him to act as interpreter. Presently he came back, and led his section to the
edge of the ridge beyond a solitary tree where
some evzones were posted. They were quarrelling
among themselves, arguing with their corporal.
Everywhere there was division in the Greek army
—of everything but labour. Varatasi was endeavouring to make them ashamed of themselves.

"What is he saying?" asked the corporal of
Mavro.

"He says, 'Do you see those ten men yonder?
they would march for three hours in a straight line
into the midst of the Turks if I told them to.'"

"That's a feather in our cap, anyway," said the
corporal ; "he's the right sort, is Very-tassy."

"I wouldn't have missed this for a good deal,"
said O'Brian to the Ulsterman, as the section
walked along, the vanguard of the Legion, erect on
the ridge in front of the Turkish army.

"'Ere, Middle Cock, bring your old bayonet to
your side for God's sake ; you'll be catchin' a
crab if you don't watch out," said the corporal.
And then it was, "Damn you, Simson! keep step,
can't you?"

"Ain't he —— pertic'lar all at oncet?" said the
section.

And Graham wondered if he were worthy to
march with these men whom Varatasi praised.
Never before had he coveted the virtues of the
simple legionary. "A self-conscious man may

I

become what he pleases," he said to himself, and he paid heed to his marching. And then at the word of command those ten men lay down, and gazed upon the plain before them. They fell to playing with the sights of their rifles. They appealed to "Mr." Graham to tell them how much longer a metre is than a yard, and then they guessed the distance of every conspicuous object before them. Graham and Mavro joined in, eager to train their eyes. Palli lay dreamily watching the end of the sun's war-pomp among the hills. He had no part in the joy of these men beside him. It is otherwise that one pays a compliment and welcomes praise in Parisian salons. Then came a cheer from below. The guns were mounted at last, and the cavalry were dragging them up the sandy road.

"So long, old man; you might have given us a chance to say, ' How d'ye do ? ' to you," said Uncle, waving his hand towards the village where the Turks lay.

It was back to Driskoli again with the heavy guns in front.

"Well, this is a rum go; damned if I ain't stiff. Got any Elliman with you, Middle Cock ? "

"Ain't you funny, Uncle ? "

"No offence I 'ope ; thought you might 'ave a bottle 'andy."

The road seemed to have spent the afternoon in wriggling. It had not been so sinuous before. The sand was twice as deep. The darkness fell, and the moors grew mysterious. Innumerable dogs barked on the hill-sides round about, and the guns were often buried in the sand. "Halt," "Halte," "'Alt," the word would run from Germans to French, and from French to English, and the column would stiffen convulsively, as though it had run its head against a wall. On in front they were straining at the traces, and men were pushing behind. The English company had "fallen out" during the pause. Palli had dropped down by the roadside; he leant his chin upon the muzzle of his rifle and bent forward. The idealism of a weary man came over him; he dreamed beautiful visions of gentle things, with a longing that had no strenuous pain in it. He saw a young girl before him, gay and blonde, with laughing eyes, and he counted the little curls that clustered round her neck.

Simson sat down beside him, and began to rub his ears.

"It's getting cold, isn't it?" said Palli.

"I'm 'ot," answered Simson, "my ears are burnin'."

"Somebody's thinkin' of Simson," said Smith.

When the march began again some instinct that he could not analyse made Palli walk beside Simson in the rear rank. They fell behind a little; they were alone together, and the heart of one was heavy, while the other's—ears burned. It was Simson who began to talk in his execrable Cockney slang, with his air of lively cheerfulness, open-hearted and familiar. He wore his heart upon his sleeve, but one liked to see it there; he was a generous, high-spirited lad, with something akin to refinement beneath his surface vulgarity. Simson was interested in the swiftness of the nightfall. He wondered what time it would be in London; how long did letters take to reach England?

"Your mother will be anxious about you," ventured Palli at last.

"Oh, it's my girl I'm thinking about," said the other naïvely.

"Tell me about her," said Palli.

And Simson told him of Annie Wells. It was a strange language of poetry he employed, the dialect of the music-halls, but his hearer touched the picture with a delicate imagination, forgave the masculine hand that drew the crude sketch, saw a woman before him.

" I think I know some one like her," he said.

" Is she a Greek laidy?"·

" No, she's a Frenchwoman."

Then after a pause: " My little girl wants me to come 'ome. She never did see no good in my goin' out. Girls mostly is like that, ain't they? Now what did your—beg pardon, I mean the French laidy—what did she think about your comin' out?"

Palli was startled. Had he given himself away? Yet he was not wholly displeased; he felt drawn towards the little Cockney, he was safe with his simplicity; it was restful to talk with him, a respite from his daily task of complicating himself. And his secret was in no danger here ; their worlds did not touch, they were not competitors in the struggle for existence. It is only to the man who jostles you in the race that you will not show your faintness.

" I didn't ask her—I never see her now."

" Does she know you're 'ere ? "

" I expect so."

" You bet she cares about it then, and wishes you was safe at 'ome." Then came another pause. " Wot maide you come out, sir, if I maiy maike so bold ? "

"Oh, I wanted a change." But this time he said nothing about the doctor.

" Il est très gentil, le petit Simson, il a des sentiments raffinés," said Palli that night to Mavromichali, as the two friends lay down to sleep in the barn.

CHAPTER X

INITIATION

THEY did not know in the Legion that it was the watch before the battle, yet the rites of initiation were afoot, without pretence or mystery. They lay secure in Driskoli, and the hill curtain was still solid that shut the Turk from view. Palli had come to Greece "for a change"; he rose at dawn and fed on black bread and coarse mutton, but it felt more peaceful here in the deserted village among the barren moors than amid the stir and rush of Parisian streets. The stagnant life of discomfort seemed a sham to the Cockneys. Simson thought of the hours he had spent flattening his nose against the railings of St. James's, watching the Guards with a ballad of Clement Scott's ringing in his ears. This did not seem like war. And they searched out the poverty of the land.

The prospect of fighting had become a dim possibility. The fighting was all in Epirus or at Velestino; diplomacy was at work too, said rumour. In the morning after the affair with the guns a note had come for Palli from Volo. No one knew

118

what it contained; he had walked about nervously, talking of irrelevant topics. Then with a sudden access of decision he had gone to head-quarters and obtained leave of absence. So even Varatasi did not believe there would be a battle. And as Graham said adieu to Palli, he had asked him to bring back a pipe with him and a book or two. The Legion was fixed indefinitely at Driskoli, it was best to make oneself comfortable. A pipe and a book would go far to make life tolerable. Palli's departure was an event, his return would be the next.

It assumed a mythological importance to Graham, this return of Palli. He discussed it with Mavromichali. The pair lay in the sun thinking of each other and talking the while of Palli. They each read the other in his opinion of the absentee. " I wonder why he came out," Mavro would say, and Graham would answer, " Cherchez la femme."

" I dare say you're right. I don't think he has any love of fighting for its own sake. He disgusts me with his jokes about running away. Of course they *are* mere jokes, but still a brave man wouldn't talk in that way."

" He's a bit of a decadent, I suppose, but I like him for his refinement. But delicacy is a quality whose value one exaggerates after living with Philhellenes."

" The Philhellenes—h'm, that's good; Uncle and the rest. But, mind you, I like Uncle; he's really witty sometimes."

" Unquotably so."

" I'd far rather have their British prejudice than
be ashamed of my own country like Palli."

" You think patriotism had nothing to do with
his coming out?"

" Absolutely nothing.   He's in love with the
Turkish bayonets."

" Poor devil!   They may serve his turn, but I
expect he'll feel suddenly sane the first time he
hears cannon.   What he wants is to be annihilated,
to 'cease upon the midnight with no pain.'   I don't
think he really has a disinterested desire to be a
lodging to a Turkish shell.   It would make a mess
of his clothes."

" Oh, he's just playing.   I've no patience with a
man who wants to die by chance.   Why couldn't
he shoot himself?"

" Still I confess to a weakness for Palli."

" Yes, I like him too; he has *style*."

And then Graham reflected for a while; he felt
that he had got the key to Mavromichali.   It lay
here in this love of style, the power of quick decision, of unhampered movement, bred of discipline and untainted by self-consciousness.   He
did not hesitate before he acted; he had an aristocracy of will that had not learnt to dread the
comment of inferiors or the carping of a critic
within.   For himself he knew that style was un-
attainable, he carried a drawing-room of dowagers
inside him.   He went about harassed by their
gossip and disparagement.

"It's an odd thing," pursued Graham, "to find style in a man of weak will. I think of it as the flower of strength and training—a rope-dancer is the perfect type of it."

"That's interesting," said Mavro eagerly; and then as swiftly and surely, "but rope-dancing can be taught, and virtue——" He was off quoting his beloved Plato again. And so the pair lay in the sun talking of eternal things like friends. And then they passed from philosophy to music, and Mavro sang the Star-song from *Tannhäuser*.

The other Philhellenes lay basking through the afternoon. Only Uncle was astir. He had got a huge pot from head-quarters, and was making soup. Half of the company was asleep, others sat talking of their old regiments at home. Morgan, who had discovered that in virtue of his Welsh name he might call himself a Celt, was listening to O'Brian, who discoursed of the new Celtic Athletic Movement; but he was unpractised in this branch of lying, and when O'Brian exposed him he vented his spleen on Corrigan, the most abject member of the company. He was a tall, lanky being, his jaw hung over his chest, his hair stuck through his ragged *képi* like a wisp of straw on a badly-thatched roof. His clothes were still covered with the hay of the Pharsala farm-yard. He had not washed since Mati. "Sure an' it was a terrible retrate," he would say, wringing his hands, if O'Brian sent him to the fountain. Graham had not spoken to him as yet. He took him for an aboriginal bogs-

man. He fled from Morgan to Uncle, and Uncle
sent him with the pot to get water. Graham came
up in time to volunteer to lend a hand. An evzone
helped him to fill the pot, while Corrigan sat on
the edge of the well, weighing his jaw. Then they
set off together to carry it back to Uncle. "Och,
now, an' it's restin' I'd be," was the burden of
Corrigan's remarks by the way. Their task accom-
plished, Graham was turning away when Corrigan
came sidling towards him, blarney in his gait.

"I think Rosebery's a finer spaker than Salisbury,
now, isn't he? He's the mimber for Edinburgh?"

"Well . . . he lives near Edinburgh."

"I think that was a great spaich he made about
Armenia, now, wasn't it? Och! and the lingth of
it, now! Sure Salisbury couldn't spake at such a
lingth. He's a beautiful spaker. I read his spaich
at Paisley about Burns. There's a sintence I re-
mimber yet. He said, 'We are borne along on
the unsophisticated stream of his eloquence.' Now
that's a sintence for ye. Do you think Salisbury
could have spoken a sintence like that? Och! an'
he's a lingthy spaker."

And then Graham was called away by Montalto
seeking a companion for a walk.

"Do ye think there'll be a battle soon?" said
Corrigan, as they parted.

"Well, it doesn't look like it."

The jaw grew lighter, the panic-dulled eyes
looked brisker as he answered, "You railly think
o?" and then he added, "and we'll be victoyous if

there is;" and so appearances were saved. He went away and washed the dust of Mati from his face, and sat down to prepare other conversations wherewith to impress Graham. He felt grateful to the man who would give him a respite from his terror. It was later in the afternoon when O'Brian came quizzingly to Graham to hear what his countryman had found to say.

"Well, it's the first word he's spoken to a living soul since Mati," said O'Brian, "and he was the smartest boy in our Celtic Club before he set out, a spick-and-span young man he was, in a bank, with the highest collars and the smartest ties among us. I don't know what's come over him— he's lost. It began in Athens. He wouldn't shave, and went about in a dream. And at Volo, when Varatasi came along to say that this was the last chance for any man to turn back who felt faint-hearted, sure he was for going. But we prevented him; we weren't going to have it said that an Irishman was the only coward in the company."

And so the day wore to evening, the passion of the sun's burning had spent itself, the sky grew blue again with a coolness of ocean in it, and men began to crawl from the shadow of the gaunt rocks where they had lain all day. In half-an-hour the evening meal would be served, Uncle would ladle the mutton broth into the company's mess tins, the burning fat would scald men's fingers, there would be a fishing for dumplings, and a curious search for tit-bits. Already these hungry Phil-

hellenes had begun to buckle their belts, to brush
the scorched grass from their sun-burnt uniforms,
to stray by common accord towards the great
oak tree near the well where Uncle was posted,
preparing his savoury mess and his cheerful
pleasantries.

Graham had sauntered towards the horse-trough
for his evening bathe. But the scene was more
bustling than usual. The Legion stood round the
oak tree. Men who had been washing clothes
left them soaking in the water, even the precious
cakes of soap were lying on the stones inviting the
thief. But even the thief was busy there by the oak
tree. The lazy air was stirred by a hum of voices,
winnowed by the Legion's tongue. Emile came
running towards the crowd, full of rumour, swift
with the speed of news. "C'est un espion, qu'on
va brûler," he shouted, as he rushed past Graham.
There he was, the spy, pinioned in the centre of
the crowd. Two evzones held him by the arms;
they were chattering, gesticulating, beside themselves. Now they railed at the spy in Turkish,
now they appealed to the crowd in Greek. They
were frontiersmen, adepts in two languages, villains
by two moral codes, emancipated thralls who held
the master, soldiers of liberty with the tyrant in
their grip. He stood erect, the spy, a squat man
of sturdy build, with short bull neck, a great chest
ready to burst the ropes around it, the square
head of a muscular man, a great *tête de bœuf*.
His dark eye flashed a sullen indignation, the

spittle of his tormentors flecked his black beard. There was no trace of terror or of yielding in his bearing. Sometimes he hissed forth a word of fearless hate with a spasm which shook neck and shoulders in their cords. Mavromichali was standing among the onlookers.

"Isn't he a splendid fellow?" he said to Graham.

"Rather brutal," was the answer. "Look at those thick lips and the flat nose. It's a cruel face; I can imagine that fellow cutting Armenian throats with great zest, or roasting Greek prisoners."

"That evzone there, the tall fellow who's shaking his fist in his face, doesn't he look fierce? He told me that he confessed that the Turks roasted thirty Greeks alive in the church at Kurtziovali. That's why they are so wild, these evzones. It was men of their own regiment who were roasted. I don't wonder at them."

"But what's all the row about?"

"Oh, they want him to give information about Edhem's movements, but he won't speak."

"H'm. If I were in his place I would tell the cleverest lies I could invent; he might do some good then, he might mislead the whole Greek army."

"So would I. But you see we're not Turks. That fellow won't speak till they torture him. Hallo! look at those Armenians in the tree. They've got a rope."

Then the sergeant-major came up.

"See old Mick," he said; "my word, isn't he a

bounder. Why he's up that tree already. By Jove, if he gets his knife in that fellow I'm sorry for him. Those Armenians have gone mad. 'Turk bad man,' says Mick. Good old Mick. Do you remember at Volo when the first rations were served out Mick wouldn't take his bread? 'No! no!' says he, 'me eat grass and Turk, me eat grass and Turk—Turk bad nation!' By Jove, he would do it too if he got the chance."

The Armenians had fixed a halter to the bough of the oak. The spy was on the ground now, silent and passive. The evzones were binding his legs. Two were at his feet pulling the cords, two at his head shaking their fists, screaming, threatening, entreating, reasoning. The Turk was silent.

Then they lifted him and placed his feet in the halter. He swung in the air, head downwards, a pendulum that measured the moments of its own torment. The bough creaked a complaint, the evzones chattered, the Armenians shouted and threatened, only the Turk was silent.

Next came an evzone carrying brushwood. He threw it on the ground, and the living pendulum swung over it, passed it, and returned again. The blood rushed to his head, his eyes started from their sockets, and again the halter swung him back over the firewood. And still the Turk was silent.

"Good God! They're going to roast him! It's sickening. I can't stand it," said Mavromichali, and he walked away.

Then came Mick with more firewood. He
looked like the portraits of Abdul Hamid with
his Armenian nose, thick under-lip, and pointed
chin.

Graham was beside himself with indignation. In
the madness of his rage he could have cut the
halter with his own hand, but a whole regiment
was ready to resist him, to seize the prisoner again
and renew the torture. At least he need not see it.
He walked off into the deserted village. But the
need of doing something turned him towards the
grocer's store, the Legion's head-quarters. Perhaps
the foreign officers were ignorant of what was going
forward. They might interfere. Thoughts of a
Press at home came into his mind. What would
Alexi's English Philhellenic papers say to this?

At the door of the store he met Chanteloup.
" Monsieur, on va brûler un espion là bas," he said.
Chanteloup turned shamefacedly away. "On ne
peut rien faire," he muttered. Then it was Ferrari,
M. le Lieutenant Dieu, as Érin called him, and he
said, " C'est juste, il ne veut pas parler." And some
one else quoted a platitude about war, "guerre"
with an Italian " r " in the middle of it. It makes
a difference in war when you trill the " r."

Under the tree the pendulum still swung. Its
path was shorter now, its vibration slower. The
throbbing eyes lingered longer on the brushwood;
at last they swung over nothing else. They saw
only firewood. The terror came closer, there was
no escape from it. And yonder was a giaour

bringing fire, an evzone with a lighted faggot in his hand, and his feet came nearer, twinkling beneath the white kilt. The Turk saw only the legs, there where he swung head downwards. He craned his neck, but he could not see the human face of pity. But the feet of the fire-bringer came nearer. And then terror overmastered him, his brain was sodden with blood, and he saw only faggot and fire. His parched throat gave a cry. Yes, he would tell everything.

It was an evzone who climbed the tree to release him, the Armenians slunk away disappointed. A Frenchman standing by tramped with delight upon the burning faggots. He was sitting on the ground now, the spy, half fainting, and an evzone was giving him *ouso* to drink.

"Damned if I can taike this soup," said Simson, "and there's Captain Birch 'as thrown 'is away, couldn't touch it. 'E was near sick, 'e was."

"Well, and wot may you think of your friends the Greeks now, Mr. Graham?" said the corporal, the burly "Big Cock" of the company. "Didn't we tell you? but you wouldn't 'ear a word against them. But you've seen it with your own eyes now. I've seen enough of ye ancient Greek, I 'ave."

"Weren't 'e gaime too, that Turk?" said Uncle.

The evening fell uneventful. Over the camp fire men talked of the day's doings. Some railed at the Greeks, some cursed the war-god, some wondered if after all the scene they had witnessed were nothing but a too dramatic threat. Corrigan sat apart, his dim mind full of Graham's assurance that there would be no battle. A halter still swung from the oak tree by the well, and from the barn came the light of candles. It was Voso who knelt confessing his sins, facing the thought of death, a sombre man with a sense of duty, who had joined the English company because it was the "most serious." "Perhaps it is my last night on earth," he said to Mavromichali. And then night descended and the wind fell. The rope hung rigid. The candles burnt to the ground, and Corrigan fell asleep contented. The day of initiation was over, the unpretentious rites complete.

K

CHAPTER XI

DIES IRÆ

IT was eight o'clock of a bright May morning. The sun had set the peak of Olympus all a-shimmer. The snow on the mountain tops glittered and sparkled till one fancied that the distant winds were dancing. On the level the hot air moved with a heavier tread. It was mere physical fact to the sixteen English legionaries. They had left Driṣkoli, drowsy and unwashed, for the most part, regretting their breakfast.

They had marched over the hills for three hours, stumbling through furze and bracken, working out military patterns against their will, cursing the trailing plants that caught their feet, and thinking of the sheep which Uncle was cooking in camp. The cicadas had stopped their singing as the soldiers went by, and once three spies had dived into the corn. Then there was a beating of bushes, a marching round hillocks, a loading of pieces, a tremor of life and a thought of danger. But the spies lay close in their lurking-place, and the company went its way.

"I'm thinking of that there sheep, and old Uncle messin' round an' toasting hisself bits of bread to 'old under the drippin'," said Middle Cock.

"Well, if that sheep's losin' more drippin' just now than w'at I'm doing, I'll be damned," quoth the corporal, mopping his brow.

Captain Birch, a brisk, gentlemanly figure, with the alert air of an old Matabeleland campaigner, called the sergeant-major to him, a tall man with the walk of a dragoon. He had been the smartest "non-com." in the Life Guards Blue, and had seen service in Egypt. They looked alternately through the field-glass which Varatasi had lent the captain for this reconnaissance. They had an air of impatience when somebody asked for leave to fall out and fill his water-bottle. "Make haste then," said the sergeant.

They flocked to the stream like cattle in mid-summer, the line existed no longer, rifles were flung on the grass, the company became a herd of thirsty animals. They soaked their handkerchiefs to make puggarees, they washed their faces and necks, they filled their water-bottles, and then drank them dry and returned to fill them again.

"Damnation," shouted the sergeant, "you don't all need to fill your bottles. Make haste with your washing there, Simson, for God's sake. This isn't a County Council wash-house. Hurry up, man. Fill Corrigan's bottle for him, somebody. Don't be a fool, Corrigan, you'll never fill it at that trickle.

Bless my soul, you're like a lot of volunteers at Brighton. Hurry up now. Fall in!"

And the company swung along again back towards the hills, some of them fitting the stoppers to their bottles as they went, some essaying to dry their necks and fasten their tunics comfortably under their bandoliers.

"Something's going to happen," said Mavro to Graham. They marched always side by side now. Palli's absence had cemented their friendship. " The sergeant's lost his temper, and Birch is twice as cool as usual. They must have seen something."

"I shouldn't wonder. There he is, using his field-glass again. Can you see anything?"

"Not yet. But I'm sure there'll be a battle before the day's done."

"Oh! do you lay claim to second sight?"

"No," was the laughing answer, "but I feel fit. There's going to be a battle."

The company had covered half-a-mile when a halt was called, and the captain and the sergeant went aside again to peer over the plain and discuss the situation.

"Hallo!" said Smith, "that road wasn't red a minute ago." It was as though a vein had been opened on the moor three miles away, and the red blood trickled slowly down, a thin streak soaking its way through the yellow dust. The eyes of the company were fixed on the dry road, greedily watching the yellow absorbing the red.

It had a fascination like nothing else on earth, this thin red symbol of terror that crept remorselessly over the sand.

"Well, I'm blowed if it ain't old Turco at last," said the company. And then with their vision sharpened they saw black squares like burnt patches on the brown heath. They seemed stationary, but while some one found a new patch nearer and more menacing, the first would move a little. And still the red line trickled down the road. Then it was the horizon that grew black, and the outline of the hills seemed ragged, confessedly irregular as the black squares came over them.

"W'y you'd think they was ants," said Simson.

A fever of curiosity seized the company. They ran to points of vantage, they competed with each other to find new squares. They lay here and there in unexpected places, and he was proudest who found one near at hand, its lines facing towards the hills, inevitably nearing the place where they stood.

"Lie down there," shouted the sergeant, and reluctantly the men obeyed. They felt a disinterested glory in the sight. It was a brave pageant, and they only prayed for more black squares and longer lines of red fezes: they were keenly conscious of each other, they felt the green of their uniforms, it subtly coloured their mood. Their blood went quickly and set their nerves afire; the flushed faces turned eagerly this way and that, and the sparkling eyes danced from the green that was English to the black masses yonder, hostile things that they were soon to meet.

"How do you feel, old man?" said Smith to Simson.

"Damn queer," said Simson; "it feels funny inside, like bein' on a swing; I'm a bit peckish, I expect that's why."

"Same 'ere," said Smith.

The passion to see possessed their superiors also. It was an adventure to stand thus in the face of an army, with a handful of men at your back. Birch was eagerly criticising the advancing hordes, trying to estimate their numbers, thinking of his report to Varatasi. He was impelled to go further, yonder to that belt of trees, the last bit of cover between the hills and the plain. It seemed as if all would be clear there, the Turks would be infinitely nearer, there would be nothing to obstruct the view, and besides it was but a quarter of a mile away.

Within ten minutes the company was among the trees, and Birch and the sergeant were still busy with the glass twenty yards away. They stood on the last ridge of rising ground among the birch trees. In front stretched a plain, all browns and yellows, ploughed fields that exposed their rich loam naked to the conqueror. A little village lay amid the hills a mile away. The advance guard of the army had just reached it. They opened out in skirmishing order, advancing warily, mistrusting the ominous silence. Behind

was the last spur of the Tekké range, a low
mamelon, with trees upon it. One could see the
red fez of an evzone moving among the branches.
The hills curved away from the spur, west towards
Tekké and south towards the Pharsala railway, a
mass of wavelike heights and hollows, with here a
farm set amid green fields of rye, and there a
naked crag, but a wilderness of furze and burnt-
up grass for the most part, deserted by the sheep
which browse there in peaceful summers.

Suddenly from the hills behind came the deep
baying of a cannon. It was a new sound to most
of the company. They had heard the old guns
captured at Sebastopol saluting on the Queen's
Birthday with blank charges, but this was a wholly
different noise. There was a resonance in it, and a
finality which could not be gainsaid. One looked
for the instant disappearance of the hostile army.
And as the report still ran echoing among the
hills a little cloud of smoke rose from the plain
and quivered for a minute, a shifting pillar hewn
by the breeze into fantastic masonry. A black
square was its pedestal, a touch of blue where it
melted in the air the only colour that varied its
creamy whiteness.

"That's shrapnel," said Smith to Mavro and
O'Brian, as they stood, the foremost of the company,
gazing on the spectacle in front of the birch grove.
He marvelled at the accurate aim of the Greek
battery as another shell fell full in the centre of
another black square. He instructed his com-

panions with all the learning of an ex-gunner in the Horse Artillery. At last the Turkish guns began their reply. One could see only the puff of smoke at their muzzles, but their target was hidden.

And then Graham joined the group. Mavro looked at him with an eager joy in the excitement which they shared, and when he moved, his muscles seemed to play with twice their wonted grace and vivacity. "Well, I told you there would be a battle, I felt it in my blood."

"Yes, it's a sight for the gods, isn't it? I feel like the man in Lucretius, who watches a shipwreck from the shore and rejoices in his own safety."

Then came a strange grinding noise as if the mills of the gods moved through the air. It seemed irritatingly slow, yet still it moved, and towards the company. There is no sound more angry or sinister, it is the rasping of iron on iron, the crunching of steel jaws, the inexorable approach of some engine of death along an iron track that strives to retard it. And at last it fell among the soft sand some twenty yards in front, the embodied noise visible at last.

Smith looked back to the company. "Pretty close shave that was, eh!" His face was flushed, he looked as if he would shout, "Come on, you damned coward, nearer, nearer," to the shell. "That was shrapnel, you can tell him by the noise. If that boy had burst 'e'd 'ave maide a mess of some of us. Queer noise, ain't it, though?"

"It's like an over'ead cash railway in a draiper's shop," said Simson.

Corrigan was sitting on the ground, his head in his hands, the picture of dejection. He had never been able to adjust himself to the strange environment of war, and here was the most bewildering circumstance of all. He gave way utterly. He felt himself already a red jelly with a thousand shells pounding his carcase. "Cheer up, Corrigan, man!" said O'Brian to him, "you've an even chance with the rest of us. Never say die!" For a moment he raised his shaggy head and closed his mouth, and then the jaw fell again. He shook himself with a sort of terror-stricken rage, and growled, "Lave me alone, will ye!" and this interference of his comrade was for a moment a distinguishable item in the massive chaos of misery and fear that lay upon him.

Voso stood beside him, silent and gloomy; his head rested on the mouth of his rifle. He was pale and agitated, but his face was set with the resolve of a man who does his duty and treats his fear as an irrelevance.

Most of the men were cleaning their rifles. There seemed to be a meaning in the act, when there came at intervals the booming of a gun from the plain or the heights behind. Mick, the Armenian, who had had himself transferred to the English company, was busy rendering little services here and there—rolling a cigarette for the corporal, or fitting a bit of rag into Middle Cock's ramrod. Mavro was still watching the plain and the movements of the black squares upon it. He was singing Wolfram's song from *Tannhäuser* softly to himself, almost unconsciously.

"We ain't got too many cartridges anyhow," remarked Smith. He stood practising a dazzling movement with his rifle. He brought it to his shoulder, pulled the trigger, and then with one turn of the wrist the muzzle was in his hand and the butt behind him, the weapon transformed into a club. He managed the heavy thing with astonishing ease and swiftness. Mavro turned round.

"What do you call that? It's *chic*. Isn't it a beautiful movement?" he said, appealing to Graham. "Show me how you do it."

"Style once more," said Graham to himself.

"It's called the last cartridge—that is," says Smith; "you fire off your last round at close quarters, and then you club your rifle, and you're ready for 'em, see?" And then Mavro practised the movement, handling his rifle deftly.

Again a shell came grinding through the air. Graham felt himself standing eagerly expectant trying to locate the sound, finding a certain pleasure in listening to the rapid acceleration of the missile as it swept down its curving path. The uncertainty as to where it would fall, and with what result, was not acuter than the interest, half pain, half pleasure, which one takes in the throw of dice. It came ten yards nearer this time, but again it failed to burst. The company breathed once more, their tongues were loosened, and they talked quickly, smiling unspoken congratulations to one another.

"That ain't a chance shot anyhow. They must have spotted us, and they've found the range, by God! The next shell will do for some of us." It was Smith's opinion, and Smith was a professional.

Then came a quick summer shower, the sunbeams danced in the rain, and the drops quivered on the leaves of the birch trees. The company curled itself up at their roots. They seemed to dread the gentle blow of the drops against their cheek. They would not willingly risk a wetting that would be forgotten in half-an-hour. They sat cowering from the rain, and fearlessly awaiting the next shell—the shell that would certainly carry some of them to a world where it is said one fears no more the heat of the sun nor the beating of the rain. They chatted carelessly, and drew in their knees lest the drippings from the trees should wet them. Such creatures of habit are we.

Mavro was theorising eagerly, wondering whether it was the firing of heavy guns which had brought the rain, when the sergeant and captain returned. It had grown too hot in the birch-wood; there was no object in exposing their men further. The company was soon in line again, making for the hill-top where the evzones were. There was a trace of eagerness in their heels as they left danger behind them.

They were hardly clear of the trees when some one chanced to glance towards the stream where they had filled their bottles less than an hour before. There were horsemen there—a long line of them still mounted, others breathing their chargers and leading them to drink.

"Well, I'm blowed!" said Big Cock. "We didn't clear out of that a minute too soon!"

On the hill-top lay a line of evzones peering earnestly in front of them. There were un-uniformed men among them—irregulars in blacks and tweeds, carrying sheepskin cloaks jauntily thrown over their shoulders. They lay prone with a low breastwork of reddish soil before them, their rifles pointed towards the stream and the hills beyond it. Their captain stood behind them with a drawn sword in his hand, nervously bending it against the ground as though it had been a cane. He wore a blue uniform with red facings. He might have been a man of fifty, he looked rough and shabby, and unmilitary, and when he spoke his voice rang thin and hoarse as if worn with much shouting amid the din of battle.

Birch halted the company. They lay watching a regiment of infantry creeping round the hill beyond the stream hardly a mile away. He addressed the evzone captain in French, but there was no intelligible response. Then he called Mavromichali to him to act as interpreter. There

was a vivacious conversation. The evzone wrung
Birch's hands, beside himself with delight, and
then he pointed to a position at the edge of the
hill a few yards away. The company lay down
there. When Mavro joined them he explained
that the whole ninth regiment was posted on these
hills. Their orders were to delay the Turkish
advance, to contest hill after hill, retiring slowly in
order to give the main army time to form behind
them. The captain's pride was unbounded to have
a company of the Philhellenic Legion under his
command, and an English officer at his right hand.
He went about explaining his dispositions to Birch
through Mavro.

There was no hope now of returning to Driskoli; and the company wondered if it would ever
see Uncle again, and the three men who had remained behind with him, sick with dysentery—
Morgan, Isinglass, and Fulton.

And now the other army was evident to the
ears and the eyes of the company. It was marching round to the left of the mamelon in which they
lay. Yonder were the red fezes which had stained
the road earlier in the morning, swinging round
the last hill barrier. Their horns sang out the
defiant advance with cheerful notes, iterating the
confidence of comrade in comrade, their readiness
to meet the infidel, their certainty of victory.

The men on the mamelon were silent, and the
hostile advance was the only music in the air. It
came unweariedly, with its great swinging gait, it

symbolised the triumphant march of the Turk. The marvel was that they tarried behind it.

Already the company was lying down, expecting the first shots of the enemy's skirmishers. When a man had need to rise permission was given grudgingly; and Graham found himself watching Mavro walking about beside Birch, erect, fearless, and swift, with a kind of awe mixed with envy. He seemed a figure strayed from some world of romance, wrapped in song and the beauty of · courage. And now the Turks were rushing a little hill. A great hoarse shout of " Hal-lah! Hal-lah!" came through the air, drowning the note of the bugles. There was a glitter of steel, of red fezes and white accoutrements, and the regiment was on the hillock. It seemed to Graham as if a god were striding towards him rending the air with his angry battle-cry—"*God is gone up with a shout, the Lord with the sound of a trumpet.*"

And when his imagination was at rest he grew aware of a stifling constriction of the chest, an intolerable strain at the base of the spinal cord, and that curious internal sensation, that stirring of suspense, of half pleasurable fear, the "swing-feeling" of one's childhood. And that mad, fanatical host came on with its cry of "Allah!" It was an incredible nightmare! It seemed a gentle, civilised, godless thing, this English company—a child lying helpless in' its dream waiting for the spring of an inspired tiger! What a fearful symmetry it had too, that tiger. It sprang clear of hills, it seemed to leap the valleys, so swift and orderly was its advance.

"They're in beautiful order," said the sergeant-major, as he stood behind the company. "That's the Aldershot attack formation. It's just like a review."

Mick the Armenian was fumbling with his cartridge-belt (his real name was Milcom M'hidarian; he had lived in America, could make signs in half-a-dozen languages, and was a member of the Hintchak).[1] He looked handsome, and pale, and ferocious. The sound of that Turkish shout had fired his blood; he could contain himself no longer. His finger was on the trigger when the sergeant saw him, and bade him wait for the word of command. Smith, beside him, was hot with the lust of battle, his face was flushed. He, too, was keen for work, but he restrained himself, and laughed to Simson at Mick's bloody-mindedness. Then Mavro joined the company, and lay down beside Graham. He was practising that beautiful "last cartridge" movement as he came up, and singing Wolfram's song in his rich tenor.

And then a volley rang out from a line of evzones posted on a little crag to the left of the company. It was ill delivered ; the report came with a rattle, and the puffs of smoke ran from one end of the line to the other as if some one had fired a train of powder.

"Disgusting," said the sergeant-major.

"This at last is a battle," thought the company.

[1] Hintchak : an Armenian revolutionary society.

The Turks replied with musketry across the valley, from their hillock, firing independently, and then their mountain guns came up and began throwing shells towards the cliff where the white and blue flag waved above the smoke. There was a hurried consultation between Birch and the sergeant, and then came the order to sight at nine hundred metres. Corrigan lay helplessly fumbling with his rifle, and O'Brian fixed it for him. And still the interchange of smoke and sound went forward across the valley.

Then the flag wavered and fell back, and the Greek company hurriedly clambered from their post, a few black figures amid the smoke. "Hallah! Hallah!" shouted those other viewless figures from under the cloud on the hillock, and the English company replied with its volley, its first challenge to the enemy since the war began. "Ready!" came in the calmest tone of the captain, the lazy prose of everyday; "Present!" with a crescendo; and at the hoarse emphasis of "Fire!" it was as if he realised already the death he was sending to the hostile ranks.

To Graham, the whole scene before him had grown vague and terrible. He could not tell which of those black masses on the hillock was bush and which was man. His hand trembled; he dreaded the recoil, though he had already become perfectly familiar with the service rifle at the Athenian ranges. But to fire with the hope and the dread of dealing death was a wholly new experience. When the deafening volley at last rang out he felt certain that his grip had slackened and his bullet fallen wide of its doubtful target. It was only slowly through a long day's skirmishing that his hand grew steady, and he learned to wait for a puff of smoke from a Turkish rifle, and to aim a yard behind it.

Then came a pause in the firing; the range was too long for the inferior *Gras* rifle, and the men had not more than seventy rounds apiece, for they had come out provided only for a reconnaissance. It seemed better to reserve the scanty store for close quarters.

But that one volley had attracted the Turkish fire. Bullets began to sing in the air above the prostrate bodies of the company. They came with a whirr like the hum of an angry bluebottle, but in a line that was awfully straight, a line that had a purpose in it, and as they passed the whirr became a hiss. At first the men ducked their heads and hugged the ground, and when the hiss had passed and left no sting behind it they would glance upwards to see which of their comrades was slain. But gradually they came to look with contempt upon the idle missiles, they would raise their heads ; it seemed laughable to lie unharmed while the air was brisk with the music of lead.

The retirement of the evzone company which had held the heights to the left made withdrawal from the mamelon a necessity. Already the old captain had gone, and now Birch gave the order to rise.

The company was standing in one long line, about to march, when a shell came singing towards them. Long before it reached them they were aware of its coming. The crescendo of sound wrought on their nerves; the line wavered, Corrigan fell flat on his face, the corporal staggered and ducked, smiling good-humouredly despite his instinctive fear. He looked as if a child had aimed a pillow at him. Some bent to right and some to left, till Graham felt a sudden stiffening in his muscles. He glanced at Mavro beside him, calm and erect, facing the danger with dignity. There was a quick interchange of smiles between them, they seemed to bow to one another, and Graham took heart, for he read in Mavro's eyes that his friend had not noted his fear, and for the rest of the day he walked erect, content to take what Fate should send him, waiting the blow with self-respect, and refusing to think of it till it should come. The shell fell harmless and buried itself in the loose sand a yard or two beyond them. It had passed between Graham and Simson.

"It's no use ducking," said Mavro to Graham. "You can't really tell where the thing is. One can't localise a sound accurately. Besides, it's bad form."

"Yes, it must be demoralising. It means that you keep your attention busied with the risk you're running. The sight of Corrigan just now was enough to stiffen every muscle in one's body."

"I feel as if it were an ungentlemanly thing to do," said Mavro.

They were marching down the hillside now
across the hollow and up the next green slope.
They went steadily, keeping their intervals of ten
paces, disdaining haste, watching the evzones in
front of them, and still on the *qui vive* for the
bullets which whistled past them. The evzones
fell back *en masse*, huddled like a flock of sheep.
Well-nigh every bullet that reached them found
its mark. Already some were limping, leaning on
a comrade's shoulder, and some went clutching
a broken arm, hugging it as if they feared to see it
drop upon the battlefield. The white sheepskin
rugs which they carried made them a tempting
target, while the English company were incon-
spicuous in their uniforms of dark green, sown
sparsely on the hillside.

At the top of the next hill they lay down again
and loaded, waiting till the Turks appeared on the
ridge they had just abandoned. At four hundred
metres they fired. They could see the enemy
clearly now. It felt at last like grappling with the
foe thigh to thigh. A passion to show themselves,
to fight square, to challenge the Turk boldly and
let him do. his worst, possessed some of them.
Smith, with the red glow of the fray in his face,
knelt to fire. He could feel the enemy's rifles
trained upon him, it seemed glory and pleasure
enough to point his own piece true, and every
minute that he survived to answer their fire was
like a victory. An officer fell as the Turks cleared
the bushes; he was shouting and brandishing his

sword, when a ball brought him to his knees. It was the company's exploit; no one knew whose rifle had done the thing. A savage exultation overcame them, a triumph that was splendid, because each man knew that the same fate might overtake himself, and deliberately he staked his life for the joy of battle and the right to destroy.

They fought on in a whirl of excitement. Their pieces grew hot, and still they fired till the skin of their left forefingers ached with the pain of burning. Their hands were black with powder, and the sweat poured into their eyes. The mid-day sun ate their backs, but they scarce heeded the glutton; it was one sensation the more in the great fulness of life that was theirs. Their right ears had gone deaf with the noise of their rifles, and when all was quiet, waves of dizzy sound beat upon the exhausted drum. They were impatient of the pauses in the fight, their life was at stake, they had need to crowd experience into an hour that might be their last.

Towards one o'clock came a long pause when they lay in the lee of the hillside. They were out of rifle range, and suddenly they remembered that they had not eaten since the evening of the day before. Graham had a sea-biscuit in his pocket, and he shared it with Mavro and O'Brian. Mick went a-begging. He came back with half-a-loaf that an evzone sergeant gave him, and he divided it among the company. Then they all stopped to

marvel at his cleverness; he had a knack of
"finding" things. He would have grown rich in
the Sahara; no hillside was so barren but his keen
eyes could find booty there. They had each a tale
to tell of his readiness. Their nerves were weary
from their surfeit of sensation; they clutched eagerly
at something of which they could talk. But even
as they lay eating their scanty dole, their sixteenth
part of half-a-loaf, a shell came singing down the
hill. Corrigan fell on his knees and hid his head
in a rabbit-hole, and Voso ducked behind him for
protection. The company laughed, snatching at
the palpable terror of the couple, that they might
forget their own hidden fear of death.

Then they looked towards the place whence the
shell had come. The battery must be yonder on
the ridge where that farm-house stood. And even
as they looked, the place burst into yellow flame.
The hayricks became angry saffron flowers, and the
fire leaped upon the thatched roof of the steading.
And then from the valley below it came a noise
like the crackling of thorns in a camp fire. It was
the field magazine of the ninth regiment which had
caught fire. The ammunition-boxes were ablaze
and spat out cartridges now in volleys and now by
twos and threes. There is a perspective of noises
in battle, and where guns are baying to right and
left, and rifles batter the air with their sharp
decisive report, the explosion of a magazine is but
an item in the wrath and turmoil of the whole.
But it put a pause in the conflict; the retreating

Greeks avoided the valley of death, and even the Turks were stayed for a moment.

And so for another two hours the fight went on. Now the company lay on a ridge and fired, now they turned as they fell back and fired standing, or again they lay waiting in shelter. It had a monotony too anxious and exacting to grow tedious. Their eyes ran along the barrels of their rifles, seeking out a black mark on the hillside. They saw nothing else, and spared hardly a glance for the serene crest of Olympus glittering to the north of them behind the enemy. As yet not a man of the company had been hit, but the evzones left a pathetic trail of dead behind them, the victims of their lack of discipline. They lay on their backs on the ploughed land, ablaze, some of them, for their comrades had set fire to their woollen cloaks. Even in the heat of battle they had time to remember the enemy against whom they fought, the fanatic Turk who destroys the wounded and wreaks his fury on the dead. They burned the corpse of their friend to save it from mutilation and dishonour.

And now the company was alone on the last plateau of the range. For six hours it had fired and retreated, to form and fire again. The last of the evzones was running down the slope that led to the great plain of Pharsala. The Turks were all about them, standing on the hilltops, charging in black masses down the valleys, and still they lay firing, in a rage of desperation, unwilling to

follow their Greek comrades. The captain was as
cool as ever, choosing cover for his men, calculating
the range, directing their volleys. He carried no
arm but his revolver, and in his hand was the staff
of his signalling flag. He had torn the white rag
away when the fight began.

They were working their way to the left when
suddenly they came to a steep gully. On the hill
across it was a black mass of men firing and cheering. It was the Legion ; they could catch a word
of French in the confusion. And their comrades
had seen them. A great cheer burst forth as they
rushed down the hillside. In the gully at the bottom
the air seemed solid with lead. Even Mavro was
bending now, for a moment ; it seemed impossible
to think of anything but the hissing deaths about
them. In the shade of the hill they formed again,
and turned. Up the hillside they marched towards
the Legion on the top. Half-way they paused and
knelt to fire. The Turks were charging down the
valley—"Three hundred metres, independent firing,
and husband your shot!" came the order, for already
their slender stock of cartridges was nearly exhausted, and those who had fired most wildly were
begging from their neighbours.

Now they could see the enemy, and every shot
was aimed at a man. Three fell in as many
minutes ; one flung up his arms and fell prone,
another rolled on his back, a third dropped on his
knees and crawled away waving a white handkerchief. And the French and the Danes above them

were pouring volley after volley up the gully. At last the Turkish fire slackened, and the skirmishers turned and ran this way and that in disorder. An illusion of victory entered the heated mind of the Legion. They forgot that they were two hundred men against five thousand, and that those they had routed were but the advance-guard of an army closing in on every side. The French had fixed their bayonets and were calling for a charge.

In the pause the captain led his men to a garden at the foot of the gully. It was a little patch planted with garlic, and surrounded by earthen walls. There they lay and fired their last shot. The Turks had taken heart again and were advancing down the gully. They came on in open order, exposing only their skirmishers. Graham had only two cartridges left; he propped his rifle on the wall, sighted at two hundred yards, and picked out his man, and paused to steady his hand. The first shot missed; at the second the man fell in the act of firing. His blood was boiling, an unholy joy surged through him, he had forgotten his own danger, he stood up to fire, it seemed the most glorious moment in his life. The world was narrowed to the issue between himself and that Turkish skirmisher, his nerves were bent to the trigger, his very soul seemed to race down the barrel after the shot, and when the man fell, it was as if the victory were won and the war ended.

But the Legion was abandoning the hill at last. The rush of the Turks, stayed for a moment, came on triumphant. The company's ammunition was exhausted, and they too were scrambling from their shelter. The bullets whistled about them, it seemed impossible that they should reach yonder lane in safety, they drank in each moment of life, snatching the minutes as they slid from them.

The sergeant and Graham were the last to dash into the lane. " Well, I didn't think any of us would get out of that alive," he said, when they ventured to take breath and to look at one another.

But there was the Ulsterman with Smith on his back. He staggered into the lane from the other end and laid his burden on the ground. Smith had been shot through the knee-cap. His face was grey, the skin taut with agony. He moaned as his leg fell limp on the earth. The company gathered round him. " Let me be, mates," he said, " go on and never mind me ; " but there were two at his head and two at his feet. For twenty yards they bore him thus till the agony grew insupportable. Their uniforms were spattered with his blood, and he groaned as they jerked his leg. There was no ambulance at hand, no chance of finding a stretcher, and the Turks were on all the heights now, pouring lead around them. It was Captain Birch who wrenched the door from the hovel which stood beside the garden. They placed him on it and carried it at first by the corners.

But the strain was intolerable, and the door offered no firm grip to their hands. Then they set their rifles under it, but still each man could use only one hand, and their arms were stretched to their length, so that the great weight of a heavy man and a thick door fell upon their wrists.

As Graham went along at the head of the wounded man, he cursed the day's work. Ten minutes before he had gloried in the fall of that Turkish skirmisher, and now he realised that the wretched fellow was in misery like this. He hated himself for his exulting. He knew now what it meant; a grey, agonised face, a brave man groaning, and comrades in misery because of his suffering. The illusion of victory was past, the vanity of the fight apparent, and the Turks were at their back; their ammunition was spent, and they were burdened with a helpless man. Three miles of open country lay before them, bare fields, with never a tree to give them shelter, and now the Turkish guns had come up. A shell came humming past the bearers, and they realised that they were a conspicuous mark for the enemy. It burst a few yards in front with a glare of yellow flame. They were sprinkled with sand and grit, but no piece of its case reached them. Graham felt the sting of the gravel on his cheek, but he staggered stupidly on, stumbling over the furrows of the ploughed land.

The torment of the wound, the loss of blood, the jolting and the tossing had broken Smith's spirit.

He lay helpless on his back, a soldier no longer, and yet death came hissing past him. "Carry me quick, mates; don't leave me. O God!" he groaned.

"Cheer up, old man," said Simson, "we'll soon be out of it; you'll be safe when we get past the bridge."

But the bridge was three miles distant. And then Graham felt a sting in his left arm as if a stone had struck him, but he only needed his right to hold the rifle under the door, and still he stumbled on. But the strain on his wrist was terrible. He envied his rude companions; he would have given all the years of life spent in studies and class-room for the muscles of a mason or a carpenter. At last he stumbled outright and fell on his knees. It rent his heart to hear Smith groan. The Ulsterman was walking behind, he begged him to take his place. He had strained his wrist carrying Smith alone, but still he bravely took up the burden again.

And then Graham fell behind and looked at his arm. A ball had passed through his sleeve, but the skin was merely grazed. He felt an insane delight in this toy danger, he turned to tell Mavro of it. There he was, a yard or two behind, walking with the sergeant. "I've just had a narrow shave," he began, but he was checked. There was the same grey in Mavro's face, and he carried his right arm thrust for support into his jacket; he had thrown away his rifle, and he leaned heavily on the sergeant. "It's my funny-bone," he said, and he tried to smile ; "yes, it hurts badly," and his skin grew greyer and he lurched towards the sergeant. His face was set and his lips tight, but his agony was only too evident. The ball had cut through the nerves of the elbow, and every motion caused him exquisite torture. Graham felt utterly rebuked, all his love and admiration for his friend rose and accused him, he ought to have been beside him, he might have shielded him, at least he should have been by to help. But now Mavro leaned on the sergeant, and there was nothing for Graham to do.

They were passing a line of evzones, men of a fresh regiment who had not yet been engaged. They lay behind a low breastwork, their pieces loaded, waiting to fire till the plain should be clear of the retreating Legion. Graham felt an impulse to fling himself beside them; it seemed better to end the day fighting, it was intolerable to march thus, whole among the wounded, unarmed, with the Turk behind him. But he remembered that his ammunition was finished, and he stumbled stolidly on.

The whole plain was covered with the fugitives, evzones and legionaries mixed together. The balls were still hissing among them. On his left he heard a shriek like the cry of a wounded hare; he turned to see Alessandrini, the Italian lieutenant, leaping in the air. Then he fell heavily, and his men ran to help. Birch was just in front; suddenly he too gave a leap, and then hopped for a few steps on one leg. Voso was beside him and took his arm, and Graham ran up to his other side. They made a chair for him with Voso's rifle. Birch was as cool as ever, and made light of his wound. "It's only a stone, I think, just a flesh wound," and he put his arms round their necks and sat on the rifle. The corporal came running up, and the men who were carrying Smith turned round. Then an Italian private dashed past on a grey horse, clutching its mane, pale and sinister with fear. A shell burst in front of the horse, and it reared. The corporal ran up and snatched the rein, the man was evidently untouched. " Get off, you damned coward," shouted the corporal, and he dragged him from his seat, and Birch was placed on the saddle, sitting sideways.

And then, in the distance, the baggage-wagon of the Legion went lumbering past. It was heaped with wounded men; some were dead already, one sat on the seat holding his entrails together. Corrigan was perched on the edge, weeping and caressing his leg. He had been shot at the same moment as Smith; his fear had left him, for the worst had come. His sanity returned to him, and he hobbled along knowing that he had met his fate, certain that no other ball would touch him. And as the cart went past he had mustered strength to scramble on to it.

And then Graham overtook the men who were bearing Smith. There was little Simson, still trudging tirelessly along. Something like shame seized Graham at the sight of him.   " Let me take a hand now," he said.

"No, I'll not leave my mate," was the answer. But the Ulsterman was exhausted, and willingly yielded his place to Graham.   He had hardly snatched the rifle from him when his wrist began to give way again.   Middle Cock in front was declaring that he could not go much further.   The men were shouting " Help ! " to the Greeks and Italians who hurried past, and then when they paid no heed to the English word, it was, " Help, you —— cowards!" and this availed as little.   Graham called to them in French, but they went their way; the sound of the shells was in their ears, and they could see the bridge and safety.   And then came the evzone sergeant from whom Mick had got the loaf.   " Call to him in Greek," said Middle Cock, but Graham was as if he had never known a language but his own.   He searched for words, he hunted for the name of help, and nothing came but tears to his eyes, and old lines of Homer to his ears, but there was no help here nor in the fragments from Æschylus that crowded after, and the evzone went past.   At last despair made him cry out; "*Kyrie— elatho—travmatisthes,*"[1] he shouted, and the sergeant turned, a bearded man with red hair and kindly eyes.   Without a word he took his place among the bearers, and their hearts were glad and grateful.

The shells still fell about them, the cry of stricken men came from right and left, but there was

[1] Monsieur—come here—a wounded man.

nothing so terrible in all that din of battle as the voice of the wounded man. His face was yellow and smeared with blood from his hand, his eyes glittered like metal things ; he rose and sat upon the door and laughed an eldritch laugh, waving his hand to and fro. And then he sang : not the note of the Turkish horns, not the cry of " Allah " had frozen the blood like this song of the wounded man. It was " Ta-ra-ra-boom-de-aye ! " Again and again he sang it, with mad glee and imbecile insensibility. And then he lay back exhausted, and groaned, and prayed to his mates to carry him out of the battle.

Then the evzone, sturdy fellow though he was, gave up exhausted, and but for the willing aid of two Danes who overtook them, the Englishmen must have dropped their burden.

But at last the bridge was at hand. The bearers almost ran in their eagerness to cross it. As they passed they saw the cart overturned by the road-side. The dead were still under it, and the wounded lay groaning beside it waiting for help. A shell had fallen near it as it crossed the bridge, and the horses had taken flight and left the road.

They were on familiar ground now. There was the railway-station, and the farm-yard beyond it where they had bivouacked a week ago. With a great sigh of relief they saw men with the red cross on their arms moving about at last. They laid Smith down, and called a doctor to dress his wound. The bullet had passed clean through the leg; he bandaged one hole and left the other open

so flurried and fearful was he. Simson stayed
behind with his friend; the rest of the company
trudged on towards Pharsala with Birch and
Mavromichali.

"Well, I never thought we'd get 'im safe in,"
said the corporal; "and old Macaroni, so he's 'it
too. Well, he *was* plucky too; did you see 'im
walking about interpreting for the captain? An'
the captain 'isself. Great Scot! And these damned
red-cross men skulking 'ere all the while, and not
so much as a stretcher for us." But the passion of
the day was over, the Legion had saved its comrades, fired its last round, and upheld its honour to
the end. Now the effort was over, and it talked
bathos in safety.

CHAPTER XII

THE BOG OF LOST CAUSES

THEY left the wounded man in the hands of a Greek doctor. Only Simson, his old friend, stayed with him. The need for self-denial was over now, they walked no longer with measured footsteps, thinking of the burden they bore. The fugitives, who had passed them and refused their help, were on in front. The Englishmen hurried to overtake them, sunk now to their moral level. The baying of the guns still sounded at intervals behind them, battering their ears, adding to that intolerable weight of sensation which lay upon them. They became mere animals, part of a scattered herd, beasts with a prairie fire behind them and safety before. They felt no resentment against the enemy, no desire to stand and die and be avenged. They were aware of their own bodies, warm, sensitive masses, doubly dear to them because of the perils through which they had come unscathed. They walked along showing each other the precious rent in their uniforms made by a ball which had rushed past towards some other target.

Some had blue patches on their limbs or faces where a ricochet had struck them, or the hurricane made by a passing shell. Graham regarded his hand with a curious awe. It was numb and bent, the fingers clung together and curved themselves in a desperate grip as if he still were holding the butt of the rifle by which they had carried Smith upon the door. He marvelled at them and tried to tear them apart and straighten them out. Then Émile overtook him with his haversack full of biscuits, for he had found a store lying deserted by the railway-station. He was exalted with the glow of battle, his bronzed face shone, he forgot that he was retreating, he did not see the wounded in the cart that went beside them, creaking out an obbligato to their moanings with its unoiled wheels. He swung his rifle, he fingered his bandolier, full once more of cartridges that he had gathered from the abandoned magazine.

"Monsieur Henri," he said—it was Graham's Christian name, he could never pronounce the sur-name—"here you are, and not wounded? Good! Ah! it was glorious this battle. Mon Dieu! I fired off every cartridge I had. *Physingia, phy-singia! oh! les braves physingia!* And the French, every one says that we had the honours of the day. Did you hear us shouting to be led to the charge? Chanteloup could hardly hold us back—and the enemy were running. And then Varatasi—it is a brave little man. Brave? Yes, I assure you. He had his horse shot under him. But you have no

cartridges ; see, here's a box for you." Graham
took it mechanically, and, as he did so, noticed the
other's sack full of biscuits. Émile was still prattling gaily. He talked laughingly of "le petit
Louis," who had turned white and sick and run
to the rear at the first sound of a rifle ; and the
Armenian company, a mixed herd of Russians,
Bulgarians, Serbs, and Armenians, led by a loud-
mouthed martinet, half Bulgar, half Greek, one
Goulonides ; they had skulked in the rear too. But
the French and Varatasi, he could not exhaust his
praise of their gallantry. Graham interrupted him
to beg a biscuit. He walked along silently for a
while gnawing ravenously. It had been more the
reflection that he had not broken his fast for four-
and-twenty hours than actual hunger that made
him ask for food, but as he began to eat a terrible
faintness came over him. His knees were like to
sink under him, a feverish heat ran tingling through
him, his wits seemed to revive in a spasmodic
struggle to retain bare consciousness. He talked
to assure himself that he was not actually swoon-
ing. Who had been wounded among the French ?
Émile did not know ; he was only sure that they
had fought gallantly and must have suffered. How
did the fighting begin ? Were they driven from
Driskoli ? But of all that preceded the battle
Émile was equally ignorant. He knew only that
he had been firing incessantly for three hours, that
the French had done gallantly, and that Varatasi
was a miracle of prowess. He thrust more cart-

ridges upon Graham, and seemed surprised when
" Monsieur Henri " demanded further supplies of
hard biscuit, and still pressed for news of the
wounded.

The causeway was crowded now with legionaries
and evzones all in retreat towards Pharsala.   They
walked like civilians, the two regiments mingled
together, officers and privates went side by side.
They had done their duty, fighting through the
long hours of the summer day to give the main
army time to form.   Their allotted task was finished,
they were soldiers no longer.   They were stolidly
indifferent now to the issue of the day.   Their
sacrifice had availed nothing.   They at least were
safe, and they moved along over the causeway,
glad that everything was over.   With a very lan-
guid interest they watched the artillery beginning
to move forward over the bog to their left, and a
regiment of infantry advancing on their right.
Some instinct told them that the battle was ended ;
the troops which had not come to *their* support,
when alone they faced the invading army, would
not give combat now.   The scene had an inde-
scribable gloom.   The Greek forces had never
looked so dirty in their blue uniforms, so dispirited
as in this laggard advance.   A gun was fired on
their left as if by accident ; they could see where
the shell fell, short of the river, within the Greek
lines.   Then they met a squadron of cavalry
leaving the town.   The men sat their horses like
unwilling lumps, many of them wore their thick

greatcoats. They walked their beasts with the reins dangling over their necks for the most part. Their only dread seemed to be lest by any chance they should get within range of the Turks before their comrades of the infantry. They felt that they were moving about the plain to make copy for Athenian journals, to supply material for the apologies of royalist tacticians, and all this could be done with buttoned greatcoats and slack reins.

The town was abandoned to lawless infantry-men who had broken from their regiments. Some sat drinking in the garden of the little *café* by the roadside, others were breaking in the door of the shop which belonged to it. From another house came a stream of evzones laden with red shoes, the stock-in-trade of a cobbler who had long since fled. Groups of men were standing by the town foun-tain waiting their turn. They arranged themselves in orderly *queues*, they kept a discipline in the supply of their private wants which they disdained upon the battlefield. When their bottles were filled they slouched off in twos and threes along the road towards Domoko.

And all this the English company viewed with indifference. Their disdain for the Greeks allowed no addition, their sense of deadening failure, of dull impotence, could not have been more leaden. There was a sigh imprisoned in their bursting chest, a sob inaudible within their throat. But these were the nervous work of battle, the rebellion of the flesh against its unwilling heroism of combat and retreat. No fresh occasion could increase a gloom that was physical. It was only when they saw a heap of stretchers standing in the middle of the street, carefully roped together lest haply any of those men swarming about with red crosses on their arms should use them, that their anger broke forth. Even then they were scarce articulate, but they thought with a rage of pity of Smith lying in torment upon his door ; their arms still ached with the weight of that clumsy burden, and they reviled the callous cowardice of the ambulance, which had skulked all day within the town and left the wounded volunteers to the mercy of their comrades, unskilful men without appliances.

"Seems to me them jokers puts on the red cross so as to keep out of the fightin' ; fine 'andy excuse that is. The —— cowards knows as much about doctorin' as I do, and that ain't much." It was the corporal who spoke. At that moment a gentlemanly youth in uniform went past with the red cross on his arm, a medical student in all like-lihood, one of the irresponsible bloods whose rioting had forced the Government into the war. The corporal turned savagely to him. "Yes, you, you —— coward with your red cross and your *zeto polemos*. That's all *you're* good for. And you think *we're* going to do your fightin' for you, do you ? I'll see myself damned first. Oh I you'd laugh, would you ? " The red-cross man had turned

and bowed with a puzzled and exaggerated smile ;
" *Ti thelete kyrie ?* " [1] he said.

"By God, if you swear at us, I'll soon show
you——"

The man bowed again and essayed French :
"*Qu'y a-t-il pour votre service, Monsieur ?* "

Another volley of oaths greeted his civility.

"*Germanos,*" he exclaimed with ineffable disgust
as he turned on his heel, as who should say, "The
man is a boor and no friend of Hellas, pah! I
smelt his nationality under his armpits, and his
hands were black with powder." For a Greek
tempers his cowardice with courtesy, and neglects
his duty with a southern grace.

Then it was a little posse of horsemen who overtook them, making towards Domoko. A cloaked
figure on a beautiful Arab rode at their head. As
he approached they could see his face in the
waning light blanched with terror. He turned
repeatedly to right and left, hoping against hope
for a salute, fearing rather to look down a rifle-
barrel levelled at his head. It was the Crown
Prince. The retreat had begun. As he passed
down the street, men turned and muttered angrily
to their companions. The Legion stared him out
of countenance, but no one saluted. He dis-
appeared, followed by red-liveried grooms and
body-servants.

In the centre of the village, opposite the fountain,
stood a large *café*. The shutters were up, and the

[1] What do you want, sir ?—What can I do for you ?

door closed. Evidently the proprietor had fled when the fighting began. A mob of legionaries, chiefly Italians, were battering down the door. While the Greek soldiery had no thought but flight, the Philhellenes, wrought to an intolerable pitch of excitement by the noise and the hazard of battle, reckless of further danger, were bent on exhausting the resources of the town; they rummaged it for drink, driven by a need to live still at battle-heat. At long intervals came the sound of guns six miles away across the river from the Turkish batteries on Tekké heights; the air still throbbed with the reverberation of battle, while the blows of rifle-stocks rained upon the door. The man shouted as the dull thud changed to a crunch of yielding wood, and then the door fell, and the besiegers rushed in. The place was almost dark, but in three minutes every bottle was gone from the shelves behind the bar; rifles, blankets, and sacks were flung upon the floor and the tables, and the men emerged unarmed, some tearing the corks from the bottles with their teeth, some drinking already. Mick, the Armenian, had secured a large bottle of cognac; he came beaming and self-possessed to the corporal to exhibit his treasure. "Me find," he said, "English very good," as he poured the spirit into the corporal's pannikin.

The company was seated now under the verandah of the *café*. Three times the pannikin had gone round, when a cheer came from the far end of the street. It was Varatasi on a little pony, riding along with half the Legion round him. "Good old Varatasi," said the corporal, "'e's come through somethink to-daiy, you bet. Shouldn't wonder if 'e'd be glad of some brandy. It's prime stuff, this is." And they all rose and crowded round him, and the corporal pressed the pannikin into his hand. He sat far back in the saddle as if he were dreaming. His eyes had a witching light in them, as if he were peering into some beyond, as if he saw, not the street thronged with common soldiers, not the village lewd with incipient debauch, but some world more dignified where lost causes wear statelier weeds, and heroism has still a glow upon it when it drops its defeated sword. He took the drink, and all he said was "*Merci*," but the gesture had a grace, the word a music in it, and the Legion cried, "*Bravo!*" and "*Hoch!*" and "*Hurrah!*" and the emaciated figure on the sorry pony left a trail of enthusiasm behind it.

"By God, 'e's come through a lot 'as Varatasi ; 'e was in the thick of it, you bet," said the company, " you could see that in his face." And the company shook its head, and deemed it marvellous that the shells which had not spared them should hiss round their commander.

And then they fell in with Uncle and Morgan, Fulton and Isinglass, the four who had been left in camp that morning.

"Well, I'm blowed," said Middle Cock, "'ere's old Uncle as large as life. Got that mutton ready,

Uncle ? I'm free to saiy it's a bit empty in 'ere.
Cut us another slice, won't you ? "

"You shut up, Middle Cock, and pass the
brandy."

" Well, an' 'ow many Turks may you 'ave bagged,
Uncle ? " said the corporal.

" Ax me another," answered Uncle, and then he
began to chuckle. " Blowed if I know, but I bet I
did for some of 'em. W'y, I up with the old rifle
and just swung her round right along the line of
'em, and says I, ' Blowed if that don't do for some
of 'em.' "

The company roared, and the cognac vanished.

" W'y, w'ot are you blokes laughing at ? I tell
you I swung the —— rifle along the 'ole ——
line."

" Fact," said Morgan, "so he did, just as if it
was a Maxim or something, and then he turned to
me and says he, ' Now I've done for the whole
—— lot of 'em.' Good old Uncle."

The laugh continued, the joke broadened into
many an obscene ripple.

" Had much sport, you fellows ? " continued
Morgan. "We caught a spy."

" Who's we ? " asked the sergeant.

" Me and old Speropoulo ; we're no end of
chums."

" Who's Speropoulo ? "

" Why, that lieutenant chap—decent fellow he
is."

" Oh ! him ! "

" This is the fez I took from him, I'm going to wear it.   I took his rifle too, but Speropoulo's got it.   I must speak to Speropoulo about that."

"Were you with Varatasi all day?" asked somebody.

" Yes, I was by him all through the battle. You should have seen him.   He's a brave chap is Varatasi.   Why, he had his horse shot under him, and he turned and asked for some one to put it out of its pain.   So I shot it through the head, and it kicked and never moved again.   I bet there's not a braver officer in the army than Varatasi. Here's a bit of his horse's mane.   I cut it off for a keepsake."

Elusive magnetism of courage!   It evades analysis, it compels belief.   The crassest vulgarian can feel it, he bears it with him, a sacred memory, and to prove the grandeur of his hero, he cites his charger's fate, and rests the marvel of his bravery on the authenticity of a bit of horse-hair.

Graham was struggling to extort a narrative from Isinglass.   The man was confused, and so eager to talk of his adventures that his desires left him no leisure to find words.   "A queer experience for a simple man like me, Mr. Graham," he kept repeating.   He had been lying all morning in the sun, ill with dysentery.   About noon there began a stir in the camp; men ran this way and that excitedly, the horses were put into the baggage-cart, and officers came to them shouting "some foreign nonsense, ancient Greek or somethink."

They put their heads together and decided to take their weapons and follow the Legion. And then came a firing of cannon, and "ye wily Turk" appeared marching down the valley. Here Isinglass' memory seemed to fail him, the rest of the day was full of nameless sensation, the prickling of heat, the pawing of fear about his heart, the hoarse rage of cheering, and the gambler's delight in standing amid the hurtling shells, with fingers itching round the trigger.

The company was merry now. The cognac went round among them briskly. It had an easy triumph over their taut nerves and empty stomachs. O'Brian and the corporal were almost at blows over the Irish question. Middle Cock radiating esteem and affection for them both, effectually parted them by falling between them. Isinglass grew patriotic in his cups. He stood up panting with emotion, rigid with fervour. "Talk of Hireland," he was saying, "and Greece (hic, hic), and Greece. *You'd* fight for Greece? I fight for Greece? Never, never (hic, hic). '*A muscle like iron and a nerve like steel*,' no, '*A nerve like steel and a muscle like iron*' (hic, hic), '*And a will once fixed no force can repeal, And that's what an Englishman's made of*' (hic, hic)," and to illustrate his point he drank more cognac and slid on to the street.

Graham endeavoured in vain to interpose. He had drunk but sparingly himself, but even as it was, he felt the terrible power of the liquor run-

. ning riot in a brain weary with battle and hunger.
An ecstasy of shame came over him.   Chanteloup
passed by, and he thought of "these new crusades."
He tried to induce the company to put past the
bottle, he reminded them of the march that lay
before them over the mountains to Domoko.
They might have to start at any moment, already
the regiments were filing past.   But the corporal
had answered cheerfully.   "Every man knows 'ow
much brandy 'e can carry (hic).   We're all ri'.
Don't you trouble your 'ead about us, Mr. Graham.
Mebbe *you've* 'ad enough, that's your affair.   'Ere,
sit down, wo't cher?   Pass the bottle to Mr.
Graham, Uncle.   A man needs a somethink after
what 'e's come through."

.   Then the artillery came lumbering through the
village, and long files of infantry followed it.
Graham turned from the company, weary and dis-
gusted, foreseeing the terrors of the long march to
come, unable to do anything.   The moral atmosphere had grown unbreathable among his fellow-
countrymen ; he turned for relief to the *café.*   It
was a large, square room with a low ceiling.   The
air was hot and foul, men lay asleep on all the
benches, wearied out and stupefied with drink.   A
few candle-ends burned waywardly in empty
bottles on the tables, and groups of wild faces sat
over them gambling.   The flickering light illuminated their passions.   Cast from beneath, it gave
inverted effects, planting its shadows in unwonted
places, suggesting a carnival of distorted emotions

unknown in times of peace. Stumbling over many
a prostrate form Graham made his way to a little
table where Érin and Émile sat talking to the
sergeant of their company. He was an old grey-
bearded man with an air of pride which he seemed
too weary to sustain. A soldier from his teens,
he had known the joy of victory, and borne the
brunt of many a wearing campaign. One ambition had sustained him, the hope of reaching a
commission at last. It was this which had brought
him out to Greece, to face once more hunger and
cold, risk, and exposure, and weariness. He carried
some half-dozen medals on his breast, won in
Algeria and Italy. Graham sat down opposite to
him. He seemed lost in a reverie of utter discontent. Occasionally he looked up and shouted
a complaint against this miserable army. He
hardly noticed Graham.

" You are sure it was he ? " he was saying to
Érin.

"Yes, it was he, I saw him driving about the
battlefield in a closed carriage."

" The man who reviewed us at Larissa ? "

" Yes, it was the Crown Prince. I could not be
mistaken. I saw the red-coated lacqueys with
yellow boots."

" *Diable !* "

He buried his head in his hands again and
relapsed into silence. One could see only the
three silver stripes of his sergeant-major's rank
upon his arm, and behind it the hair grown white

as the stripes in gaining this poor distinction. He felt now that the whole campaign must end in disaster, his last hope of winning the promotion that had been the goal of his life was blasted.

"*Tenez*," said Érin, "you were at Solferino? Was it like to-day's battle?"

"It was a victory," said the sergeant.

And then all three were silent. They envied the wretched old man. They feasted their eyes upon his medals; they would have sold long years and bartered hardships for the flush of victory, the pride of counting a triumph among the moments of their life. They felt themselves the victims of a hard chance; the sacrifices, the heroism, the danger are not greater when victory is the issue. They had toiled, and only the shame of defeat rewarded them.

One of the German company strolled up to Graham presently. He was a tall man, with a great brow and dreamy eyes which seemed oppressed by its weight. He had the exquisite Slavonic mouth, a pouting, sensuous upper lip which all but hides the lower, and gives to the whole face the expression of one who has made too great demands on life, who recognises their vanity, yet cannot leave desiring. He was a Pole by birth, an exile from his country, one of a band of revolutionary students who plot, and drink, and dream in Zurich, and wake up some morning from a mist of wine and fancy, in a burst of explosive energy, and rush to their death, trusting still to the studied illusions of a lifetime. He too was bitter in his outcry against the Prince and the Greek army. He hoped some day to fight for Poland's independence. He talked of secret societies, of a network of volunteer organisations throughout Europe. There were twenty thousand men in England alone, he said, pledged to march against Russia when the hour for uprising shall strike.

"I never heard of them," said Graham.

"Of course not, the thing is a secret. We have learned the value of discipline and organisation. Our preparations are almost complete. I shall be in command of a regiment from the Swiss Universities. I came here to prepare myself, to learn something of war. But it's so much time wasted. I shall learn nothing here. The Greeks were unprepared, they ought never to have risked this campaign."

"And you, will you wait till you have a force equal to Russia's, and victory is certain?"

For reply he only detailed their organisation— secret committees of young men who met to make speeches amid the fumes of beer and tobacco. He was pitiless in his criticism of a failure that was palpable, proved to his ears by the echo of the marching of an army in retreat. But the other cause, that was bound up with every breath he drew, he refused to criticise or doubt, and all his sorrow was for the collapse of the enterprise to which he had looked for a military training.

The candle-ends were flickering out now. The gamblers were pocketing their winnings and rolling themselves in their blankets upon the floor. Graham flung himself beside Érin under a table. His blanket had been left behind in Driskoli, but he was too weary, too full of the day's tragedy to think much of his loss. But the air of the *café* was foul and stifling, and the men around him groaned in their sleep. Isinglass made one corner hideous with his drunken ravings; he was on the verge of delirium. At last Graham rose and lay down on the flagstones under the verandah. The air was bitterly cold, and the pavement beneath him made his bones ache. The cognac which he had drunk had left his brain heated and fevered. Half-way through the night he rose and bathed his head at the village fountain. He stumbled in the darkness, and he fancied that he must be drunk. A sickening shame overpowered him ; he lay flogging himself for his weakness. He vowed that he would not taste strong drink till the war was over. To be drunken in the hour of crisis and disaster, to stagger in the uniform of a sacred cause—it was the crowning humiliation of the day. He lay absorbed in his selfish musings. He mourned over this blot on his honour, while inside the *café* the sergeant wept over his shattered hopes of promotion, and the Pole nursed his disillusionment, and planned desertion.

Towards three in the morning he fell asleep. The last Greek regiment went past him, and the

N

echo of its footfall entered his dreams. He thought
that he was in some large town at home. It was
Saturday afternoon, and armies of working-men
hurried through the streets. He noted their air of
gaiety and content. A week of hard work was
behind them ; they hastened as from some battle
where energy, and discipline, and care of minutiæ
had won the day. They lit their pipes, making
careful breastworks against the wind with their
hands or with their coats. They husbanded their
matches as if they had been cartridges. The cars
went by, running smoothly on rails prepared for
them. It seemed a marvel of organisation. Each
man was going home too ; a gentle selfishness
possessed them, a private selfishness which no one
shared. An old man was fiddling in a side street.
A score of busy wayfarers passed him as he drew
his bow over the wet strings. He was blind, and
no one regarded him. Graham stood and watched
him in his dream. The old man's face moved with
some emotion, the bow rose and fell, the gnarled
fingers wriggled painfully up and down the strings,
but no sound was audible. The melody died in
the fiddle, only the broken musician heard it. It
was drowned by the footsteps of the passengers,
each hurrying home. Graham was like to weep at
this type of futility, and then he looked again and
saw that the blind fiddler wore a blue uniform and
top-boots. It was Varatasi.

He awakened as the last company of the
defeated army filed past him. The legionaries

began to rise and shovel on their accoutrements. They were pale and bent, and their eyes were red and blear. Varatasi was arranging the order of the companies. He was trying to make the sergeant-major understand him by means of signs. And then Graham rose, and a great joy filled him. He saw a duty before him, and from that moment to the end of the war he acted as interpreter to the English company.

An hour later the Legion filed out of Pharsala. As they mounted the hills behind it, they looked back on the great plain of calamity, the bog of lost causes. The white tents of the Turks shimmered in the morning sunlight. They were the tents which the Greeks had abandoned at Larissa. They followed the defeated army, a badge of old dishonour, presage of fresh disaster.

CHAPTER XIII

A COMEDY IN FIVE ACTS

I

IT was on Tuesday morning, the day before the battle at Pharsala, that a legionary returning from hospital in Volo had handed Palli the mysterious letter. A lady had given it to him, he said; she had been visiting the wounded in company with the wife of the French Consul. She had written the letter on the spot, hearing that he belonged to the Foreign Legion and was about to rejoin it. Palli recognised the hand. It was that of "the French laidy"; a faint perfume clung to it still, it recalled many sprightly little notes of invitation received in the happier days before his "doctor" sent him to Greece "for a change." With a trembling hand he opened it. It seemed no miracle that she should be here; he had dreamed of her in camp; he had carried her image through the Mati battle and the Larissa retreat. He had heard her voice while Mavromichali or Graham talked to him, and its tones had been more real than theirs. She was the sole centre of emotion to him, the only tangible thing in all the world. Nay, long ere this, passion's reasoning had all but convinced him of her presence. He read her note with no surprise.

> " *Volo*,
> " *Monday, May* 3.

"DEAR M. PALLI,

"Why don't you come to see me? You are very neglectful. We have been here with the *Hyacinthe* for nearly a week. I am dying of *ennui*. This place is full of nasty peasants, and dirty officers and wounded soldiers. Besides, I want to see you in your new *rôle*. You are the last man I would have expected to be bitten with a love of soldiering. But that only shows how little I knew you.

> "Yours in haste,
> "EUGÉNIE BLANC."

Through the long morning he paced about, debating what he should do. Sometimes he thought of her wish to see him, her playful accusation of neglect pleased him, and he was fain to go. Sometimes he gave way to his pique at her raillery, and he decided to stay. And then he would read the note again, and the last sentence would puzzle him anew and stimulate his curiosity. She admitted that she had not known him when she rejected him. Things might go differently now, and so he walked swiftly to head-quarters and got his leave of absence, hurrying lest a new aspect of the case, less flattering and hopeful, should strike him. And while he weighed the end and the beginning of her letter, and passed over the middle with a gesture of impatience, Eugénie Blanc sat sunning herself on the deck of her father's yacht, brooding on the tedium of her existence. Palli appeared to her as a possible relief from boredom.

The military train which should have taken him from Pharsala to Volo, had stopped at Velestino Junction amid Smolenski's army. The delay would be indefinite; he decided to stay and visit the scene of Friday's engagement. By good luck he might even see a battle, and return to Driskoli the object of the Legion's envy.

He left the station and strolled up towards Velestino village, a pretty hamlet framed in olive groves and mulberry plantations, with gently sloping hills behind it. An ornate mosque, with an old stone bath beside it, rose in its slim grace beside the barn-like church; a few houses of red stucco with the woodwork painted a crude green, stood among the yellow mud huts of the peasantry, vaunting their gay colours in the bright sunshine. The left wing of Smolenski's force lay camped with its mountain batteries in trenches on the hills. The guns were covered with leathern cases on their mouths. The men strolled about unarmed, smoking cigarettes. The Turks had withdrawn since Friday's battle; the great plain lay clear, between the low hills that sloped towards Tekké on the left and the outworks of Pelion on the right. Between them was Karla Lake, blue and peaceful and cool, stretching into a misty distance where it seemed to merge in the snowy top of Olympus.

Palli made his way to head-quarters. As he strolled past the groups of evzones and linesmen who stood chatting with irregulars by the road-side, he became aware of a spiritual climate different from that which prevailed in the Prince's army. These men were victors ; they had confidence in their commander; the commissariat served them better; they recognised the tactical skill which had disposed them in their trenches on the hillside. They eagerly awaited another battle; the honour of Hellas was in their keeping, and this responsibility wrought a subtle change in their bearing, nay, even in their dress and in their carriage. Above all, they had no reproachful memories of rifles flung upon the Larissa road ; they had kept aloof from the rout, and their General had been with them in retreat.

Outside Smolenski's tent, Palli was astonished to find another man in the uniform of the Legion. It was Coletti. He had made his way leisurely to Domoko and so to Velestino. He had cut down his trousers to knickerbockers, he was now a free man. He had wrung Smolenski's hand, and the General's tent was open to him, the sole " English " volunteer in the brigade. He was standing outside now, chatting with a staff officer. The pair were discussing the points of a score of horses which stood tethered to a fence beside the General's tent. They were Turkish chargers found riderless on the field after the mad cavalry rush on Friday. Coletti and the officer received the new-comer effusively. They greeted him at first as a foreign legionary, and then as a bearer of a name known all over Greece, for ancestors of his had fought bravely at Suli against the great Ali Pasha, and what was perhaps of more consequence in the eyes of modern Greece, they had founded a firm whose banks are trusted all over the Levant.

Coletti and he were soon on easy terms. The "Englishman" showed him the stores of Martini rifles gathered on the field; he had discarded his *Gras* since Saturday, and went about exhibiting his Turkish weapon to every one he met, longing for a chance to use it against the Turk himself. Now he insisted on arming Palli with another of the captured weapons, and then, mounted on Turkish chargers, the pair set out to inspect the battlefield.

They visited the battery which had withstood the rush of Moslem horsemen. It was planted on a plateau, and its pieces, gagged now with their leathern covers, were pointed down the long slope which led to the plain. It was dotted with little mounds, the graves of the troopers who had sold their lives so gallantly. Coletti and Palli went about poking in the fresh earth of the little heaps looking for trophies, rewarded now and again by the discovery of some bit of torn blue cloth, or

perhaps a hand or a foot projecting from its tomb.
They went about prattling, like children let loose
in the greenroom of a theatre, playing with the
properties of last night's tragedy.   And round
them the bees hummed among the heather, grass-
hoppers plied their busy music in the sunlight, and
the wind that had toyed with the smoke of shrapnel
three days before, babbled among the reeds, and
blew its rustic perfumes into the nostrils of the
sight-seers.   They trampled the dead under-foot,
and desecrated with their prying the memory
of that Moslem sabbath, when a cloud of dust had
swept over the slope, and a shout of " Allah " came
from it, bidding defiance to the guns which bayed
against it.   Bravely it swept on while the shells
cut lanes through it, and the bullets of the evzones
who assailed its flank made ruin in its columns, till
at length, its war-cry silenced, its ranks broken, it
turned and galloped back.   One man alone reached
the battery, staggering along in a splendour of
fanatical rage till, wounded and dismounted, he fell
across the gun on which his eyes had fixed while
his comrades were still around him, and their
shouting fired his blood.

"You're a sensible fellow, dear friend," said
Coletti to Palli, as they mounted their chargers
once more and slung their Martinis over their
backs.   "You did well to leave the Legion.   You'll
see life, I tell you, as an irregular ; you're your own
master, free to come and go, and every one respects
you.   Look at me : Smolenski treats me like a

gentleman, I sleep in his tent; he lent me his rug the other night; and there are no damned Italian officers to bully you and send you errands."

II

On the evening of the following day the pair were standing again together near the head-quarters tent. The Turks had returned in force, a simultaneous attack was being made on Pharsala and Velestino. Their efforts had been concentrated on Smolenski's left wing; could they but turn it, they would cut the communication with Pharsala, and isolate the two armies. All day the Greek artillery had played on the advancing squares, again and again the Turkish infantry had attempted to rush the heights where the Greeks lay behind their breastworks. Again and again they had retired, discomfited by the accurate practice of Smolenski's gunners, and the enthusiastic volleys of the evzones. Now they were massing across the valley for a final effort.

Smolenski rode along his lines, received everywhere with enthusiastic cheers. The dark eyes glowed in the powerful square-cut face, a face that bespoke inflexible determination, an almost brutal force of will tempered by a quick gift of foresight and calculation. He addressed his men in terse, vigorous sentences, instinct with magnetic confidence. It was the critical hour in the day, his own reputation was at stake, and the fate of Greece perhaps depended on the effect of his words.   He bade his troops remember of what stock they came, urged them to quit themselves like men, to stand firm even if the sacred soil of Thessaly should be drenched with their blood.   With a cheer that was half a sob of passionate devotion the men responded; afire with heroism, they hardly saw the disciplined line which advanced against them.   The batteries played upon it, the infantry fired volley after volley into it, until at last it wavered.   Leaving their trenches with a cheer the Greeks charged down the hillside, and the advancing host broke and vanished in the hills.   The battle was won.

Palli had fired his Martini at intervals throughout the day, lying down in the remotest trench, and sighting at eighteen hundred yards.   He knew that the range was too great, yet at last he would be able to say that he had potted the Turks.   He even fixed his bayonet when the charge took place.   He fell gradually and gracefully to the rear, and waited for a moment, watching the rout of the Turks. Then with a sigh of satisfaction and a smile of self-complacency he turned and made his way to Velestino station, with the air of one who has watched a thrilling melodrama from a comfortable box, seen the curtain fall on the death of the villain, and now saunters off to catch the train which will carry him to his suburban villa.   Two hours later he stood on the quay at Volo, waiting for a boat which would take him to the *Hyacinthe.*

III

The yacht *Hyacinthe* lay at anchor in Volo harbour.   The bay was crowded with men-of-war ; there were the cruisers and battle-ships of the Greek Eastern Squadron, with Prince George's torpedo flotilla nestling under their bows.   There were the gunboats of the Powers, quietly waiting events, and here and there a smart Glasgow-built passenger boat which the Government had impressed as a troopship or hospital boat.   Alongside the *Hyacinthe* lay the *Albania*, almost deserted save for the dirty bare-legged blue-jacket who paced her deck on sentry duty with bayonet fixed. Native *caïques* flitted hither and thither, poised on their graceful wing-like sails, and flat-bottomed lighters plied between the merchantmen and the *Mole*, carrying army stores.   The Greek boatmen stood up in their bows, swaying backwards and forwards, rowing with a sort of back-water stroke.

On the *Mole* blue-jackets from the foreign warships strolled to and fro, laughing to the impassive refugee women camped there with their children and household belongings, waiting for a boat to carry them in safety to the islands.   The town lay round the bay, an uneasy motley thing, with its churches and its mosque, its handsome hotels and public buildings, its squalid lanes and oriental bazaars topped by tall chimneys of brick, which mark the sites of factories where they turn out

"Egyptian" cigarettes or "French" cognac.
Behind the town is the heavy mass of Pelion with
its terraced hamlets and its villas, flat-roofed and
girt with vines.

On the deck of the *Hyacinthe*, under a striped
awning, two girls were sitting on American folding
chairs. Eugénie Blanc, the elder of the pair, was
a pretty blonde, about the middle height, and
some twenty-five summers old. Her figure was
full and mature, and her pink blouse and short
walking skirt displayed it with little reticence.
She seemed to vaunt her sex, to luxuriate in her
womanhood. Her hair was auburn, and curled
with a charming waywardness over the smooth
characterless forehead. One noted rather the ears
and the neck than the clear blue eyes and short if
shapely nose. The features were those of the
average pretty girl, inoffensive, negatively pleasant,
but there was a waxen delicacy about the tiny
ears, and an alluring suggestion of grace and
slightness in the white neck and the lawless little
curls that caressed it. The lips were habitually
parted ; one forgave that suggestion of weakness
for the vision of pearly teeth between the sensuous
curves. Anne Beaulieu, her companion, was still
in her teens. Dress and features alike ran to stiff
lines and angles, but there was a charm of merry
abandonment, of almost naughty gaiety in the
dance of her eyes ; her nose was long and straight
and her chin pointed. They promised something
vigorous and eccentric in her character. The pair

had been reading during the sultry afternoon, but now their books lay idly on their knees, and Anne was chatting vivaciously. Eugénie seldom spoke much to women, with men she was more demonstrative.

Anne got up and sauntered round the deck; as she returned she gazed fixedly at her friend.

"Oh, but you do look cross, Eugénie; what on earth is the matter?"

"I'm only bored."

"*Only* bored; as if that wasn't enough. Now if I were bored I should fly into a great rage, and make things interesting. That was what I used to do in the convent, till the abbess took me into her cell, and said, oh! such funny things, and then I ran away to my room, and laughed, and laughed, and laughed!"

"Oh, you quaint child! I could endure an abbess, but that Mr. Wilson—that's quite another matter."

"How often has he proposed?"

"Let me see, how long is it since we left Constantinople?"

"One, two, three, four—oh, how brown my hands are getting—five—ten days."

"Then say ten times for a rough estimate. He does it every day at dessert. What a sad world it is, to be sure! You can calculate all that's going to happen. At seven we shall dress, we shall be ten minutes late for dinner, the soup will be cold, father will be cross, Mr. Wilson will blush and apologise for me; then there'll be razor-fish, and chicken, and lamb, and oranges."

"'As it was in the beginning, is now, and ever shall be,'" said Anne, intoning the quotation; "and Mr. Wilson will propose to you while you're helpless and at his mercy, fighting with a banana. Why can't he do it every second day for a change? And then we go to our cabin, and he sits talking to your father about his travels in South Africa, no doubt—how much he paid for a cigar in Pretoria, and how bad it was, or how his eleven nearly beat the English embassy at cricket in Constantinople, or how he wondered if he could trust the Armenian porter to carry his silver dressing-case ashore. Would you like to marry that silver dressing-case, my dear?"

Eugénie only fanned herself languidly, and watched the sentry on the *Albania*.

Anne rattled on.

"And then they'll come into our cabin, and Mr. Wilson will sit with his hands on his knees, like an old Egyptian god, gazing at your beauty. And when we can stand him no longer, we'll pretend that it's time to go to bed, and we'll both have headaches in the morning until he's gone off with your father. Oh, dear, do they never change the tunes on this barrel-organ? I wonder will M. Palli come?"

"I don't. I'm certain he will. Just as certain as that Mr. Wilson will make one of his proposals to-night while I'm skinning my banana."

"Then don't take one."

"But I like them."

"Which? Oh, you dear old hypocrite! And I suppose you don't care whether M. Palli comes or not?"

"No. I'm quite indifferent."

"Eugénie," the girl spoke solemnly, "I'm going to say *things* to you. Now don't pout. If I were you I should just adore M. Palli. I never heard of anything so romantic. To think of his going off to get killed, all for you, because he couldn't have you. Don't you feel vain—just a little bit?"

"No."

"I know you do. You're only shamming. If I were you, I would—I would go down on my knees to him—from sheer vanity. You needn't try to deceive me. Why did you send him that invitation?"

"Oh, I want to be amused. You can't think how funny he'll look in uniform. I can hardly imagine it."

"You mean you can hardly imagine whàt a man looks like who's dying for you."

"Oh, yes, I can. I've seen it often. They generally dress very badly."

"You don't deserve to be so beautiful, Eugénie. It isn't fair. You've got no idea of romance. Oh, if I had half your beauty! And I've tried so hard! For a whole year I went to bed at eight and slept round the clock, just to get a good complexion. I hate pale, interesting people. I want to be big, and red, and healthy, like the girls in tobacco shops, you know. And the only person who ever made love to me was a little boy at school, who wanted to elope with me and join a circus troupe. And you—men fling away their lives for you, and you don't care *that!* But, I—am—quite—sure— that you're—shamming, miss, You *do* care. I should *hate* you if you didn't."

IV

Towards six o'clock on Wednesday evening Palli arrived in Volo. As he walked through the streets of the town, he found himself regarding them in other wise than he had done three weeks before when the Legion landed there from Athens *en route* for Larissa. His standard of comparison was changed. His memories of Paris, or Havre, or Marseilles were obliterated, the place seemed vast when he thought of Driskoli or Velestino. The houses were palatial ; in the wares in the windows of the sorry shops he recognised culture and civilisation once more. The sight of a bookseller's show-case made him gape. He felt all at once twice as dirty and unkempt as before. He paused before a photographer's booth, uncertain whether to go in and perpetuate his disguise; but a barber's pole beckoned to him across the street, and he ran to it with a nervous thrill of delight. He washed his face and brushed his hair before he

o

would submit to the scissors.   At a neighbouring
shop, a queer compound of drapery and iron-
mongery and grocery store, he bought a white
linen shirt, and went to an hotel for a bath.   He
lay half-an-hour in the warm water, luxuriating in
a new sense of cleanliness.   On his way to the
quay he was assailed by the sellers of oranges and
lemons.   He bought some fruit, and despite his
nascent passion for respectability, ate it on the
spot, and went back for more.   He could have
gorged on lemons, they were ambrosia to him, his
blood cried out for them after the diet of lamb and
sour bread to which he had been reduced in the
Legion.   Verily abstinence makes strange luxuries.

It was already the dinner-hour when he reached
the *Hyacinthe*.   Victor Blanc, an old friend of his
father, greeted him warmly.   He was a tall, handsome man, with alert but courteous manners, grey-
haired, but still vigorous ; he had been a politician
of some note and a senator, until some breath of
scandal from the Panama affair forced him to
retire.   But he was still a keen financier, and a
traveller, and he loved to match himself with
younger men on the Bourse and the high seas.
Palli was silent over the table ; he felt his brain
move sluggishly, he could not keep pace with the
talk of these people round him, who had not
dwelt in the wilderness among savages.   Words
came slowly to his lips, he could hardly think
except of his animal wants.   He dallied over the
modest dainties of the meal, the soup, and the fish,

and the salad. To taste unresined wine of France
was experience enough for an evening, and he felt
an insane pride in rejecting the lamb. Mr. Wilson,
who had been dismayed at first by the advent of
such a formidable rival, plucked up courage when
he saw Palli's silence. He devoted himself to
Eugénie, and talked loudly in the most blatant
manner of the British philistine, of the sorry show
which the Greeks were making in the war. Victor
Blanc was annoyed with him, but neither his
sympathy nor Wilson's jibes roused Palli from his
lazy, sensuous dream.

The ladies rose early from table and went on
deck. It was nine o'clock before Palli followed
them. The cool air braced him, he was satisfied
now, and began to feel at home in this strange
environment of comfort and elegance. Eugénie
was sitting down and Anne was standing beside
her. She was listless, and hardly noticed her
lover's approach; his silence had annoyed and
disappointed her. It was Anne who began the
conversation. She assumed the exaggerated, uneasy manner of a young actress who is trying to
play the part of an eighteenth-century coquette.
She bowed to Palli as he came up; she threw
herself into quaint alluring postures; she was full
of graceful apology. Wouldn't he tell them something about the battle? She knew he must be
tired, and she was sure he had fought very hard,
but she would *so* like to know. And she leaned
back against the taffrail at an angle of sixty

degrees, casting her eyes at Palli. He had not time to reply before Eugénie sat up in her lounge chair and began to talk; the coquettish advances of Anne had piqued her. She seemed suddenly to realise the æsthetic value of this man, who would fling away his life for her. She felt Anne's interest as a challenge to herself to claim him. Her dormant vanity was roused.

"Come into the light and let me see you," and she waved to him to stand under the lamp that hung from the rigging.

"I'm really not fit to be reviewed by my Empress Eugénie."

"Oh! you don't know how picturesque you are. But you don't look hungry enough."

"I have feasted. Mademoiselle sat opposite to me."

"You've lost half your buttons. You've got a beard. Your boots have not been cleaned for a month of Sundays. This is capital. And you have one—two—three rents."

"There is another which Mademoiselle cannot see."

"Then turn round."

And so she inspected him, laughing at his clumsy uniform. She made him show her his arms, and she played with the rifle. He took her little hand in his, thrilling at the touch, and showed her how to work it; and then she would have him stand behind her, leaning over her shoulder while she raised the heavy weapon and tried to hold it in position.

And next she spent her curiosity on the details
of camp life. She did not ask Anne's question
about the Velestino battle, she would not adopt
another's interest, and accept the lead of a school-
girl; she pressed rather for details about food and
quarters, and the *personnelle* of the Legion. She
gave a frigid shudder when she heard of nights on
the bare hillside, and to Palli they seemed twice as
cold and comfortless as before. He talked of the
lamb coarsely roasted over a wood fire, greasy and
ill-cooked, which one tore with one's fingers after
removing the straws and grit that adhered to it.
She shook her head, looked down, and gave a
gurgle of disgust.

"Oh! I don't know how you can be so nasty,"
was her comment; "no civilised man would endure
it; don't talk about it, please. The men, are they
all impossible?"

"Most of them. I hardly know anything about
them. Half of them are old soldiers discharged
for drinking. Two of them hail from the Austra-
lian diggings. There's a little Cockney shop-boy,
a few Irish savages, and a pair of cattle-drovers
recently escaped from an American liner. I sus-
pect one man of being a card-sharper, whose trick
has been discovered—I mean universally adopted—
or a bookie down on his luck. He's the corporal."

"Oh! I thought every one was an officer in the
Greek army."

"Pretty nearly—it comes to that—every man
his own officer."

"And are there really no civilised people in the company?"

"Well, it's nominally an English company."

"But you're not English."

"Thank you." He was delighted, he consented for a moment to drop his cynicism. "Well, now that I think of it, there are two educated men among them, and even education is something among the unwashed—*faute de mieux*. They've both been at college, one of them very much so. He's a well-trained prig, I think his name's Graham. The other is a gentlemanly boy called Mavromichali."

"And your commander—is he *class* at all?"

"Hardly. An odd little man—" Palli hesitated.

"Cavalry?—any dash about him?"

"H'm. I think he was a Professor in the Military School. He's very learned, I believe."

"Horrible. Hasn't he one redeeming feature? What sort of a moustache has he?"

"Red and bristly."

"Ugh!" said Eugénie, and turned her head with a pretty disdain. The lamplight flashed upon it, and Palli noted the little ears, and the provoking curls like dainty vine tendrils.

Then Mr. Wilson strolled up to the pair with an after-dinner glory in his inside.

"So you're an ardent Philhellene, M. Palli, and an enthusiastic soldier?" he said.

"Oh! nothing so tedious, Mr. Wilson, I assure you," answered Eugénie.

"Indeed," said the Englishman ; "are you what
the French call *blasé* ?   One gets over that.   Now
my motto is, 'Whatever is worth doing, is worth
doing well.'"

"A very moral precept," Palli retorted.   "In
our set we invert it.   Whatever you can do well is
worth doing."

"Yes, he is amusing," thought Eugénie as she
undressed in her cabin.   "I'm glad I sent for him."

•

V

It was about six o'clock on the evening of the
following day.   The broad eternal sunlight still
brooded over the bay.   Victor Blanc sat on deck
talking to the lieutenant in charge of the hospital-
ship *Albania*.   He had few duties to perform, and,
a rough, sociable seaman, he had already struck up
a cordial intimacy with the owner of the *Hyacinthe*.

"Tell me now, lieutenant, why is it that the
navy has made such a poor show in the war ?   We
all thought it was the one chance for Greece.   I
had my first disillusionment on the day war was
declared—a Sunday, I think.   We had spent a few
days off Corfu.   Well, early on Sunday morning
we heard the firing of guns somewhere down the
Turkish coast.   There was immense excitement,
and they told us you were bombarding Prevesa.
We set off that afternoon.   I can see the old place
still—the quay thronged with folk fêting some

English nurses and Italian volunteers—bands play-ing—flowers everywhere ; and the last sound we heard was a bugle from the old fort summoning the reserves to mobilise.   We had a charming sail. I never remember the sea calmer, a lake of glass would be rough compared with it.   Well, when we got to Patras, I asked why the cannonade had stopped, and our dragoman got a paper and read an official telegram which explained that firing had ceased on account of the 'terrible storm.' What did that mean, I wonder?   The Gulf of Arta is a land-locked bay, remember."

"Oh, probably ammunition had given out. Our boats and our ordnance are all right, but we're short of coal and short of shell.   On my last trip to Athens, I met Ralli in the Piræus going round to all the private merchants and ship-owners beg-ging a ton or two from each.   Then as for shells, they had to set a private foundry in the Piræus on to the job ; moulds had to be made expressly, and you can fancy what amateur affairs those shells were."

" It's a sad affair, certainly, but still you have the islands and the Turkish coast-line at your mercy.   What about Salonica now ? "

"Well, of course the official explanation is that any attempt to take the islands or the coast towns would have been revenged by a massacre of all the Greeks throughout Turkey, but *entre nous* that's nonsense.   The real fact is, that the Powers have imposed inactivity on the Greek fleet."

" But I thought you did try to capture Salonica ? "

"Not a bit of it. We arrived off Salonica one fine night, and decks were cleared for a bombardment. But before morning a despatch reached the Admiral with the news that the Powers had intervened. I think they said that Salonica was a valuable port, and that any damage done to it would have to be made good. I'm not sure if that was all, or if they would actually have fired on us. So you see Greece has never had a free hand." [1]

"Have you done nothing at all then?"

"Well, the Western Squadron banged away at Prevesa for a time at a three-mile range. We landed at Caterina and took the place after a stiff fight, but it's no use to us now. Beyond that we've nothing to show for ourselves but a few prizes. It's a miserable business. Somebody will have to pay for it, I assure you."

And then the pair sat smoking gloomily in silence. The lieutenant was tired of impotent grumbling. The navy had stopped that long ago and taken to planning revenge, wildly and indiscriminately, against Delyanni for making war, against Ralli for thinking of peace, against the King because he was supreme, against the Minister of Marine because he was not. Victor Blanc too was silent, pondering the price of the Russian Alliance which had dragged France into virtual league with barbarism, shrinking with the delicacy of the guilty from offering his sympathy.

And then a Red Cross orderly came on board in

[1] See Note C. *ad fin.*

hot haste seeking the lieutenant. They talked a
while excitedly in Greek, and then the officer
turned to Blanc and explained the situation.
There had been another battle at Velestino.
Smolenski's force had resisted till sundown; all
that generalship could suggest and bravery ac-
complish had been done. But the odds against
them were overwhelming, the little army had been
engirdled by invading hordes, and its centre forced
in by sheer weight of men and lead. And after
the Crown Prince had evacuated Pharsala without
a blow, save for the long resistance of the Legion
and the Ninth Evzones, and that one shot fired at
a venture by the artillery, there was no longer an
object in attempting to hold Velestino. Smolenski's
brigade had already begun its reluctant and orderly
retreat across the hills, and now Volo lay at the
mercy of the Turk. Its hospitals were crowded,
and a train of wounded had just arrived from the
scene of the day's conflict. All of them must be
carried into safety before nightfall. The *Albania*
would not suffice for the purpose; the lieutenant
was in dismay. With an impulse of generosity,
prompted as much by shame as by humanity,
Blanc placed his yacht at the lieutenant's disposal.

The sun had dropped behind the hills, red and
angry over the battlefield; the night came on
apace. Long streams of wounded debouched from
the streets upon the quay, the dismal harvest of
the hospitals. The men who bore them fought
their way through surging crowds of fugitives.

They thronged the quay, refugees from Larissa, townsmen of Volo. Stealthy brigands began to creep among the deserted houses, looting as they went, and when flames shot up from a street hard by, the crowd lurched towards the water, wailing "*Tourkos.*" For an hour the stream of wounded ceased to flow, the place was abandoned to the thieves and the panic-stricken. Men fought for possession of the boats, the gangways of the merchant vessels were besieged, and the light *caïques* in the harbour all but swamped by their human burden. And then order was restored by some hundreds of French blue-jackets. They swept the quay and patrolled the streets, and at last the pulse of panic beat something slower.

And then came a blaze of white light from a Greek warship in the bay. It fell upon the quay, and showed to Palli and Eugénie, sitting speechless in the yacht's bow, a slow train of wounded wending towards them. Then it swept over the town, and the factory chimneys stood out black and solid above the demoralised chaos. They talked of energy and bourgeois virtues, prudence and self-control, of resolute purpose and narrow aims; they preached the gospel of Samuel Smiles. And finally the search-light lit up Pelion, the black mass that had loomed over the town like some Sinai ready to fall. Groups of horsemen galloped across the illuminated track, and the fugitives on the decks of the steamers cried "*Tourkoi!*" Up and down ran the light, and then for a while it was steady, and its lower arc made day on a little reach of the quay. Slowly the wounded filed into it, now a man with bandaged head, now one laid rigid on a stretcher. Incessantly they came, from a blackness peopled with horror into the brutal glare, and so to the dark again, and one shuddered for their fate. Once the pair on the *Hyacinthe* saw the bearers lay down the stretcher and lift a corpse from it. They paused for a moment before returning for another load. One of them looked round him and recognised a friend; it was Sandeman, the engineer of the *Albania.* He had been drinking to keep up his spirits, as an undertaker will. He grasped the hand of a tall soldier.

"Man, Coletti, is this yoursel'? Who'd ha' thought o' seeing you here? A bad penny's aye turning up. Man, it's a terrible business this, an awfu' stramash. But I tel't ye, man. It's the finger o' God, sure as death. It's the sins o' the fathers, unto the third an' fourth generation. It's thae Cretans, as I was saying, but ye wouldna' believe me. Man, ye're a damn fuil, Coletti. As I was saying, it's a' they Cretans, a parcel o' damned liars, as Paul said, evil beasts, slow bellies. It's the finger o' God, I'm telling ye," and he began to sing to the *Old Hundred*—

> "For why? the Lord our God is good,
> His mercy is for ever sure,"—

but another stretcher hurried into the light with

its ghastly burden, and, Sandeman was elbowed aside.

The *Albania* was full at last, and the wounded were coming to the *Hyacinthe*. Coletti was on board, interpreting for a brave English nurse, a delicate girl in a blue cloak, with a red cross worked upon it. Anne Beaulieu was with her, and between them they tended the wretched men lying in every berth and on the sofas of the saloon. Anne had gone lightly to the work, thinking of romance and girlish heroism, but she did not tremble when the real task began, and she saw the grey faces and blood-stained uniforms. Only Palli and Eugénie huddled together in the bows, driven into each other's arms by their selfish terror of pain.

'By midnight the yacht was under weigh. As her screw churned up the water, and sent a tremor through every nerve of the sufferers, a drunken voice carolled under her bows, merrily now. It was—

> "Duncan Gray cam' here tae woo,
> Ha! ha! the wooin' o't."

The moon rose low upon the waters, the sea was calm, and the breeze balmy. The yacht leapt across the silvery track. The pair in the bow were talking gently.

"Yes, it was for love of you."

"I don't deserve it."

"You! Oh! far more than this—Eugénie."

" I wish I did."

At that moment Anne brushed past them, seeking something for a patient. Coletti, quaint cavalier, was at her heels, and she talked pleasantly to him. She cast a contemptuous glance at the lovers. " Aren't they well matched ? " she muttered between her teeth; but presently she had forgotten them, cooling the brow of a wounded man with her own sponge, and prattling to him gaily, prettily, forgetting that he understood no word of what she said.

CHAPTER XIV

DEMORALISATION

"'ERE, I saiy, Mr. Macaroni, what the devil does the old joker want? 'E keeps pattin' me on the shoulder an' pointin' to that shop there. 'Ere, you—it's Greek to me; I'm blowed if I know what you're after, but I'll come with you. You've got a screw loose, take my 'appy Davie on it."

"Johnnie," said the other, a shabby old Greek, and leered again. "Johnnie good ; Johnnie! Johnnie!" and he pulled Simson after him into a wine-shop in the square of Lamia, and treated him to *ouso*. "Mr. Macaroni," otherwise Mavromichali, followed, his arm in a sling. Presently the old Greek was busily talking to him; he plied him with *ouso*, a reward for his bravery. He must be brave, this tall young legionary, for was he not wounded? And to Simson too he gave *ouso*, for he was an Englishman, and he himself drank *ouso*, for there was a war on hand, and he admired bravery. He asked a few questions about Pharsala, and before they were half answered, he retorted with a tale of heroism which had come his way before, about an officer who had shot himself, shouting "We are betrayed," when the order to retire had reached the troops advancing against Damasi, earlier in the war, in the days when men still dreamed of the conquest of Macedonia and a triumphant march on Salonica. And then he ran off to retail his news to the other gossips in the wine-shop, the Prefect, and the grocer, and Madcap Demetri, who still carried his bandoliers. He had but half heard Mavro's story, but what did that matter? Any intelligent man can fill in details.

They had halted here for a few hours, Smith and Simson and the rest, on their way back to Athens. Their wounds still carried the rough dressing of the battlefield, and they were weary beyond speech for want of rest and food, and sick with the jolting of the cart that had carried them over the mountain roads from Pharsala to Domoko and from Domoko to Lamia. Their progress had been incredibly slow; it was now Friday morning. All through the night of the battle the cart had jolted along, Smith and Mavro lying side by side, Simson walking behind. Smith had become early insensible, and Mavro was left alone in his torment. Often he groped about in the cart for a rifle to end his sufferings, and felt round the belts of the other wounded men for a pistol, but there was none at hand. Then he had tried to converse with Simson, but the little fellow was frightened by his wild talk, spoke a soothing sentence from time to time—"There now, Mr. Macaroni, don't you taike on so; you'll feel better in the mornin'," and finally moved on in front to avoid him, giving way to the terror which the simple feel at the sight of madness or delirium. For a moment Mavro abandoned himself to his misery, and then the memory of the battle came to him, and he recollected his delight in standing upright among the shells beside Graham, while the corporal and his mates ducked to avoid them. He nerved himself with an effort, and when the wild thoughts and ghastly images rushed again upon him, he paused and regarded himself with a smile, and fell to translating each phantasy into all the languages he knew. The suicidal impulse grew very abstract when it had passed from Greek to French, and from French to English, and from English to Latin. The self-conscious effort served as a brake to his emotions.

Simson had gone with his wounded friend, hardly counting the cost or weighing his motives. Habits of discipline were of very recent date, it was an old loyalty that bound him to Smith. "Me desert!" he would have exclaimed in surprise if you had questioned him, "see myself 'anged before I'd leave my maite!" He had had some notion of staying in Domoko to await the Legion, when he started out with Smith, but he found himself isolated there in an army which could not talk his speech; to stay alone among chattering Greeks in the quaint crowded streets of the ancient town

would have required more heroism than to stand
unmoved beside comrades on the battlefield amid
the bullets. Besides, Smith required his attentions;
he was crying for water constantly, and the Greek
soldier who led the cart-horse could not understand
his wants. He would go with him to Athens, and
return in time for the next battle. And then
following the cart through the strange scenery of
the Phourka Pass, alone, with no one to speak to
—for the wounded were not talkative—he fell to
repeating that letter from Annie Wells. He saw
her on her way to school—the fresh open face, the
tender brown eyes, the neat dress, the air of cheerfulness and content as of one who loves and is
beloved, or he surprised her in her apron, dusting
the parlour some evening when he had arrived
before he was expected, and she had run off with
a pretty show of discomposure to doff her apron
and put away the duster. A thousand trivial
details crowded in upon him. Her shoe-lace came
undone in the Park, and he fastened it for her and
told her what little feet she had. He created an
environment around himself that spoke only of
Annie and of love, and when at the head of the
pass they camped and lay down till dawn, he
thought of her postscript, "*I just lie in bed at night
and stretch out my arms, and pray to you to come
back.*" He blushed in the darkness, a flood of pity
and shame came over him. Desertion, desertion!
was he not a deserter every hour that he stayed
away from Annie? He fell to planning how he

should return. The Volunteer Committee had
guaranteed his return fare, but perhaps he would
forfeit it by going back now. But that obstacle
delayed him only a moment—he could go back
before the mast, or he could earn his passage ;
as a last resort he could write home for money ;
but however it turned out, Annie would be satisfied.
She would no longer dream of him dead upon the
battlefield. He sat now reading over her letter,
and then he asked Mavro if there would be a post-
office in Lamia.

"Yes, but your letter will probably go sooner if
you keep it, and post it in Athens."

"Oh, damn ! I don't care. I want to write it now
and send it off and be done with it. A postcard 'll
do. S'pose I can get one at the office. Costs three-
'apence don't it ? "

"Yes, fifteen lepta."

Simson rose and went to the door. A carriage
drew up, and Victor Blanc got down, followed by
Palli and Coletti. He had sent the *Hyacinthe* on
to Athens with orders to return as soon as possible.
The girls went with her, Mr. Wilson had found
shelter on the *Albania*, and he himself was driving
up to Domoko in order to see something of the
Prince's army. Palli, of course, went with him, and
Coletti, a handy, energetic fellow who spoke every
language of the Levant, was made welcome in the
carriage they had hired at Stylis. As for Palli, he
had been surprised into the expedition. Through
the night of love and terror he had never once

thought of returning to the army, he had lived in the moment, struggling to grasp this joy long postponed, shrinking into Eugénie's arms to escape the horror at his side. They had talked of love to drive out fear, no word had been spoken of the future, of war and death, of peace and marriage. A couch had been made somewhere for Eugénie in the morning, and she had gone to rest without so much as saying farewell to her lover. The wounded could not be delayed, and Blanc was reluctant to spend three days on the way to Athens and back with such a gloomy ship's company. He assumed that Palli was anxious to return to the Legion, and fancied that he was conferring a favour on him in offering him his company on the way to Domoko, and a seat in his carriage. Palli acquiesced without a word ; he was dazed and sleepy after his vigil, he seemed to doubt the reality of what had passed.

And now he was confronted with Simson.

" W'y, it's Mr. Palli ! You may thank your stars you was out of wot we've bin through. My word——"

" Oh! were you engaged at Pharsala ? I heard there had been fighting."

" Just weren't there ! There's four of us wounded 'ere. Cap'n Birch, 'e's pretty bad ; you should 'a' seen 'im, and Smith too. My eye, but we'd a work to get 'im safely out of it. An' old Corrigan too, but I expex 'e's mostly shammin'. And Mr. Macaroni——"

" Who ? Mavromichali ? "

" How are you, old man ? " It was Mavro's voice,

with a ring of the old cheerfulness, but it sounded
like irony speaking through a tragic mask. "You
must be content with my left hand. You see I've
had my wish. I used to think it would be picturesque to be wounded. I wish it hadn't been in
the first battle though. You went away a day
too soon."

"Not at all. I was at Velestino and assisted at
a victory. Had some capital shots at the Turks
with a Martini. But I hope this isn't serious?"

And then followed introductions, and Mavro
lunched with Victor Blanc and Palli. Towards
midday they parted and went, some to hospital at
Athens, some to the camp at Domoko.

It was already dark when the carriage reached
Domoko. The place was in confusion; hotels there
were none, and the *cafés*, their store of food and
coffee long since exhausted, were thronged with
soldiers drinking *ouso* and resined wine. Palli and
Blanc wandered round the square helplessly looking for rooms; it was Coletti who had the bright
idea of inquiring for the quarters of the English
company. A man of the Ninth Evzones showed
it to him, talking enthusiastically the while of the
exploits of the strangers at Pharsala. Presently
he came back assuring his friends of a welcome.
Together they walked through the narrow streets,
elbowing their way among the motley crowd to a
tall but dilapidated house in a stinking lane. They
had to stoop to enter the doorway, the boards of

the passage threatened to spring when they trod upon them. A turmoil of quarrelling came from the left, where the German company were housed, a music-hall chorus from the right. They entered a room some twenty feet square, with two tiny windows and a low roof, against which Coletti nearly knocked his head. The remnant of the English company were inside, fifteen in all, but there were strange faces present in fresh green uniforms.

"Welcome to the Black 'Ole of Calcutta," said the corporal. The remains of a sheep lay in a lid of a great copper on the floor, and the familiar Barmecide dainties were produced by the imaginative Middle Cock for Palli's benefit. Blanc spoke no English, and presently Palli and he separated themselves from the rest and sat talking to Graham, listening to his narrative of recent happenings. He recounted the reconnaissance and the long skirmish over the Tekké hills, the terrible retreat to Pharsala and the night in the *café*. The Legion had lain in the village till long after the last Greek heel had left it. The road to Domoko was already in Turkish hands, and the Philhellenes had made their way perforce over the mountains, the rear-guard of the army.

It was a day of blazing heat. They marched sullenly with unregarding eyes over the marvellous hills. Gay colours flashed around them, red earth that the sun had bronzed, rocks and crags that bewildered the eye with their brilliant detail, vivid

in the clear air.   They felt a beautiful world around
them, could they but have seen it.   No rations had
been served for two days, and the cognac drunk in
Pharsala had wrought havoc on the overtaxed
nerves and empty stomachs of the men.   The road
lost itself in a dry torrent bed, and for miles they
stumbled on, burdened with rifles and cartridges,
searching everywhere for water, while heavier than
their arms the gay sunbeams weighed them down.
As the hours of the morning wore on, all semblance
of discipline was lost, and every man picked his
way as best he could among the rocks.   They overtook men lying asleep on some arid patch of shade
under a rock, but the sun sped swiftly overhead,
and the short shadows followed him spinning on
their stony axis, and soon the glare and the prickling of heat awoke the sleeper and he went on his
way more weary than before.   Once they passed a
little group of Italians gathered round a comrade
who had died, exhausted by the long fatigue, and
fevered for want of water.   Eight hours of desultory
marching lay behind them, before the rocks opened
out and showed to Graham and O'Brian a grassy
plateau with fugitive peasants and their flocks
resting under trees.   They shouted to those behind,
and men who had barely crawled before fell into a
double.   For two hours the Legion lay there,
drinking and washing at the well and then lying
down to sleep, only to return and drink again.
That night they slept in a village two miles from
Domoko, but the retreating army had eaten every

loaf before them, and it was not till next morning that rations were served again.

And then came the entry into Domoko, the dressing of ranks, the attempt to preserve appearances. Graham was initiated into his duties of interpreter, there were lists to be made of the wounded, requisitions for bread, negotiations about quarters. The company was gloomy, and hungry, and tired, and quarrelsome; only for a moment did it revive and give a hearty cheer when Varatasi came round with a copy of an Order of the Day published that morning by General Macris, and Graham translated it to the company. It thanked the Foreign Legion " for the conspicuous gallantry and bravery they displayed in the battle of Pharsala," and "especially the English company for the invaluable assistance rendered by them to the Ninth Regiment of Evzones."

The groups in the tiny crowded room shifted like the colours of a kaleidoscope. Men came and went, running out for wine or for water. A new company under another sergeant had arrived that evening. They had been sent out by the Volunteer Committee in London. They had all served in some armed force before; there were troopers from the hussars, privates from the infantry, artillerymen from the Chartered Company's forces who had worked Jameson's Maxims at Krugersdorp, there was a half-bred lad from the Egyptian army, some English sergeant's merry-begot, two came from the Ceylon Police, one was a Cockney volunteer, and another a yeomanry man from the home counties. The three "Cocks" were posting them up in the Greek character, talking of the Larissa panic, dilating on the torture of the Turkish spy at Driskoli, the shortcomings of the ambulance and the commissariat, the cowardice of the Crown Prince and his officers. The new-comers, not to be outdone, told of scanty rations, marches on boggy roads, bivouacs in the rain on the open hillside. The air was heavy with discontent, he condemned the Greeks and their cause who would be righteous, he talked of desertion who would be hopeful. The wine went round without stint, and urged men to bickering.

Morgan was full of a private adventure, a grievance more romantic than that of his comrades. He had fallen behind on the retreat from Pharsala, footsore and fevered. He had slept for an hour in the shade and wakened to find himself alone, "when up comes two Greek brigands," said he. "Up they came, looking damned villainous, I can tell you. They planted themselves in the road before me, and one of them began fingering my cartridge-belt. He said something in Greek and pointed to the belt, and then he tugged at it. Next he pointed to his rifle, and I saw that he was going to murder me for my cartridges. Well, thank goodness I kept my presence of mind, slipped a cartridge into the breech of my *Gras*, and pointed it at him. He made off fast enough, I can tell you. These mountains are just full of brigands, and they'd murder you for a few drachmas, though you came out here to fight for them. If I hadn't been in Texas before, and seen a bit of life——"

"You might have told the truth," said O'Brian. "Sorra a bit did they want to murder ye. They were just begging a cartridge from ye, as any gintleman might. They pointed to their rifles just to show what they wanted. Devil take you and your brigands."

"Hallo, Morgan, what's the latest? Got any new lies?" was Middle Cock's cheerful inquiry. And so they wrangled until a new affair distracted them.

This time it was Mick the Armenian. He sat on the floor cunningly cutting tobacco leaves, which he had "found" on the march, into clean long shreds for cigarettes. An admiring group watched his dexterity. Some brought their own stock of dried leaf. "Me makee for you," reiterated Mick cheerfully. And at that moment an Irishman who had been leaning against the wall in a drunken sleep awoke and caught Mick's words. "You'll make for me, ye Armenian devil? Will ye? I'll make for your ugly face first," and he rushed upon him. They closed, and a knife was raised in the air before the bystanders pulled them apart.

And then Palli discovered Middle Cock discussing bread and honey. Mick was giving his opinion of the dainty. "No good honey," said he, "bees no makee that honey. There is honey that bees make, and honey that men make. That no good, that man-made honey." It was indeed a queer compound of sugar and butter. Mick's explanation raised a general laugh and all eyes were turned to Middle Cock, and then Palli noticed that he was licking up the honey from a silver spoon of his own. "Excuse me," he said, "I think that's my spoon you're using."

"Sorry to contradick a nice gentleman like you, but it's mine. I found it on the piano."

Palli turned away in disgust. His face flushed and his lips curled. "Ce sont des bêtes," he said to Graham, "des bêtes, des menteurs, des voleurs." He was not wont to use such simple language.

He sat down beside Graham and they talked awhile in French, but the noise, the rude laughter, the snatches of ribald song, interrupted them and gradually they lapsed into silence. Palli tried to think of Eugénie, her delicacy, the dainty graces of speech and manner, the little curling locks, the white neck with the thread of gold around it. But ever and anon some foul word broke upon his musing and defiled the image in his mind. "How brutal the immodest words in English are," he remarked to Graham. They were fresh to him in their hideous grossness, he had heard only soft Greek vowels and musical French rhythms for the past four days. And at intervals came vivid glimpses of an unashamed animal, the soul of these men.

"W'y, yes," the other sergeant was saying, "it's a good enough bunk that laundry is. The work

ain't too 'ard, the rations—well, I don't know as
I've much quarrel with them, meat twice a day,
and beer or porter, whichever you 'appens to fancy.
And the girls is a jolly set, too, and mostly let's
you do what you wants with 'em. It's a good
enough bunk that laundry. I don't quarrel with
my life. 'Praise God from whom all blessin's flow,'
says I. Pass that cognac, corporal."

And then it was a red-haired fellow named
Ginger, who had served in some line regiment, who
interrupted to pursue a thread of reminiscence.
"Any of you blokes know Sergeant Williams?"
he asked.

"'Im that was in the Engineers, at Woolwich?"

"That's the man. Beastly bounder he was too."

"W'y yes, I know him well enough. He's in
Canterbury now, an' married. Jenny Brough, the
girl's name was."

"Jenny Brough!" exclaimed Ginger. "Strike
me pink. W'y I've mashed that tart many a time
myself. Wot her an' me 'aven't done ain't worth
doing. So 'e's married Jenny Brough! Serve him
jolly well right."

Eugénie, Eugénie! He hunted down the sunny
glades of memory for some pure image, and when
he found it he cast it from him in horror, ashamed
to drag it to the light in that foul atmosphere.

And then conversation flagged and some one
proposed a "sing-song." Uncle was called to the
chair, and one of the new-comers gave a "'armony."
He was a tall, lank fellow with vacant eyes, hanging

jaw, and long arms that dangled about his knees in gorilla fashion. His song had a parody refrain, *O dem golden kippers*. It was a lyric of the London slums. The gawky figure threw itself into every undignified posture, every attitude that can describe what is mean and degraded. The voice was harsh and strident, the words played with jingles and assonances. Of melody there was little, of emotion less. Hints of vice, suggestions of trickery, were the burden of its slender meaning, mockery and disillusionment its mood, if one can use words that imply thought of an effect conveyed by a jaunty string of senseless syllables. Graham listened fascinated by this masterpiece of ugliness. It was greeted with rapturous applause. He turned round to find Palli lying sobbing beside him. He was almost hysterical. Graham offered him cognac, but he turned away and hid his face, sobbing and laughing. "C'est la beauté qu'il me faut," he gasped, "la beauté, la beauté!" And Graham remembered the first night that *he* had spent with the Legion in the guard-room at Lamia, and his own silent cry for beauty. Now he could afford to gaze steadily at the pollution round him, he had found his own place in this chaotic world, he regarded it with a certain stoical pleasure in his own pain. "I felt as you did, at first," he said next morning to Palli. "Now I've come to make a *luxury* of necessity."

"Why do you emphasise that word?' answered Palli. "Virtue and luxury, they're all one. Virtue is spiritual velvet." He had utterly given way to his misery, and Graham, despairing of calming him, announced that he was ill and appealed to Uncle, to stop the concert. There were murmurs, but Uncle peremptorily closed the "sing-song." "And I'm sure, gentlemen, you'll all join with me in 'opin' that Mr. Palli will be quite restored to 'is usual robustious 'ealth in the mornin'."

"'Ear, 'ear," said the Philhellenes with one voice, and then the new-comers went off to their quarters and the men of the old company rolled themselves in their blankets and parcelled out the floor among them.

And when the room was quiet and the candles had flickered out, there still came a miasma of demoralisation about the sleepers. The air was rank and poisonous, it reeked with the odours of the insanitary camp. The rain pattered on the roof and forbade one to think of sleeping outside. From the room to the left came a continuous uproar. The Germans were mad with drink. For two days they had drunk *ouso* incessantly, and now they were fighting among themselves. The Englishmen were wakened by the noise of their wrangling, they seemed to be dragging some poor fellow across the floor, they were threatening to murder him. O'Brian got up and went to the door, and others followed. The Germans released their victim at the sight of the spectators. From midnight till one, and from one till two the din proceeded. Palli and Graham lay awake side by side, and every

few minutes some one of the company got up to
swear at the vermin which were devouring him, or
at the unholy din in the Germans' room. Towards
three it grew worse, and the Englishmen were for
invading their neighbours' quarters in a body.
Graham foresaw a bilingual altercation, a confusion
of tongues and a free fight. He persuaded the
men to wait and allow him to go as deputy. He
entered the filthy room, it was ablaze with candles,
some of the men were ill or asleep, some played
cards, others sat gloomily gazing before them,
drinking silently. He used his most polite and
circuitous German, gently hinting that his countrymen would like to sleep, but the Berliner ordered
him out, and the Schweitzer snatched up his rifle,
slipped in a cartridge, and levelled it straight at his
chest. He was unarmed, but one blow from his
fist sent the drunken Swiss staggering into
the corner ; he left the room and returned to
Palli. " It's no use speaking to them, they're
hopelessly drunk," was all he said to the company,
but he told Palli in French what had happened.

" I can stand it no longer, I can't endure it," was
the other's comment.

By day it was the spectacle of the town and the
army which took the place of that nightmare of
excess and ugliness. Palli and Graham used to
wander about together. At first Graham tried to
fight against the despair of his companion. He
tried to discuss questions of ethics or letters as
they had done in Driskoli, but from hour to hour

and day to day Palli grew more listless and more gloomy. The army lay around them, angry and desperate, waiting for its next retreat. They had not the energy even to fortify the place or build breastworks and rifle-pits along the precipitous terraces. It was a position of appalling strength, a resolute force might have held it indefinitely against an enemy vastly superior in numbers. An old Venetian fort crowned a precipitous crag, and the squalid town huddled behind it for shelter. A long flat valley rolled away to the west, dotted here and there with villages and groves. High hills walled it in to right and left, curving like a horse-shoe. Domoko stood in the middle of the curve and commanded the whole expanse. As yet there were no signs of the enemy, he still lay quietly beyond the hills at Pharsala, celebrating the Feast of Bairam in the old ruinous mosque, relic of his former sovereignty.

The army talked incessantly of peace. Victor Blanc had visited the Crown Prince and came back with a personal assurance that the Powers were about to intervene and that the war was virtually over. He had left immediately for Lamia, tired of the dirt and discomfort of Domoko, and all the European war correspondents had followed his example. Only once did the town put on a martial bearing. A village in the plain was on fire and the loiterers on the Acropolis had seen it. The rumour ran through the narrow streets, a hurry of footsteps rushed along all the ways, men put down their

glasses in the grocery stores and *cafés* and came to
the doors. "*Tourkoi!*" shouted the fugitives, and
the stampede swept onwards. Cavalry and infantry,
evzones and linesmen, all were running from the
town.   The streets were blocked near the Legion's
quarters, where the human stream lapped about a
train of camels laden with biscuit which was entering the starving camp.   And then when the place
was cleared, the artillery set to work. Graham and
Palli went up to the Acropolis.   On the way they
met a horse-battery dragging its guns with incredible labour up streets where no wheel had ever been
before.   Men pulled in front with ropes and the
horses strained at the traces.   An officer directed
them ; they dragged the gun a few yards at a time
and then rested, putting forth all their strength
again at the word "dynamis." [1]   Graham joined
them and pulled with the rest, delighted to find
any occupation, any work that offered temporary
relief from his gloomy brooding. Palli stood behind
him and watched him curiously. And then they
went up to the citadel. There again everything was
bustle. A big Krupp gun had stood below it for
days, but no platform had been made for it. Now
boards had been brought, and men ran to and fro
carrying earth in baskets to make a level area for the
recoil. Others beat down the earth with heavy
beetles such as roadmakers use. Graham snatched
one up and fell to work. Palli stood by smiling,
noting the play of the muscles of his neck as he

---

[1] Literally "force," *i.e.* "with all your might !"

raised the beetle and then dropped it. He took an
indolent delight in watching them swell and flush.
When the work was over he looked Graham full in
the face,—"Ah! yes, I thought so," he said; "you
have blue eyes, that accounts for it, you are a
northern." And then came the officer in command
of the citadel, and scrutinised the plain through a
telescope. "It's only our men burning a village, in
order to destroy cover for the Turks when they *do*
come,—if they ever mean to come," he said; and so
everything assumed its normal lazy tranquillity and
the Krupp was left at the bottom of the hill. It
would be time enough to drag it into position when
the enemy appeared.

They were sauntering off when an artillery sergeant stopped them, addressing them in French.
He thanked Graham for his help, and invited
them into the guard-house, and offered them wine
and cigarettes. He talked with passion of the
betrayal of the army.

"You were at Pharsala, were you not?" he said,
in his simple way, struggling with an unfamiliar
language.

"Ah! yes. All day we lay idle before the town,
cleaning our guns again and again, and listening to
the Legion firing among the hills. But the word
never came to *us* to advance. I remember it well;
I wept in desperation. And you, you were in the
English company, facing the Turks alone. Oh! I
do not know how we can ever thank you, you
foreigners, who have fought bravely for a country

that is not yours.   How can we ever thank you ? "
There were tears in his eyes.

" Mais, mon ami," said Graham.   " It is we who
owe everything to Hellas, everything."

The sergeant smiled through his tears.   " Ah !
—And you must think that we have done nothing
for our country.   Oh ! the shame of it !—But it
is not so, it is not so.   There is not a Greek but
would die to save her.   Perhaps you do not know.
I will tell you.   There are twenty thousand troops
in Athens even now chafing to go up to the front ;
but the Government has no arms for them—no
rifles, no cartridges, no uniforms.   It is not the
people who are slow to sacrifice themselves.   Why,
there are two regiments of volunteers here in
Domoko formed from the eldest sons of families
and the children of widows.   They are exempt by
law from conscription, but they are ready to give
their lives.   See, here is a letter from my brother
in Athens.   He is a priest, and exempt from
service.   But he is in barracks now, waiting for a
rifle.   There is a whole battalion of them—young
men and old—who have thrown away their black
robes and donned a uniform, and fastened up their
long hair with pins, as women do.   Oh, he is mad
with shame ! but what will you ?   There is no rifle
for him.   Then my other brother is in Crete, a
volunteer with Vassos.   He is a medical student.
I have not seen him for two months.   Perhaps he
no longer lives.   Ah ! my friend, you have come
to help us, and you have seen our shame ; but do

not believe that the Greek people are unwilling to make sacrifices. No, no; the common folk are heroic."

It was the officers who were to blame, he continued, and above all the Crown Prince. There was no lack of readiness or courage on the part of the men; but the officers were lazy, indolent, luxurious. One could not respect them, one disdained to obey them. The abandonment of Larissa and of Pharsala—it was treason, and the Prince should suffer. "See you here, my friend," and he pulled a cartridge from the pocket of his trousers, "I am keeping my last cartridge for the Crown Prince." And then he went on to rail at the Royal Family at large. "Do you know what I shall do as soon as the war is over? I shall fling off my uniform and march straight to the Palace and make a revolution. The whole army will do the same." And so he sat talking politics and tactics, lecturing with the aid of a little map that he carried in his haversack. And the Krupp lay at the bottom of the hill.

It was noon now, and Palli and Graham still strolled about seeking some occupation. The time went slowly, and the town was vacant of resources. They hunted for books in all the shops, but there was nothing to be had but school primers, geography text-books, boiled-down summaries of the ancient classics in a colourless modern prose. Graham used to read aloud from a prose version of the *Iliad* to Varatasi's servant, who corrected his pronunciation, in return for lessons in English, for he was an engineer by trade, and his great ambition was to go to London and perfect himself among the wonderful machines he had heard were there, but he soon grew weary of such arduous work, and ran off to gossip in the *café*.

To-day the place seemed more vacant than ever, the life more hopelessly futile. Suddenly they ran against Coletti in a side street; he carried his rifle and all his belongings. "Good-bye, dear friend," he said, "I'm going off. I've quarrelled with that Italian officer. I won't stay in the same army with a coward. I offered to fight him with swords or pistols, whichever he wished, but he turned his back. 'Well,' says I, 'you're a damned coward, and I'll tell every one behind your back what I say to your face.' That's square anyway, sure as I'm an Englishman." So he said his adieus, and returned to Smyrna.

They strolled back to their quarters and found the "Cocks" with Uncle and Isinglass, gambling round a blanket laid on the floor. The stakes were large, and some hundreds of drachmas were in the pool. They wondered where the money had come from. It was O'Brian who explained the mystery. The corporal had a little phrase-book of Greek and English in parallel columns. His method was to enter a prosperous-looking store, march up to the proprietor, produce the phrase-book, and point to a request for a penny-worth of sugar or some such trifle. The book excited the wonder of the Greeks; every one in the shop flocked round to discuss this ingenious substitute for a dragoman. And then while every eye was busy, Middle Cock would quietly slip his hand into the till. They amassed booty in kind with equal effrontery. The room wore the appearance of an old-clothes shop; there were handkerchiefs, socks, trinkets, even watches; some of them they sold, some they used themselves, most were left behind when the next march began.

Yet these were the men who had carried Smith for three miles under fire, and faced the Turks, raw soldiers that they were, like veterans through half a day. They had caught the infection of the camp. There was no longer a cause to fight for, no longer a General to trust. All confidence was at an end, all hope had vanished. And the helpless officers sat still and babbled of an armistice.

It was slowly melting away, this army. The Greeks left by scores, unmolested. Desertion was a term unknown in the vocabulary of the Prince's troops. Every man was his own strategist, and often the better opinion was that the true line of defence lay not at Domoko, but at Thermopylæ, or Marathon, or Athens, and the patriot who came to this conclusion was free to act upon it. Even the Legion became a prey to this spirit. The Italian company dwindled to half its size, and when the Domoko shops were emptied, some four of the Englishmen had left, Middle Cock and Isinglass among them.

"I think they're worse than ever, these Phil-hellenes," Palli remarked one evening. "Of course I've been away for a while, and before I went I had got used to them, but it isn't wholly that."

"No ; I think they *are* worse," answered Graham. "It's that affair of the spy and the bad behaviour of the Greeks at Pharsala that I blame for it. Demoralisation is an infectious disease."

"Yes ; after all, morality is a striving to be no better than one's neighbour. And I'm no exception to the rule."

"Who is my neighbour?" quoted Graham dreamily.

"Eugénie," answered Palli within himself. He was weary of the iron bondage of honour that kept him chained to his post in this miserable army. And he thought for ever of Eugénie; he fled to her a fugitive from duty; from her at least he need dread no condemnation, and if conscience called him deserter, her lips would still part as winsomely, and the blood course as daintily under her delicate skin.

CHAPTER XV

TEN days had passed since the Pharsala skirmish, and once more the Legion was on outpost duty. They were at Amarlari, a pretty village on the extreme edge of the army's left wing. They were part of the force which guarded the mouth of the Agouriani Pass, and the road to Lamia. It was Sunday, but the little church was abandoned to the ambulance and the engineers. The doctor's cook made soup in the shelter of the consecrated walls, and the engineers wrote official documents on the reading desk, resting their papers on the thick slabs of wood covered with holy pictures. The village was abandoned to the foreign soldiery ; they slept in the little mud huts, they washed at the well, they lay under the great tree beside it, and smoked, and grumbled, and drove bargains with the peasants who came selling home-made wine in black goat-skins, *ouso* in earthen jars, and tobacco.

On the knoll behind the church a company of evzones lay in the trenches with a pair of field-

232

guns among them. A telescope stood there, and the Legion, weary of inaction, would clamber up among the fragrant thickets to scan the white line that skirted the hills across the plain. The Turkish army was camped there now. Through the glass one could see horsemen cantering among the tents, or wagons bearing rations from regiment to regiment. Palli and Graham had been there this Sunday morning. The line was longer than before, it sent branches up the valleys and rootlets that twisted round the hills, and the camp was busy as ever with horsemen and carriages. The spectacle rebuked their own sluggish life. And those too were the tents which the Greeks had left behind them at Larissa. "Be sure your tents will find you out;" the perverse misquotation echoed in Graham's mind.

Then when they had said a good-day to the evzones, and examined the guns, and admired the trenches for the twentieth time, they sauntered back to the church, and searched in the mulberry trees for the luscious berries, white or red, with their nutlike flavour. A company of evzones occupied the terrace, working a heliograph. The instrument clicked, keeping time with the dazzling flashes that lit up the battlements of Domoko Acropolis. Palli chatted with the man who was working it; he was a gentlemanly fellow and spoke French. Yes, he admitted that the message was important and exciting. Was it about the armistice? Well, he would not say no. Now one of the men was spelling out the message letter by letter, and another took it down on paper. Graham was allowed to stand by unmolested ; he was a Frank, of course he did not know Greek ! Palli was courteously dismissed. Intently Graham listened, till presently he had heard enough—"*Armistice expected to-day, Powers have intervened.*" He ran back to Palli with his news. They walked about feverishly debating what they should do. The clear bright air grew delicious to them ; the morning breeze fanned their hopes ; it blew keen and sanguine, unwearied as yet by the tyrannous sun. They went with elastic steps, talking of the cheerful march across the hills to Lamia and the sea ; they would get leave of absence from Varatasi ; they would go down to Athens, and revel in civilisation for a week, for the armistice could not well be for a shorter space. Their skins tingled at the prospect of a bath, of clean linen and the sheets of a bed ; they talked fondly of reading books once more, of converse with gentlefolk in drawing-rooms. And here came Varatasi walking from the church ; he must have got the news by this. " Do you speak to him for us both," said Palli ; " I've bothered him so often already about this armistice."

Graham went up to him, saluting. He met the tired eyes with their look of hopeless but unflinching resolution. The face was thinner than it had been earlier in the war, the skin yellow, and freckled, and

covered with a three weeks' stubble. "Well, well,"
he said, with his tolerant courteous smile, "are you
getting impatient, young man? War is a very
slow game, you see."

Graham could hardly bring himself to speak;
he hesitated until Varatasi began to move away.
Already he felt that strange exultation, more coura-
geous than courage, which comes when an accident
has saved one from oneself. Yes, he would accept
Varatasi's imputation; it was impatience that he
felt; it was another battle that he longed for;
surely he had been going to ask, even that moment, what chance there was of fighting within
the next few days. He had had no right to over-
hear the heliographic message; he had acted dis-
honourably; he would make amends by forgetting
what he had learned and waiting patiently, ignor-
antly, for a battle, or for peace.

And then he chanced to look up and saw Palli
strolling along in the field beside the road; his
head was bent; he was gnawing his finger-nails in
suspense; he looked desperate, miserable, reproachful, as if he saw his last hope fading from him.

"Excuse me, sir," said Graham, "is there any
truth in the rumour that an armistice has been
concluded? M. Palli—and I, thought of asking
you for leave of absence for a few days during the
cessation of hostilities. We should like to go down
to Athens "—Graham noticed a shade of displeasure
on the brow—"or Lamia, if you would permit it."

Varatasi reflected for a moment and then seemed to accept the situation. "Yes," he answered, "it's quite likely that there will be an armistice, but I have had no official intimation of it. I'll let you know as soon as I hear from head-quarters, and you and M. Palli shall have leave to go *to Lamia*."

"Thank you, sir." Graham saluted, he felt grateful, rather because no official news had yet come than for the promised leave of absence.

"Well?" said Palli, on edge with apprehension and suspense.

"He says that he has no official intimation as yet, but he will let us know when he gets it, and give us leave to go to Lamia."

"But the intimation came by heliograph! What does he mean? He knows how to lie, that little man."

"Well, I could hardly remind him of the heliograph, could I? There may have been something throwing doubt on that message immediately afterwards. The thing has been clicking incessantly."

"Ugh!" said Palli, "it's miserable, but one must wait I suppose," and he flung himself down in the shade of the mulberries. Ugh! the tones of a silvery voice shuddering its disgust returned to him; it was Eugénie's surely. He saw the pretty .head in profile, he feasted again on its sunny colour, its genial lines, its smooth contour that was all an invitation and a joyous assent. And again it said "Ugh!" and shivered, that winsome memory. It had been her comment on his own description of Varatasi. Life grew gay and irresponsible around that recollection ; it banished severity ; it made honour less desirable. It brought with it a climate of content, wherein men may laugh at duty, and mock brightly at great causes. Yes, Varatasi's moustache was red and stubbly.

Graham had gone into the mud hut where the company had its quarters, to discuss the situation with the sergeant. It was already ten o'clock, but some of the men lay still on the floor, rolled in their blankets, pretending to themselves that they were asleep. One or two were ill with dysentery or fever. A tall Welshman, named Griffiths, lay on his back with his arms strapped to his side and his legs roped together. He had been drinking *ouso* incessantly for three days until his maddened brain gave way, delirium seized him, and he had attempted to run amuck with his bayonet. In self-defence the company had bound him, and now he lay slowly coming to himself, gazing about him with a stupid defiance in his black eyes. Uncle was cooking outside, the sergeant sat smoking and making up his pay list. He called Graham to help him.

Presently the doctor entered on his rounds, followed by Palli. 'He was a young surgeon from Guy's, who had come out as a volunteer. He had arrived only two days before, but already he had organised an ambulance company for the Legion, and made rough stretchers for use on the battle-field. A clever French cook had joined him from Chanteloup's section, and between them they attempted to feed the sick into condition. He was a cultured, sensitive man with curiously shy manners and a strange drawl, which the English company resented as a piece of *side*, an aristocratic affectation. He moved about among the sick, administering medicine to one man, bidding a second send up to the church for soup, questioning a third about his symptoms. His patients were surly and ungrateful. He had just given Ginger some medicine to be taken after meals. "And look here," he said, "I'd advise you to be very careful with that *ouso*. It's very coarse stuff."

"W'o told you I'd been drinkin' *ouso*?" said Ginger.

"Your breath," said the doctor quietly.

"Damn you," said Ginger, "you ain't a doctor, you ain't. You're a —— parson. Think I'm drunk, do you? Look 'ere, parson, don't answer me; look me in the face, and think before you speak. Who stole the black kid gloves? Yea, verily!"

The doctor passed out and went his rounds to the French encampment.

"Taike it aftah meals in a little watah! haw! haw!" quoted the corporal. "W'o's 'e, I'd like to know? An' 'e calls 'isself a volunteer. Don't you believe un. Came out 'ere just to get a case of

instruments free gratis. That's about the size of
'im. An' a nice sort of Englishman 'e is. 'E's too
thick with them Greeks for my taste. Goin' about
with that there Palli. Mighty swell 'e is to be
sure. Oh! beg pardon, Mr. Palli, didn't know you
was 'ere. No offence, I 'ope, but I do like a man
to stick to 'is own countrymen. Taike it in a little
watah! haw! haw!"

"Come and let us look for Varatasi," said Palli
to Graham. "Perhaps he has received that official
notice, by now. I can't endure those Philhellenes.
My nerves will give way altogether if I stay much
longer."

So they went out and strolled about the camp
seeking Varatasi. Palli was silent and moody,
clinging to one idea, hugging the single hope that
remained to him of leaving this intolerable life
without loss of honour. Graham, with a like
thought in his mind, looked about him with a
certain regret. He surprised the life of the Legion
in its habitual simplicity, saw it unconscious of impending fate, untouched by high movements, open,
rude, and genial. They passed the French quarters;
the company numbered some fifty men now, for a
strong force of French Greeks had arrived from
Marseilles a day or two ago. Chanteloup sat at a
little table outside their hut chatting with the
doctor. The men were gathered round two burly
fellows who were wrestling; they cheered and
laughed and chaffed. Only the old sergeant stood

apart, walking about with heavy head and lips that
spoke of bitterness and disillusion, while on his
breast glittered the Solferino medal.

The Germans were busy cooking. They sat
grilling tit-bits from the lamb that hung at the
door of their hut. Some were making toast and
soaking it in the fat of a neighbour's frying-pan.
One man was plucking a fowl. The Schweitzer
was talking busily, he was still in a state of perpetual intoxication. He espied Graham, and
greeted him with effusion, he had totally forgotten
that midnight incident in Domoko; he seized his
hand and introduced him to the bystanders as *ein
(hic, hic) ausgezeichneter guter Kerl.* He forced him
to sit down and share a piece of toast. The Berliner sat by the fire on a log, naked but for his
shirt. He was engaged in hunting in the lining
and seams of his uniform for vermin, *die Raubthiere
Thessaliens*, as he called them. He expended
many a pleasantry upon them, and sighed for
Wurst and *Speck* and *Weissbier*, when the savoury
smell from the frying-pan came to his nostrils.
Graham was busy trying to find out what had
become of Hauff's *Märchen*, which the little Norwegian had carried with him from Lamia to
Pharsala, but it had been lost or stolen. And
then the Berliner put on his clothes and fell to
cleaning his rifle.

> "*Spielet nicht mit Schussgewehr,*
> *Denn es fühlt wie Ihr die Pein,*"

he muttered to himself, mixing his moral ditties with whimsical effect, and presently he was talking of the bright May weather, and he grew sentimental,—ah! to be walking with his little Else in the *Thiergarten*, gazing at the *Siegessäule* and the statue of *der jute Jöthe* !

And so they passed on to the Danish quarters, the Germans were sure that they would find Varatasi there ; some row was going on, they thought. And sure enough, there they found him with Lieutenant Speropoulo, laughing grimly. The Danes had taken the baptismal font from the church, a big copper vessel like a huge saucepan save for the cross on it. It was not that they had a baby to christen, but they were tired of the daily roast mutton, and the font would serve admirably in lieu of a pot to make soup in. Varatasi laughed at the joke, but ordered them to replace the holy vessel at once. As for himself, well, he was amused ; he was not a man of prejudices; but if the evzones heard of it, they would swoop down and massacre the whole Legion. He was turning away when Palli intercepted him—"Ah! yes, you are anxious about the armistice. No, I have positive news that there will be no armistice, and we may have a battle any day." And in a moment he was gone. The curt answer seemed a comment on the triviality of the issue at stake. One volunteer the less in the Legion, of what import was it ? The fate of a nation was at stake. Palli strolled off by himself to meditate, overwhelmed by the blow.

R

Graham found himself once more among the Legion, a soldier again. The broad current of life lapped about him, its motley passions absorbed him. He forgot himself in its little patriotisms, its private wrangles. He chatted with Montalto under the oak tree and admired his pocket Dante, and then his acquaintance bade him farewell, his furlough had expired, and he must return to Italy. And then he joined a group of legionaries who were bargaining with a tobacco merchant. Ginger was among them, and Graham noticed him slyly conveying handfuls of tobacco to his sleeve—until the peasant saw him and broke forth in rage. "Italos?" he said with contemptuous interrogation. Ginger nodded. "Yes, old boy, I'm an Italian. Me Italian. Italos. Right you are. Had you there, dear boy."

· And then the peasant ran with his complaint to Varatasi. Ferrari was sent for, but disowned the man, and waxed indignant. The Italians gathered round. And then Varatasi appealed to Graham. Yes, the accusation was true, he feared, and the culprit was an Englishman. And then Graham had to translate a scathing rebuke and demand the restitution of the tobacco.   . .

"God damn *you*," said Ginger heartily to Graham when all was over. "A —— skunk, that's w'at you are. I don't see w'at call *you* 'ad to come messin' round with your cursed interfering. I didn't do *you* no 'arm anyway. Strikes me you ought to lie low ; your countrymen ain't got no

great cause to be cocky." And with many a
Parthian arrow of invective the man withdrew.
Graham's face flushed; he would have challenged
the man but for a lingering tradition of gentility
which still clung to him and made him ashamed
to wrangle with an inferior. He had never been
addressed in this way by the old company, and
the reference to his " countrymen " puzzled him.

A dash of red had mingled with the Legion's
green by this time. It was the Garibaldians with
their scarlet shirts who had strolled over from
Agouriani to visit their fellow-volunteers. The
new legion was posted some five miles nearer
Domoko. It had but just arrived from Athens.
It numbered some eight hundred men under Riciotti
Garibaldi, the son of Italy's liberator. There were
veterans who had fought in Naples and in France,
beardless lads who raved of Anarchy, Socialist
deputies from the Italian Chamber, gaolbirds and
deserters, all the flotsam and jetsam of humanity,
the ragged edge of society swept up by the broom
of the war-god. Some five hundred were Italians,
the rest Greeks from Turkey and Marseilles, fugitives, adventurers, enthusiasts from every nation of
the earth. There was an English company among
them, thirty strong, under Major Short, a retired
officer of infantry. They had donned the red
shirt in order to leave Athens the sooner. A
deputation was in the village now, talking to the
Philhellenes. Fulton and a new-comer were on
their way to Domoko, deserters. The Philhellenes

provided a sympathetic escort; only the sergeant had protested. The debate had grown heated when Graham joined them.

"It's a nice waiy for Englishmen to be'aive," Fulton was saying, "and in a foreign country too. You ain't Englishmen, you ain't, puttin' on the uniform of a lot of brigands and joinin' a regiment o' cut-throats an' Socialists. W'y didn't you come to us in the Foreign Legion?"

"'Tain't an English Legion is it?" said the Garibaldian. "We're just the saime as you. An English company under an English orficer in a Foreign Legion. An' 'e's an infantry orficer is Major Short. Your sergeant's all right for cavalry but 'e's no go for infantry."

"If you've anythin' to saiy against our sergeant, you just saiy it to me," put in the corporal. "He's a gentleman 'e is."

"Dunno nothin' about your sergeant," said the Garibaldian. "Dessay 'e's all right, but——"

"Look here," said O'Brian, "I'm not an Englishman and I don't like Englishmen, but if I were, I'd stick to my own countrymen."

"'Ear, 'ear," said Fulton the deserter, moving off; "God saive the Queen. And w'at do you saiy to it all, Mr. Graham?"

"Well, Fulton, I say this, that I'd rather serve with the Garibaldians than desert from the Legion."

There was a silence and Fulton turned away. Graham felt astounded at himself, he had never taken part in the disputes of the men before. Now he was one of themselves.

He turned away and sauntered back to the village, past the still wrangling legionaries, past the Italians shouting in their musical tones, "*Guerra* or *Rivoluzione*"; he caught the brave alternative as he went by, the motto of the Garibaldians in distracted Greece. And then he met Palli with Montalto, each with his rifle, his blanket, and his haversack.

"Good-bye, Graham, I'm off; I can't stand it any longer."

"But Varatasi expects fighting. You'll be all right when you hear the guns again. It's this *ennui* that's so hard to bear."

"Oh! I know. I'll come back if there really *is* any fighting. I think my nerves have gone to smash."

"Have you told Varatasi?"

"No, I couldn't bear to see him . . . . Good-bye. I'm off." He broke into tears and turned to hide his sobs.

So he was gone at last. Graham was not surprised. He had watched his moral strength running down like clockwork. He had grown every day more sensitive to insult, the rude life had sapped his endurance, the coarse environment had seemed to tell him that the ideal lay elsewhere. The foul atmosphere of the camp had choked him, he had cried for beauty and failed to find it, and all the while an alluring memory beckoned him from duty. Graham knew that he would never return. The last of his educated comrades was gone; he returned to the mud hut of the company ten times more lonely than before.

"So 'e's gone is Palli," said the corporal that evening. "'E ain't much loss neither. Damned coward 'e was. An' 'ow does 'e expec' us to staiy when he can't stick to 'is post like a man, an' fight for 'is own country? I saiy, Uncle, shouldn't wonder if there's goin' to be a battle to-morrow. 'E's got some one who tips him the wink, you bet 'e 'as. Do you remember 'ow 'e 'ooked it just before Pharsala? Sly dog 'e is."

"Don't you be so 'ard on Mr. Palli, Big Cock," answered Uncle. "'E ain't like you an' me. W'y, bless you, you could see that by lookin' at 'im. Not much of a constitootion 'e 'adn't. W'y, I always maide a point of givin' 'im the biggest dumplin', w'en I was servin' out the soup. 'E needed it did Mr. Palli."

And then Ginger came forward to Graham with outstretched hands. He had been drinking and his face beamed with cordiality. "'Ere, Mr. Graham," said he, "there was some words between you an' me this mornin'. Well, I ax your pardon and I 'ope you'll forget it. Now I can't saiy more 'n that, can I? I thought you was a —— Greek, blowed if I didn't. I wouldn't 'ave spoken saime as I did, if I'd 'a known you was English."

"Thank you," said Graham. "It's all right. I thought you'd made some mistake," and they shook hands.

"Well now, if that ain't a feather in your cap, Mr. Graham, I don't know w'ats w'at," quoth Uncle. "Took you for a —— Greek, 'pon my word! Well, I must saiy this, you 'ave bin comin' on with your Greek somethin' wonderful lately."

"Why do you call me 'Mister'?" said Graham.

"I dunno. Ain't you Mr. Graham?"

"No. Private Graham of the Foreign Legion."

"Lights out," said Lieutenant Speropoulo at the door in French, "and there's to be no singing or shouting till dawn, by Captain Varatasi's orders." Graham translated the order.

"Come now, that looks somethink like business, don't it," said Uncle, as he blew out the candle.

"Good-night, Uncle."

"Good-night, Graham."

CHAPTER XVI

A HAPPY WARRIOR

THE battle had begun vaguely and without ceremony, as battles will. The Legion had been marching in from their position on the extreme left since ten in the morning. But everything was uncertain. Once they lay in a ploughed field and watched a squadron of cavalry that seemed to be sweeping towards them. For an hour they squatted behind an earthwork on a ridge. A great black square seemed to be advancing upon them; it faced now east and now south, wriggling as it were under the steady gaze of the big Krupp gun on the Acropolis. Shells fell in its centre and the smoke curled over it. An intermittent bellow came from the centre of the horseshoe, but it failed to blend with the landscape. The damp voluptuous life of the marshes sweltered in the midday heat, and one felt that here was the appropriate music to the scenery which the sun had staged. The baying of the cannon was an irrelevance, thunder from a clear sky. Once a white ring of smoke danced gracefully up the

wind, it came from an ammunition wagon that
had exploded; it wandered through the blue air
lonely as a cloud, and one did not question its
origin. The black sunburnt rocks across the plain
moved as though Orpheus had played to them.
It was only the veteran sergeant who knew them
for battalions wheeling to the notes of their
bugles.

It was near three in the afternoon. They were
still marching inwards. The guns were calling
them, the air was light with their expectancy, their
cartridge-belts felt like a lady's favours, they stepped
jauntily, for they had just paraded past a company
of the Ninth Evzones who lay waiting by the
roadside. The old captain, spirited as ever, had
come running to their sergeant. He had grasped
both his hands and crowed over him like some
proud father, and then he gripped Graham's right
as he walked by the sergeant, ready to interpret
Varatasi's orders. The men of his command had
cheered, and the remnant of those who had fought
at Pharsala had turned to the new-comers and
explained that these were their old comrades in
the earlier fray. It was an omen that made for
pride and gladness. And then Varatasi, walking
ahead of the English company, had turned and
called Graham to him. His face was bright and
joyful, a gaiety of courage laughed in his eyes when
a volley of musketry rang out across the hillock in
front of them. "Tell your sergeant to march at
the double, we are just going to take part in the

fighting yonder." He had the air of one who says, "See, I have kept my promise at last. Had I not a great surprise in store for you?"

With a run the company was over the hillock in time to see a thin line of Greek infantrymen rising from their positions and running to the rear. They found themselves inside a bay of hills. A bold slope ran down towards the flat plain, spurs of higher ground strewn with volcanic rock flanked the bluff to right and left and narrowed the prospect. For some forty yards behind the ground was a flat terrace, and then the hills ran up in bewildering billows. It was a place to hold with steady endeavour. One saw only the enemy in front, one's comrades to right and left were forgotten, the issue was narrowed to a duel. The Englishmen were posted at the edge of the bluff to the left. They lay down flat, some thirty-two strong. The sergeant stood behind, and Graham was the last man on the right. A dwarfed thorn tree hung solitary over the slope in the middle, and the Italian company manned the edge, continuing the English line. The tree was between Graham and the first Italian. The French were on the bluff to the left, the Danes and Germans on the right. The Greek and Armenian companies were posted behind the Englishmen as a reserve, while the doctor took up his post among the hillocks in the rear.

There were puffs of white smoke on the plain which marked the position of the Turks. Bullets were spitting on the slope and whistling overhead when the Englishmen took up their position. They had hardly time to dispose themselves on the earth, before the sergeant shouted his orders for a volley. A quickening of the pulse, a bewildered desire to call a halt, was all that Graham felt, and then his fingers were working mechanically at the breech of his rifle. He felt himself acting ever a little ahead of his thoughts, the word " Ready " rang out always a moment before his reflections had finished their work on the previous volley. His imagination was at rest, there was nothing to stimulate. A puff of smoke that one fixed with one's eye, a quick calculation as to where the Turk behind it was standing, and then came the word to fire. The sergeant's voice grew hoarser as it struggled with the din, the Turks crept closer, and still the volleys rang true and clear, with unfailing regularity. The Italian beside him was pierced through the chest ; his neighbours carried him to the rear, leaving his cloak and his haversack upon the ground, but in a moment the incident was forgotten. " That tree is a good mark for them, you'll get their attention next," was all that he said to himself, and he went on firing, determined to use every moment that was left to him. O'Brian staggered up at the far end of the line, shot in the shoulder, then it was Uncle, and then one of the new-comers, but each time he only muttered grimly, " Your turn next, my man." He was completely at his ease, he felt as though this work of sighting, and aiming, and firing had been his daily vocation since boyhood.

For an hour the mechanical firing of volleys went on, broken only by the scarce regarded cry of a wounded friend. He was carried to the rear and borne off by the doctor's men with stretchers ; his comrades ran back at once and dropped into their places like machines. It seemed as if only one living man were on the battlefield, Varatasi, who walked about behind the company. Once and again he called Graham to him for an order directing the sergeant in his firing, or cautioning him to husband his shot. The company's ammunition was giving out. The Ulsterman beside Graham was begging for cartridges, and his own store had grown perilously small. He bethought him of the Italian who had fallen. He rose and rummaged in the man's haversack. A strenuous haste took possession of him, he felt as if all the fire of the Turks was upon him as he stood up alone, fronting them. A ball went through his sleeve and another tore his boot. And then, as he fumbled excitedly, Varatasi came up to him. His face wore the same melancholy smile as ever, he took up the Italian's sack and calmly examined it. It was full of cheese, and garlic, and bullets, there were socks and letters, and, strangest sight of all, a book. "Regardez ce que le pauvre garçon a porté," said Varatasi. And then he examined the book. "Qu'est-que-c'est que ça ?" he asked, and handed it to Graham. It was an Otto's English-

German Grammar. Varatasi laughed, and then a ball whistled between them, and passed through the captain's blanket which hung in a roll over his shoulders. He smiled again and went on exploring. Graham returned to his place, and distributed the hundred rounds he had gathered among the men nearest to him. And now in the intervals of the volleys his eyes followed Varatasi, strolling about, watching the enemy through his glass unconscious of danger.

And then the sergeant called him again, and sent him to tell Varatasi that the company's ammunition was all but exhausted. The Turks were wavering. They had advanced under the cover of a huge trench that drained the marshy soil, to within four hundred yards of the Legion's line. Six of the Englishmen had fallen, but the Turks were beginning to retire. It was the moment when every rifle should be busy. It was the time to persuade the enemy that the air around him was made of lead.

Varatasi was behind, standing beside the Armenian reserves, talking to his Italian adjutant. Graham rose and went towards him. At first he was inclined to hurry, his blood was boiling, there was a briskness in the air as the bullets whipped it into motion. And then he felt the captain's eye upon him. He straightened himself and walked gravely. "Sir," he said, "the sergeant sent me to ask if we can get more ammunition from the rear, we have hardly ten rounds apiece."

A look of agony crossed the adjutant's face, he bent double and put his hand to his leg. He had been struck. "Assistez-le," said Varatasi quietly, and Graham took his arm and helped him to hobble up to the rock behind which the doctor knelt, busily dressing the men who were borne to him. He returned, and Varatasi told him to go and gather what he could from the pouches of the dead and wounded. And so he wandered over the field. A Bulgarian lay on his back at his feet, rigid in death. His face was bloodless, and the sun-burnt skin showed yellow and ghastly. His eyes were closed and his mouth open. There was a hole in his left temple with a filigree pattern of blood frozen round it. Graham hardly paused to shudder, he was full of his new joy of working under Varatasi's eye alone in the open among the bullets. He emptied the Bulgarian's pouches into his haversack, and went off searching for the bandoliers of the wounded which the ambulance men had taken from them as they placed them on the stretchers. They littered the ground, a pathetic witness of the carnage. And then he noticed a handful of Greeks cowering behind rocks, their bandoliers full of unused cartridges. They were a remnant of those who held the slope when the Legion came up. Their officers had fled, they lay terror-stricken and inactive in their cover. A touch of rage was added to his recklessness as he noted their eyes following him over the bullet-swept terrace.

Back to the line again, past a group of Italians
bearing a wounded man who sang madly as they
carried him, into the din that almost drowned the
hoarse shouts of the sergeant, and then began
again the mechanical serving of volleys.   Once
the ammunition was exhausted and the men lay
flat, resting. They had the air of those who have
struggled through a fire, their hands were black
with powder, the barrels of their rifles had scorched
their fingers.   And then came Varatasi, sauntering along the line. He rolled a cigarette in his
fingers, he looked with a caressing glance upon
his men as if he walked invisible through peril,
and pitied those whom the enemy could see.
" Ask what we are to do now," said the sergeant.

"Now—now—" answered Varatasi, and he smiled
the beautiful smile of a brave man. "*Maintenant il
faut se reposer.*"   The sentence sank into Graham's
memory. The smile of the speaker and the music
of the voice haunted him, he knew not why. They
were the last words that Varatasi spoke to him.
" Now it is time to rest."

The men peered over the plain anxiously. The
other companies were still firing, and though the
Turks were falling back, the hail of bullets had
scarcely slackened. Suddenly a flash of red lit up
the yellow corn to the left in the lee of the hill,
and then it lengthened to a line. The Italians
leaped to their feet and cheered. There was a
brisk stir on the ridge. It was the Garibaldians
who had come up. On they came—a thin red

line blazing among the golden grain, striding intrepidly. The very colour of their ranks was a challenge to the enemy, their posture an inspiration.

Varatasi was among the Italians now, their officer shouted his order to Graham. "Let every man who has cartridges advance and fall in on the right of the Garibaldians!" Mad with the shouts of the legionaries and the spectacle of the red line pressing triumphantly onwards, he hardly knew what he did. He rifled the pouch of a dead man of its cartridges, and rushed down the slope among the Danes.

And then the scene was all of fury and forgetfulness. The scarlet line advanced slowly and steadily, firing as it went; men fell wounded, but still the line pressed forward undismayed; the officers rode up and down on their maddened chargers, some bareheaded, some with their *képis* crushed on with the peak behind. The Turks, too, were standing, they also firing at intervals, and then falling back. Once crossing the ditch Graham stumbled over a dying Turk, and a few yards further on, buried in the corn, lay a bearded old veteran with scars on his cheeks and a bullet-wound in his brow. The Danes were hurrying onward, led by a Swedish officer with a Scottish name, Adjutant Sinclair. He ran on ahead shouting the range. It began at six hundred yards, soon it was four hundred, and then three hundred. There was an earthwork on a low mound a little way in front. The men who held it were firing

busily upon the Danes and Germans, but with
execrable aim.   The order to charge was given,
bayonets were fixed, and the company ran forward ; but the enemy left their cover long before
the legionaries reached it, and a shell from a
battery on the hills pursued them, followed by the
triumphant exclamations of the volunteers.

And then the companies converged on the abandoned breastwork.   The flag came with them,
swaying and fluttering in the hands of a German
corporal.   It moved like a thing tossed by con-
flicting passions.   There stood a crucifix beyond
the trench and a well of clear water beside it, and
here beneath the symbol of Christ's army militant
the Legion halted.   A great cheer went up as
Riciotti Garibaldi—a burly figure on a brown
horse—dismounted and crossed himself.   The flag
was laid against the crucifix, while its bearer
drank at the well.   "*En touto nika*," it seemed to
say, as its folds caressed the cross—"In this pre-
vail." They crowded round, a motley group ; Greeks
and Italians bent their heads, and made the sacred
sign on brows moist with sweat, and their fingers
left a stain of powder—strange token of fierce
baptism.   And· even the northerners uncovered
reverently, and forgot Luther in the common
impulse.

The night was falling now.   A bar of orange
cloud made a gate to the plain.   A pearly light
hung wistful and reluctant over the great strath
with a troubled air of disappointment, as though

S

the predestined glory of the summer's day had somehow failed; while wreaths of powder shrouded the hills, draping their harsh outlines into tone with the vagueness of evening.   Dark masses of Turkish troops manœuvred uncertainly to right and left among the corn, like black reefs at sea, with whose contour the waves made sport.   No order to halt had been given, but the quiet spirit of twilight caused men to lose the lust of pursuit. The cross had been wrenched from the Moslem; the drama had found its own *dénouement.*

The companies began to mass again.   "*Die Deutschen!*" shouted the Berliner, and the Germans formed and fell back together.   "How many have you lost?" asked Graham as they passed him.

"Two or three," answered Baumgarten.   "I don't know exactly; but our officer is terribly wounded, and Varatasi is killed —*juter braver Kerl!*"

Then came the French, Émile in the front rank. "Ah! Monsieur Henri," he said, "and you are safe!" and he wrung his hand joyfully.   His face shone with the joy of battle.   "*C'est la vie!*" he exclaimed, and he kicked a dead Turk from his path.   "This is life, is it not?"

"How many have you lost?" asked Graham again.

"Five or six, and Chanteloup is wounded.   He fell into my arms.   And they say that Varatasi is killed."

He was dead — the man whom each nation

counted as a brother, whom every company reck-
oned as a comrade. Graham waited no longer;
there was nothing more to hope for or to do. One
thought filled his mind. He hurried on, striving
to realise what had happened, careless of the victory, thinking only of the Legion's loss. And
when he passed an acquaintance, Dane or Frenchman or Italian, he told him the news, anxious to
find consolation in another's grief.

He found the English company drawn up on
the terrace. They had got scattered in the charge,
and the sergeant had lost them. The other sergeant was there, flurried and disturbed. Had the
sergeant-major been wounded? Where was the
Legion? Where were they to camp for the night?
Graham snatched at a chance of doing something
that would drive the thought of Varatasi from his
mind. He offered to run and see whether the
Legion were in the little hamlet, a mile away,
which they had passed in the morning. He ran at
his best speed, heedless of aching limbs and hunger.
He found that it was as he had guessed, and returned and led the company to the *rendezvous*.

On their way they passed a group of wounded
Garibaldians. They lay in a hollow of the hills,
where an old Danish doctor had dressed their
wounds, and now they were waiting to be carried
to the great barn which served as a field-hospital.
Graham noticed one struggling to rise; he was
a Frenchman, and he had been shot in the side.
A bearded Italian was helping him. His voice

sounded strangely familiar. It was Grassini, the Socialist óf the Lamia guard-room, who had deserted on the first day of the march to Pharsala. He had gone back to Athens, lived like a free patriot in the best hotels, and come up with Garibaldi in time to see the last act of the tragedy. Graham went to his aid, and between them they lifted the wounded man. In the dark they could not see his face, but he spoke with a pure accent, absurdly grateful for their help. They put their arms about him ; his shirt had been cut over the wound, and Graham could feel the warm flesh under his hand. A strange sense of tenderness and comradeship came over him in the darkness. He felt that he had often seen him before, this wounded alien ; all the familiar suffering that he had known from childhood was here within his arms, and he talked to him gently with a caress in his voice. The support that he gave him became an embrace. It was that thought of Varatasi stirring within him, which melted the hardness and austerity that had grown upon him during the campaign in his struggle with a hostile environment. They were using the "*tu*" and "*toi*" of brotherhood before they had gone many yards, this pair who had not even seen each other's faces. The wounded man was panting, "Tu es bien fatigué, n'est-ce-pas ?" Graham said, "Il faut te reposer un peu."

"Mais oui. Il me faut reposer un peu. Tu es bien gentil !"

The iteration of the word *reposer* brought a picture before Graham's mind. It was Varatasi who walked in front of the line. "Now it is time to rest," he said. He rested, indeed, dead in the hour of victory, and Graham shuddered with a half-repressed sob, while he set the wounded man by the roadside to rest ; and as his arm went round him again, he spent on him the tenderness that he felt for his fallen commander.

"This blanket is in his way," said Grassini, removing the rolled-up *couverture* from his shoulders. Two minutes later when Graham looked up, he had vanished, and call as he might he never returned. And then Graham remembered that he had had no blanket of his own.

With redoubled tenderness he lifted the wounded man to his feet. They were alone now on the road. The night was dark, and a biting wind blew down from the mountains. A random shot came whistling past them, evidence of a Turkish picket somewhere near. They struggled on with what speed they might, Graham half supporting, half carrying his companion.

The Legion was quartered in an old farm-house beside the road. The yard was one seething mass of men talking in half-a-dozen languages. A light burned in the parlour of the house and officers went in and out. Varatasi lay there, mortally wounded. He had been shot as he was joining in the charge on the right of Garibaldi's line. "Where are the Danes—the Italians—the English—the Germans ?"

said the buzz of questioning tongues in the dark farm-yard, and then it was, "Is Varatasí killed? Will he live?"

Graham brought his charge to the door of the barn. A Garibaldian sentry stood there with fixed bayonet. He sought to prevent Graham from entering. He shouted to the man in all the languages he knew, but still he stood stupid and immobile. Graham gripped his rifle at length, and forced a passage. Inside, the long room was carpeted with wounded men in their red shirts or green tunics. The English doctor moved from case to case, doing his work quietly, skilfully, swiftly, the one calm man in that nervous place. A huge red-shirted surgeon was dealing with some desperate case at the far end of the barn. The wounded lay silent and impassive for the most part; some were asleep, some smoked cigarettes· Their hurts had been washed and bandaged, and a sense of ease and comfort stole over them as they lay at rest on the soft straw with four walls round them, and the keen wind and the Turkish bullets far away outside. Graham made a place on the straw for the Frenchman, propped up his head and shielded his wound from the air. And then the door opened, and the bitter mountain wind rushed in. The fevered patients turned and groaned, and Graham remembered the stolen blanket. The Frenchman shivered. "My blanket?" he said feebly.

For a moment Graham hesitated, till the memory

of Varatasi came to his aid ; he was there beyond that wall dying, and he stood to Graham for a symbol of all that was heroic in this sordid war.

"Here it is," he said, and he gave him his own.

"Water!" exclaimed the wounded man again, and then Graham sought out a bucket and went out to look for the well. It was half-a-mile away. When he returned he had another struggle with the sentry. The Garibaldian seized his arm and flung him back. A great rage of pity possessed him. "Je ne veux pas laisser mon—*camarade*," he shouted as he forced his way inside. He had ceased to think of the duty of an educated man among the unschooled. And presently he was kneeling by his unknown comrade, washing his face and moistening his lips, and as he rose, the man took his hand and kissed it.

Outside Lieutenant Speropoulo was calling for him to act as interpreter. There was everything to be done. Quarters had to be found for the various companies, a messenger must be sent to head-quarters, and a company of bearers organised over-night to carry Varatasi into safety in case the battle should be renewed. Hour after hour went by, and still he was busy fetching water for the hospital, carrying messages between Varatasi's deathbed and the English doctor busy in the barn. Towards two in the morning he lay down at the door of the outhouse where the English company was sleeping.

At half-past three a Greek sergeant awakened

him. "The army is in retreat," he said, "and we shall have to escape over the hills.[1]   Wake up your wounded ; we have ponies for those who can ride."

The world was chill and dreary outside.   The morning star shone in the cold blue sky, and the dawn crept wearily over the hard earth.

"Shall I wake the bearers for Varatasi ?" asked Graham.

"No.   He died half-an-hour ago, just before the messenger came from head-quarters."

For an instant Graham's eyes were hot, and his breath escaped him like a sob.   And then he straightened himself and smiled.   The man he loved had died in the hour of victory.   He had led his men triumphantly, he had died ere he knew that the battle was lost, the war ended, and his country's cause betrayed.   He had not seen the shame that waited for lesser men.   He had gone out alone, a proud light in his eyes, the only victor sent from Greece to join the heroes.

[1] See Note D. *ad fin.*

CHAPTER XVII

LES REVENANTS

DROWSY, unwashed, unrested, the Legion set out upon its last retreat. Round the farm-houses lay the wounded, waiting to be mounted on mules or placed on stretchers. Graham served out a sack of biscuits, but most of the men refused to carry anything. Goulonides, the Bulgarian lieutenant, was wrangling for the possession of a pony destined for a wounded Frenchman. Speropoulo shrieked at him, reasoned with him, spat upon him. Once and again they were torn apart. Ultimately they mounted their beasts and rode at the head of the Legion, shouting and gesticulating unweariedly. Slowly the dejected train, whole and wounded together, crept along the dusty road. Once they halted at a village. Ginger raided a wineshop, and came out staggering. Mick went up to a little wooden shrine in the market-place with its alms-box and its gaudy Madonna and Child in blue and gilt. "Ha! Jesu's photograph! Jesu no want money, Jesu rich," quoth he, as he pocketed a handful of pence.

The sun blazed unrelentingly upon the wounded. Peasants in flight bustled about the cross-ways, and, unregarded, the pageant of hill and valley unrolled itself. Over the low hills, and their boots galled their feet; through the interminable woods, and they thought they had lost their way; over torrents on fallen trees, and they staggered from faintness; up wonderful terraced slopes planted with vines, and the noonday heat made cowards of them; into the fastnesses of the mountains, and their brains grew numb.

Sometimes they halted and moistened their biscuits in the brawling stream. The Germans had shot a little pig, and they adorned its mouth with festoons of leaves. "That is not good," said Speropoulo, in his quaint practical French. "That is not good, when our officer is dead." And then he looked at Graham gloomily, and shook his head in misery, and talked of the death of Varatasi and the abandonment of Domoko. They grew very kin and very kind on these halts, but Speropoulo only sighed and said, "He is dead, it is impossible," and then he shrugged his shoulders and groaned, "It is treason." Up and down the hills they went companions, and when they mounted they said, "He is dead," and on the slope they set their teeth and muttered, "It is treason."

The company vowed that Speropoulo had lost his way; and indeed he had. At last they met an old shepherd who guided them. And so through the evening they wound ever higher upon the

heights. Night fell, and still they skirted a pre-
cipice; fallen pines had torn the road, the loose
flints went rolling into black abysses. A great red
glare shot up on their left. The mountains showed
black in its shadow, and the rosy light filtered
through the mists that rose from the valleys.
Away towards the sea the last glimmer of daylight paled flickering on the snows of Othrys, and
glinted on the green sea hard by Thermopylæ.
" It is Domoko that burns," ran from company to
company. Men shivered and sighed for the wasted
heat. The cold breath of the night pierced their
thin garments, they chafed their hands and thought
of the wounded in the hypocrisy of their selfishness.

And then one by one they said, " I can go no
further." For seventeen hours they had marched
over hill, and mountain, and stony valley. The sun
had beat upon them, and now their arms grew
heavy. The Englishmen lay down in a body
beside the path on the edge of the cliff. Graham
still stumbled on with the Danes beside Speropoulo,
determined to hold on to the end. The other companies, save for a few stragglers silent among men
of alien speech, had fallen out by the way and
wandered off, each on some different track.
Another hour and they had reached the camp
of some Greek infantry regiment high on the
hillside. Peasants herded among them for protection, and stared incredulous at the flames of
Domoko. The snow was just above them. The
reluctant twilight that lay ghost-like on the plain,

revealed the black outline of a great Venetian fortress towering on its crag. It had been a Greek citadel when the frontier line had run through these mountains, giving Thessaly to the Turk. And now Domoko burnt through the still night, a bonfire of vanities.

Graham lay sleepless and shivering beside the camp fire, thinking of the war. How beautiful it was, that rosy splendour in the cold blue air. Liberty and Freedom were there. A bonfire of vanities! It held all that men loved, home and faith and fatherland. The war was over; an infinite bitter sadness shrouded all his memories. Patriotism and devotion, all the bright aims of Hellenism,—the words came lightly to his ears mixed with a chatter of frivolity. It seemed better to watch the triumph of a stern and serious barbarism than to dream of the lost ideals of a people too futile to guard them. He sat up and stared at the glare in the sky. He divined the scene around it in the Turkish camp. He saw the white captured tents pitched in the illuminated plain. And yonder were the Krupps abandoned in the Acropolis. He pictured their black mouths till they leered at him with the grin of a disillusioned gargoyle.

And then he turned, and hugged the hard earth and thought of sleep. He warmed his numb hands at the fire and thrust his feet among the ashes. He longed for the blanket that he had given to the wounded Garibaldian, until the grave face of Vara-

tasi came before his memory and smiled upon him.
He thought too of that other night after the battle
in Pharsala, but he could remember little of his
sensations then.   They seemed to him remote,
and somehow different, but he was not curious
about them.   He thought only of Varatasi as he
had ridden on through the ribald village, thinking
of lost causes, and now he unconsciously attributed
his own reflections to the man he had loved.

And then an old peasant staggered wearily up
to the fire.   "*Kalen nycta*," [1] he muttered mechanically, as he warmed his hands.   And in the strange
light Graham thought that he recognised the face.
It was old Alexi, the shepherd of Domoko.

"Alexi!   Is it you?"

"*Malista*. [2]   And you—the stranger who slept in
my house?"

"The same."

"Ah! I have killed them.   A sergeant and five
men.   I shot them with my own hand from behind
a rock as they entered Domoko this morning.   A
sergeant and five men!   And you?"

"We chased the Turks for two miles."

"*Kala*," said Alexi, as he rolled himself in his
rug.   "Nay, simple shepherd.   It is not well,"
thought Graham.   "Six Moslem mothers are
desolate in Anatolia, and Varatasi has fallen, and
all that true men loved is lost, and there is none to
heed.   And now there is joy in all the Chancelries,

---

[1] Good-night.   [2] To be sure.

and the Philistines make merry." And he envied Varatasi.

> "Who is the happy warrior? who is he
> That every man in arms would wish to be?"

And then as the grey dawn defined the outlines of the hills, blackened the great fortress and revealed the snows, he fell asleep and dreamed.

And in his dream he was at rest. He lay on his back on the plain of Domoko, dead, and Varatasi was near him. A blaze of white light illumined the hillside. It shone till the blood danced as to the noise of a trumpet. And men in shimmering armour swept up towards him, with a song in their mighty throats and a purpose of victory in their tread.

> "Hail, Saviour, Prince of Peace,
> Thy Kingdom shall increase."

They sang the brave words to that old crusader's tune, with the clang of arms in its rhythms, the resistless ardour in the throbbing of its accents. And he knew that every man who had fallen in battle against barbarism was among them. They had the terrible joy in their faces that men wear who have not outlived defeat, they sped to instant conquest, and the wind of hope played with their pennants. Godfrey de Bouillon rode at their head on a white charger, and he touched with his lance the dead legionaries at his feet, so that they lived and swelled the troop in its irresistible advance. Varatasi rose in his turn and went beside him on

his puny pony, great in his courage. And then
Godfrey approached him where he lay, wistfully
gazing like Adam waiting for the breath of God.
But Godfrey passed, and he cried to him in his
agony—

"Mon Sire! Mon Sire! Moi aussi!"

And then he saw Varatasi's eyes upon him, the
tired eyes weary of commanding lesser men, and
the musical voice spoke gently with an accent of
pity, the same old words—

"Mais maintenant, mon enfant, il faut se reposer."

And then he woke. The lieutenant stood by
the fire with his white horse, he stirred the dying
embers to a blaze, and he said in quiet tones, "We
must start in an hour. You had better go back
and wake your countrymen. They must keep
with us. It is not safe to straggle on a retreat."

Wearily he rose, rubbing his eyes, for he was
fain of victory and the magic wrought by courage.

He noticed Alexi peacefully resting. He looked
more closely and saw the stain of blood on his
sheepskin cloak. He had been shot in the side,
and had died quietly as he slept.

And then he turned and went without a word to
his thankless task. As he tramped the three
miles in the grey light and the bitter cold along
the mountain path, he thought of his dream, and
found comfort. For there is a time to fight and a
time to rest. He took up the great burden of

peace and dishonour; he thought no more of the madness of the charge; he ceased to long for a death among the enemy. The time for fierce energy was past, the light of ideals had faded. For there is a time to fight and a time to rest, a time for resurrection and a time to acquiesce in death. He trudged along accepting the mortal prose of failure.

NOTES.

A.

Note to page 70.

CAPTAINS VARATASI AND BIRCH.

IN other cases where my characters are drawn from life I have changed their names. But to alter that of a man who at least in Greece was a well-known figure, seemed to me to savour of pedantry. I have also referred to Captain Birch, the English officer, by his real name. To make a living man a figure in a romance seemed to me an impertinence, and I have accordingly made but scant reference to him throughout the book. I wish that I had been at liberty to write with less restraint of his gallantry as a soldier and his capacity as an officer.

B.

Note to page 71.

THE WAR.

In an interview published in the *Acropolis* (September 9) the Crown Prince remarked, "I need hardly tell you that when I went to Thessaly, I did not believe that we were really going to war." It is now abundantly clear that the King and Delyanni were playing a game of bluff, as they did in 1878 and in 1886. The war was an appeal not to arms, but to the nerves of an over-drilled Europe. In this light the half-hearted defence of the frontier, and the withdrawal from Larissa, and then from Pharsala, become explicable. It is now known that it was only after a protest from the Thessalian deputies that any force was sent to Velestino. A serious resistance was not in the programme of the King and his Prime Minister, however much in earnest the nation as a whole may have been.

C.

Note to page 201.

THE INACTIVITY OF THE GREEK FLEET.

In a book recently published in Athens, *Foreign Rule and Monarchy in Greece*, by M. Philaretos, the deputy for Volo, it is stated on the authority of M. Levidis, formerly Minister of Marine, that the instructions sent by the Ministry to the Fleet were constantly met by contradictory orders emanating from the Court. He had prepared an aggressive programme, but the King co-operated with the European Concert in "localising the conflagration." This certainly tends to confirm the theory that King George had some understanding with Russia.

D.

Note to page 264.

THE BATTLE OF DOMOKO AND ITS SEQUEL.

It is necessary to say something here 'about the battle and its issue. The Greek line was at least sixteen miles long, and the attack was general. In the centre the Greeks held their own, thanks to their splendid position. On the left the Turks were everywhere repulsed, and with notable success at Katagouriani, where the foreign troops under Garibaldi and Varatasi were posted. But the right wing under General Macris was driven in, and reinforcements came too late. The Prince abandoned Domoko about eleven at night. How far he was justified I cannot pretend to decide. It is still a mystery why Smolenski lay all day at Halmyro, a position from which he might easily have come to the succour of the right. Certainly the Greek officers were indignant that no effort was made to retake the lost position. But with a necessarily extended line, and an army that numbered only half the force at Edhem Pasha's disposal, the sequel could hardly have been different. The position at Domoko seemed at a first glance impregnable, but its safety really depended on holding the Agouriani Pass on the left, and the various roads on the right which Macris had been compelled to surrender. To hold so long a line perhaps required a larger force than the Prince had at his disposal. Nevertheless, Riciotti Garibaldi, a man trained in war from his youth up, who knew the ground and the resources of either side, was loud in his indignation. He declared in the Athenian press that " he or any other European general would have prolonged the resistance to four days." (*Soteria*, May 29.) It is not unlikely, however, that the army at large was without ammunition for another day's battle. Certainly the Legion had hardly twenty rounds per man. This was the Nemesis for the stores abandoned at Larissa, and the reckless waste of cartridges indulged in by the irregulars and the raw recruits at every stage of the campaign. I have referred to the bad behaviour of the Greek troops in the vicinity of the Legion during the battle. It is only fair to say that, judging by the accounts of correspondents, their conduct cannot have been typical.

The battle of Domoko decided the issue of the war. It was the last engagement in Thessaly, with the exception of some skirmishing in which the rear-guard was involved in the Phourka Pass, and at Taratza. An armistice was concluded on Wednesday, May 19, two days after the battle. The Foreign Legion was disbanded a week later.

THE END

Richard Clay & Sons, Limited, London & Bungay.

www.ingramcontent.com/pod-product-compliance
Lightning Source LLC
Chambersburg PA
CBHW031344070726
47496CB00017B/1722